D0050734

THE THING
I'M MOST
AFRAID OF

Also by Kristin Levine

The Jigsaw Jungle
The Paper Cowboy
The Lions of Little Rock
The Best Bad Luck I Ever Had

THE THING I'M MOST AFRAID OF

KRISTIN LEVINE

putnam

G. P. Putnam's Sons

G. P. Putnam's Sons

An imprint of Penguin Random House LLC, New York

Visit us online at penguinrandomhouse.com

Library of Congress Cataloging-in-Publication Data
Names: Levine, Kristin (Kristin Sims), 1974– author.
Title: The thing I'm most afraid of / Kristin Levine.
Other titles: Thing I am most afraid of
Description: New York: G. P. Putnam's Sons, [2021] | Summary: In 1993, twelve-year-old Becca, who struggles with a anxiety disorder, visits her divorced father in Vienna, Austria, where she befriends a Muslim refugee fleeing the Bosnian genocide.
Identifiers: LCCN 2020058463 (print) | LCCN 2020058464 (ebook) |
ISBN 9780525518648 (hardcover) | ISBN 9780525518655 (ebook)
Subjects: CYAC: Anxiety disorders—Fiction. | Refugees—Fiction. |
Yugoslav War, 1991–1995—Bosnia and Herzegovina—Fiction. | Vienna (Austria)—History—
20th century—Fiction. | Austria—History—20th century—Fiction.
Classification: LCC PZ7.L57842 Th 2021 (print) | LCC PZ7.L57842 (ebook) |
DDC [Fic]—dc23
LC record available at https://lccn.loc.gov/2020058463
LC ebook record available at https://lccn.loc.gov/2020058464

Manufactured in Canada
ISBN 9780525518648

1 3 5 7 9 10 8 6 4 2

Design by Eileen Savage. Text set in Adobe Caslon Pro.

To all my friends in Vienna, and to Julia

I Have (Not So Much) Confidence

IT WAS JUST a metal detector. You know, the normal kind they have at airports to make sure no one smuggles a gun or a bomb or an iguana onto a flight. Millions of people go through them every day without a problem: old people, babies, pregnant women. But I couldn't shake the feeling that it was actually a cancer-causing death trap.

Come on! you're probably saying. *Everyone knows they're safe.*

But everyone used to think that X-ray machines at shoe stores were safe. My dad told me this story of how he took a bazillion photos of the bones in his foot one summer. And then that fall, his left baby toe got a wart, and he had to have surgery. Coincidence? I think not.

Okay, so maybe that's not the best example. In Dooms-day Journal #2, page 14, I have a section on how warts are caused by viruses caught by touching contaminated surfaces, such as a locker-room floor—or an X-ray machine used by every kid in town. And metal detectors don't use X-rays; they actually use non-ionizing radiation, but that's beside the point.

The point is, I wanted to go visit my father in Austria. He'd moved there four months earlier. I missed him. A lot. But if I wanted to see him, I had to walk through the metal detector.

Unfortunately, my brain overreacts sometimes. It tells me that many, many things are dangerous, and not things that lots of people think are scary, like making new friends or public speaking or math tests. I'm actually okay with all of those. No, *my* brain tells me I should avoid certain things that most people believe are safe. Like metal detectors.

Of course, logically I understood my fear didn't make much sense. But I still didn't want to walk through that beeping monstrosity. I could practically see the rays zapping each person who walked through, mutating harmless freckles into skin cancer. The line got shorter and shorter. I started gulping down air, trying to catch my breath.

"Are you all right, Becca?" my mom asked.

She was flying to Austria with me. Not to see my father—they'd been happily divorced for years—but so she could take a summer backpacking trip through Europe. I was glad she was traveling with me, but I was also a little embarrassed. I mean, I was twelve. I should have been able to get on a plane by myself. All I had to do was sit there. My friend Chrissy started flying to Atlanta by herself each summer to see her grandparents when she was eight. But we all knew there was no way I'd be able to get on a plane alone.

Planes. Sometimes they crash and explode. No, I can't think about that now. I have to get through the metal detector first.

"Yes," I squeaked. "I'm fine."

Mom knew I was lying. She took my hand and squeezed it. It was clammy and cold. I tried to distract myself, like Dr. Teresa told me to do. Focus on Austria. Austria. *The Sound of Music.* Happy children frolicking in the Alps. *Doe, a deer, a female deer* . . . and . . . and . . .

Suddenly, we were at the front of the line. Mom moved smoothly and efficiently, like a cat, carefully putting her purse and backpack onto the conveyor belt. My joints felt stiff, my arms and legs suddenly too long, as I struggled to pull off my backpack and place it in the bin. I lumbered back to our spot in line, as if I were Pinocchio right after he came to life.

"Do you want to go first, sweetie?" Mom asked.

I shook my head.

"Come on, ma'am," the guard called. "Please step on through."

Mom squeezed my hand one last time and walked away. A moment later, she was through. My mom stood ten feet in front of me, her black slacks job-interview crisp, her dark hair as sleek as if she had just come from a salon. We were separated only by a stupid metal gate, but it felt as if she were a million miles away.

"Kid!" The guard sounded less patient now. "You're clear to walk through." I had pulled my curly hair back into a ponytail, but I could feel how wisps in front had fallen out and were now sticking to my forehead. There was sweat running down the small of my back; it was July and hot outside but so cold in the airport the air-conditioned air made my teeth hurt. And my heart was beating louder than a jet engine. I kept gasping for air, but I couldn't seem to get any oxygen. I started to feel dizzy.

"Come on!" There was a teenager behind me, clutching a skateboard. He rolled his eyes. "You're holding up the line!"

I saw my mom gesture to the guard and whisper something to him. I stared at my Keds. I knew what she was saying. *My daughter has an anxiety disorder. Sometimes she has panic attacks and . . .* It was so embarrassing!

The boy behind me gave me a push. I stumbled and almost fell, and by the time I regained my footing, I realized I had taken the few steps through the metal detector and it was over.

I burst into tears. The boy behind me started laughing, and I ran toward the bathroom. I locked myself in a stall and leaned against the cold metal, shaking, not quite sure if I was going to throw up. A minute later, I heard someone else walk in and my mother call, "Becca! Becca!"

"I'm here," I whispered, peeking out through the cracks in the door. My mother was struggling to carry both backpacks and her purse. One strand of her hair was out of place. The bathroom was mercifully deserted.

"You did it," Mom said.

"I made a huge scene!"

"It doesn't matter," she said. "You're through."

"But . . ." I sniveled. "Do I have cancer?"

"Oh, Becca." Mom sighed.

I knew it was ridiculous. But the thought kept bouncing around in my brain. Mom was really good at being patient. She looked in the mirror and combed her fingers through her hair, straightening the one strand. The thought bounced and bounced, like a motorized Ping-Pong ball, until finally, it ran out of steam. I unlocked the door and came out of the stall.

"Here." Mom fumbled in her purse. "Let me give you your Benadryl."

She pulled out a small pill and handed it to me along with a bottle of water. I didn't have a cold or an allergy attack, but, as listed on page 3 of Doomsday Journal #1, Benadryl was sometimes also recommended for anxiety. Especially in kids. It was 1993, for goodness' sake; you'd think they would have invented something better by now! I didn't like taking it—it made my head feel fuzzy and my mouth dry—but I wasn't even on the plane yet, and I was already freaking out. I really didn't have a choice.

I felt better as soon as I'd swallowed it. I knew there was no way it could work that fast, but . . . it was part of the plan we'd written out with Dr. Teresa last week. And I wanted to see my father.

So I splashed some water on my face and patted it dry with a scratchy paper towel. We went to McDonald's and each got a Quarter Pounder and fries and a Diet Coke. And as we ate, I tried not to think about the next thing I was afraid of—getting on the plane.

CHAPTER 2

Pancakes and Peanut Butter

THIS HAD ALL started last February. Dad and I had gone out for brunch, like we did every weekend I was at his house. It was Valentine's Day; I remember because I ordered heart-shaped pancakes with strawberry sauce. The bacon was too raw, so I had to send it back, but the next batch was nice and crispy. I was just pouring syrup on my pancakes when Dad cleared his throat and announced that he had gotten a job at the International Atomic Energy Agency in Vienna.

"Vienna?" I asked, stuffing a pancake into my mouth. "Isn't that near Tysons Corner? Can I walk to the mall from your new office?"

"Not Vienna, Virginia," Dad said. "Vienna, Austria."

I kept chewing. Truthfully, I was trying to remember if that was the one with Mozart or the one with kangaroos.

I should have paid more attention when we did world geography in social studies. Finally, I swallowed. "Oh."

"That means," Dad said slowly, "I'll be moving overseas."

I looked up at him. I liked my life just how it was. I liked my dad with his short haircut (he wasn't military, but a lot of the people he worked with were) and how he traded the suits he wore to work for jeans and an old T-shirt on the weekends. I liked our schedule: Mom's house on Monday and Wednesday, Dad's on Tuesday and Thursday, and switching off on the weekends. It worked great! My stomach suddenly hurt.

"I know it's sudden," Dad continued, "but I'm really excited about this."

I didn't say anything.

"I've been waiting for years for a position to open up. And this is my dream job!"

I knew he wanted a response, so finally I mumbled, "Yay. And you'll get to see some koala bears."

"That's Australia," Dad said.

"Oops." I stabbed my heart-shaped pancakes with my fork.

"Sweetie," Dad said. "Austria is beautiful. It's known for Mozart, Schubert, and Beethoven. It was the home of Sigmund Freud, has amazing coffeehouses and architecture, and was a center of intellectual engagement and—"

"Didn't it also have Nazis?" I asked.

Dad sighed. "Yes, that's true. Hitler was also from Austria."

I folded my arms. "So why would you want to go live there?"

"Maria von Trapp was from Austria."

"*The Sound of Music* is Mom's favorite movie. Not mine."

"Rebecca." I could tell Dad was upset, because usually both my parents just called me Becca. "Think of what a great opportunity it would be. To live in another country. Doesn't that sound interesting?"

"But you and Mom share custody," I pointed out. "How are we going to handle that?"

"I've already spoken to your mother. You'll stay with her for the rest of the school year and then come visit me for eight weeks in the summer."

Living in another country for eight weeks sounded a lot more exciting than my normal summer routine of watching TV and hanging out at the pool. And I was lying about *The Sound of Music*. It was definitely in my top ten. But there was one problem.

Last time I'd gotten on a plane, I'd been seven and we'd been going to see my grandparents in Chicago. I'd totally freaked out, started crying and screaming until I was so hysterical, I threw up. After the visit, Dad had rented a car and we'd driven the two days home. It had been shortly after that plane ride that I had started seeing Dr. Teresa.

"Do you really think I can get on a plane and fly overseas by myself?"

Dad smiled. "That's what is so perfect about this plan! Your mother has always wanted to go to Europe. And since she's a teacher, she doesn't have to work in the summer. So she's going to fly over *with* you, drop you off with me in Vienna, spend eight weeks traveling, and then pick you up on the way home."

What?!

"Isn't that a great idea?" Dad asked.

I felt dizzy. Why couldn't I have *normal* divorced parents who fought with each other instead of worked together to create a secret plan to turn my life upside down?!

"I'll even hire you a nanny. So you'll have someone to take you sightseeing when I'm busy working."

I thought about that. I wasn't sure if I should be offended that Dad thought I needed a babysitter or excited about having my very own Mary Poppins.

"Becca, I know this is a lot to take in," Dad said. "And I'm gonna miss you like crazy! But this is a once-in-a-lifetime opportunity for me. I can't pass it up."

I didn't want Dad to pass it up. I wanted to be brave enough to go. "When are you leaving?"

"Two weeks."

"Two weeks!"

"I know, it's really soon! But I'll call and write as much

as I can. And you won't come until school's out, so that gives you four months to get used to the idea."

"I'm not going to get used to the idea!"

"Sure you will. Look, for now all I'm asking is that you work with Dr. Teresa on a plan."

"Fine," I agreed. "But if this actually happens and you end up hiring me a nanny, she'd better be just like Julie Andrews!"

"Absolutely." Dad laughed.

After that, we pretended everything was okay. Dad finished his eggs; I drank the rest of my juice. Dad told me all about this old movie starring Orson Welles that was set in Vienna. "You have to see it!" he said. I nodded politely.

But there was another problem. I knew Dad loved me, and we had fun when we were together, but I'd seen how he'd sighed when I sent back my undercooked bacon. I knew he got frustrated when we had to leave the movies because there were too many people. And a couple of months ago, I'd overheard him telling my mom that they shouldn't buy me tickets to see *Les Misérables* for my birthday because I'd probably be too nervous to stay for the whole thing and he didn't want to waste the money. I couldn't help wondering if maybe Dad sometimes wished for a daughter who didn't worry quite so much.

The thought rattled around in my head, like a gumball in an almost empty machine, for months. It was still there as I sat in the airport McDonald's and finished up my Diet Coke. "Penny for your thoughts?" Mom asked.

"Groschen, Mom," I told her. "Pennies in Austria are called groschen." Dad had sent me a few coins in the mail. I wanted to tell her my worries about Dad, but I was already so embarrassed about the metal detector. I wanted to say I was going to miss her, but I couldn't say that either or I'd start blubbering again. Instead I asked, "Do you have your AT&T calling card? With the country codes? No matter where you are, you just dial the number for that particular country and—"

"And it will automatically charge my account. Yes, I know." Mom rummaged in her blue backpack and pulled out a brown paper bag, which she handed to me. "I brought you something."

Inside the bag were apple slices, peanut butter and crackers, and three soft-baked chocolate chip cookies. This was the lunch Mom had packed for me every single day of elementary school. Every. Single. Day. In first grade, she'd tried to give me different things, put in a turkey sandwich, or an orange, or Oreos instead of chocolate chip cookies, but I'd always given the offending food away and come home complaining of being hungry. Finally, she gave up.

This lunch screamed *home* to me like nothing else. The peanut butter smelled so good. Dad had promised to have some peanut butter for me in his kitchen when I arrived.

"I thought you might like some comfort food on the plane."

"Thanks." Okay, so maybe a tear or two sneaked out. And I guess Mom noticed, because she wiped them away with her thumb.

"Becca . . ."

"I'm fine!" I said.

"You're going to have fun."

"I'm going to miss you."

Mom came over to my side of the booth and whispered, "I'm going to miss you too."

We sat like that for a minute, and I started to feel a little better, at least until I heard the announcement over the PA system. "Austrian Airlines Flight 743 to Vienna. Boarding now."

"Time to go." Mom wiped her eyes, her voice falsely bright.

"Yeah."

"I bet you're excited to see Dad."

"Yeah." Thump, thump, thump went my heart. Dad had been methodical about staying in touch (he wrote twice a week, and we talked on the phone every Sunday), but it wasn't the same as being together. What if he liked it better this way? What if he liked *me* better when he didn't have to deal with all my worries?

"I can't do it," I cried. "I want to see Dad, but I'm so scared."

"Oh, sweetie, we've discussed this. Flying is safer than driving!"

I hadn't been talking about the plane—but now I was worried about that too!

Mom pulled me into a hug and sang softly into my ear, *"I've always longed for adventure, to do the things I've never dared. Now here I'm facing adventure. Then why am I so scared?"*

I knew that song. It was from *The Sound of Music*, when Fräulein Maria is leaving the abbey for the first time.

"You're going to be just fine," Mom said firmly. She grabbed my arm and marched us both over to the gate agent.

"We are going on a grand adventure!" she announced.

I was so embarrassed, but the gate agent just looked at us blankly. "Boarding passes, please."

My mom handed her our tickets and then pushed me onto the gangway. I looked back. "Right behind you, sweetie."

And so I didn't have a choice except to turn and start walking. I imagined Maria from *The Sound of Music*, starting out so hesitantly as she leaves the abbey, then gaining strength and courage until she's literally skipping down the road.

I tried to channel her. I strode more confidently down the walkway toward the plane.

But I didn't skip.

CHAPTER 3

The Doomsday Journal

A T THE DOOR to the airplane, a woman in a red dress with white trim and matching heels smiled at us. "Grüß Gott!" she exclaimed cheerily. "Welcome to Austrian Airlines." She looked a bit like Little Red Riding Hood, minus the cape. Mom beamed at her, and we stepped into the plane.

The Benadryl had started to kick in, and I felt a little woozy. I didn't remember planes being quite so *big*. There were two aisles, the seats arranged in a two-five-two configuration. We had seats 22A and 22B, but we picked the wrong aisle to walk down, so we had to continue to a little galley kitchen, then cross over to the other side. Finally, we reached our seats.

"Do you want the aisle or the window?" Mom asked.

"The window." Dr. Teresa had suggested that since I wasn't scared of heights, maybe being able to see the ground would make me feel a little bit more in control. It was worth a try.

Mom nodded and stowed her backpack overhead, while I shoved mine under the seat in front of me. I tried not to think too far ahead, focusing on putting the bag lunch from my mom in the seat-back pocket, right next to the bag for motion sickness, and pulling on my anti-nausea wristbands. Next, I kicked off my Keds and dug out my compression stockings. Now I'll admit, they're not particularly attractive, being long black socks that go up almost to my knees, but blood clots are nothing to mess around with. And sitting around on an international flight increases your risk of developing one by almost 50 percent! I was not taking any chances.

Finally, I pulled out the airplane safety card. I tightened my seat belt firmly across my lap, checked under my seat for the life jacket, and looked for the nearest exit. When I was done, I pulled out my journal so I could write everything down.

I guess I'd better explain about my Doomsday Journal. After we had to drive home from Chicago, my parents started to notice how I seemed to have more fears than the average kid. I worried about the mean sixth grader on the school bus, falling off the jungle gym, learning my math facts, forgetting my lunch, getting kidnapped, nuclear war, finding a razor blade in my Halloween candy, getting a Tylenol bottle with the safety seal removed—you get the idea.

My parents didn't know what to do. They told me again and again that I didn't have to worry about those things, but it didn't help. Finally, they took me to a child psychologist, Dr. Teresa. I liked her. We'd color happy pictures or build safe places with blocks. As I got older, she taught me about deep breathing and distracting myself when I started to feel anxious. And she was the one who came up with the idea of the journal.

Dr. Teresa didn't call it a Doomsday Journal; she just said maybe I should write down my fears and think about the worst-case scenario and how I would handle it. My parents thought that approach sounded a little weird, but my mom drove me to the store, and I picked out a hot-pink diary with a unicorn and rhinestones on the front. (It's a little embarrassing to look at now.) Truthfully, I was pretty doubtful too, but my parents promised me a chocolate-vanilla-twist ice cream cone with rainbow sprinkles if I tried it for one week.

And the funny thing is, it worked! Well, mostly. Once I wrote down my math facts in my journal, I didn't worry about forgetting them anymore. If I wrote down a bunch of different comeback lines I could use if the mean sixth grader teased me on the bus, I could relax and talk to my friends. (I was a little disappointed she never bothered me after I wrote them down—there were some real zingers!) Once I made a shopping list of all the nonperishable food supplies I'd like to have on hand in case there was a nuclear attack by the Soviets, I didn't have to worry about it anymore.

But some of my fears, especially the ones about illness or getting hurt, were harder to get rid of. Sometimes I'd get over my fear of choking on an apple, only to discover I was really much more afraid of popcorn getting stuck in my throat. It felt like a never-ending game of Whac-A-Mole. As soon as one fear was gone, another would pop up. So I kept writing.

In fifth grade my friend Chrissy nicknamed it my "Doomsday Journal," and the name stuck. By the time I turned twelve, I had filled three diaries, creating my own little reference collection of worries/survival guides. The old journals were packed in my checked luggage, but I had my current one (#4) with me in my backpack. Chrissy had given it to me for my birthday, right after she had heard I was going to Austria for the summer. It had an old-fashioned map on the cover and the words *Don't be afraid to get a little lost.*

That quote made me laugh because I *was* afraid of getting lost, but that was covered in my rainbow diary, otherwise known as Doomsday Journal #2, on page 47 (DJ #2, p. 47). Anyway, I pulled out my map journal, flipped to the first blank page, picked up a pen, and started writing.

International Plane Flight Safety Procedures

Nearest exit: 25A, wing exit.

If that exit is inaccessible, nearest exit is at
front of plane.

In case of a water landing remove life jacket
from under seat.

I drew a little sketch of recommended crash positions for an emergency landing.

And so on. When I finished, Mom asked, "Did that help?"

"Yeah," I said, even though I wasn't quite sure if it had. I focused on the flight attendant's safety spiel (I already knew everything). We hadn't even left the ground yet, and I already felt like I was going to throw up. I must have looked a little green, because Mom gestured to the motion-sickness bag in her seat-back pocket, but I waved her off.

We turned onto the runway, the engines roared, and I grabbed Mom's hand. *Well, if I'm going to die, I hope it's quick. Would dying in a plane crash be quick?* I thought it probably would. We accelerated, and the speed pushed me back into my chair. I closed my eyes, and suddenly my stomach dropped as if we were on an elevator. I gave a little shriek.

"It's okay," Mom said, squeezing my hand tighter. "We just left the ground. Look out the window."

CHAPTER 4

On the Plane

OBEDIENTLY, I OPENED my eyes and looked out the window. It had been five years since I had been on a plane, and I'd forgotten how cool it was to see the cars and buildings and trees from a different perspective. Before I knew it, we were in the clouds, the ride smoothed out a bit, and takeoff was over.

I'd done better than I'd expected. I was glad, but it was also frustrating, because I never knew exactly what would set off an attack. I mean, going up in an airplane was a lot scarier than a metal detector, and yet here I was, absolutely fine, while in the airport I had been a sniveling mess.

Mom and I watched *Sister Act* until dinner arrived. As I peeled back the plastic from the tray, I saw a beef pot roast, a few tiny potatoes, a cup of clear-broth soup, and a hot roll with warm, melted butter. It actually tasted pretty good! But when I put the meat in my mouth, I started to worry. It was only lukewarm. *Did they heat it up properly and it just cooled down? How do they heat meals on an airplane? Is it possible their microwave isn't functioning correctly?*

"Is everything okay, Becca?" Mom asked.

"Fine," I said, "fine." I wanted to ask if she knew the proper cooking temperature for beef, but I was pretty sure she didn't. Mom didn't worry about stuff like that. And I didn't have a meat thermometer, anyway.

I carefully covered the rest of the meat with a paper napkin. I ate the soup and the roll, gobbled down the vinegary green bean salad (vinegar is a very effective preservative), and then pulled out the peanut butter and crackers.

The familiar taste of sticky peanut butter on salty crackers almost made me cry. All the thoughts I was trying so hard not to think came rushing in at once. I didn't know anyone in Vienna except for my father, and I hadn't seen him for four months. What if he had changed? I mean, he *had* changed. He'd sent me a pic, and he had a beard now. He also had a girlfriend.

That was news he'd dropped on me just last week, on our final phone call before my visit. "Katarina is a newspaper reporter. She's Austrian and lives two doors down from me."

"Oh," I said. I mean, I assumed my parents dated from

time to time, but I'd never met anyone they were seeing before.

"She wants to come with me to pick you up from the airport."

"Okay," I said politely. "It'll be nice to meet her."

"And get this," Dad continued on. "She has a son your age. His name is Felix, and he loves to read. He's a bit on the quiet side, but I'm sure you'll like him a lot. The au pair will be there too."

The French term *au pair* is basically a fancy word for *nanny*, a glorified babysitter, usually from another country. It's really more of a cultural exchange than a traditional childcare arrangement. I only knew what one was because Dad had told me a few days before.

"What's her name again?" I asked.

"Sara Tahirović. I believe she's Muslim."

"How old is she?"

"Nineteen, I think."

"Where's she from?" I asked. "England? Scotland? Australia?"

"Sarajevo. That's in Bosnia."

I didn't know where that was either. "Does she speak English?"

"Of course, Becca! I'm not going to hire you an au pair who doesn't speak English."

"Okay." I didn't know what to do. Dad sounded exasperated, but I had a million more questions. Before I could ask any of them, Mom came in to confirm our arrival times, and then it was time to hang up.

On the plane, the flight attendant came down the aisle to pick up our dinner trays. Mom pulled out a book while my thoughts continued to swirl. *What was Felix like? What TV channels did my dad get? Would Dad remember to buy me a jar of peanut butter?* The stewardess came back again, handing out pillows and thin red blankets this time. Mom and I both took one of each.

"Time to get some rest," Mom said, closing her book and placing it in the seat-back pocket. "I love you, sweetie. Sleep well." She kissed her fingers and, like always, pressed them to the worry crease between my eyebrows.

Mom took off her purple glasses and tucked them in next to her novel. She draped her new "travel" sweater (*Never wrinkles! Wash in hotel sink!*) around her shoulders and tucked the red blanket around her legs. Her eyes closed, and a minute later she was snoring—small, soft, dainty snores. Mom could sleep anywhere, anytime—bus, train, automobile. Sleep was another thing I wasn't very good at.

I sat there, staring at the illuminated seat belt sign, trying not to imagine the oxygen masks popping out. I forced my eyes closed and tried to count sheep, but my thoughts would not keep still. *Why does it have to be sheep? Could I count kittens? Or pigs? Or baby rabbits?* Finally, I ditched the animals and just counted backward from a hundred.

I had almost drifted off when we hit a patch of turbulence. I grabbed Mom's arms so hard, I was sure I had woken her up. But she just mumbled, "Feed the gerbils" and turned her head the other way. That was weird. We didn't even have gerbils.

I thought about counting gerbils, but instead, I pulled out Doomsday Journal #4. Reading it sometimes helped me to relax when my thoughts wouldn't stop spinning. Unfortunately, the first page I opened to was page 7:

How to Prevent Blood Clots
on Long Plane Flights

1. Get up and walk around as often as possible.
2. Wear compression socks.
3. Make sure to stretch.

Okay, then. I guess I'd forget about sleep and do some stretches.

I crawled over my sleeping mother and walked down the aisle. The bathroom was next to one of the galley kitchens, and there was a bit of room in the aisle between them. I bent over and touched my toes, feeling the blood rush to my head.

"Nice socks," said a woman in the seat closest to the kitchen.

I stood up so quickly I felt dizzy for a moment. The woman wore a white shirt and a blazer. I could see gold hoop earrings peeking out from her shoulder-length hair. She looked vaguely familiar, but I couldn't figure out why in the world she was complimenting my socks. "They are compression stockings," I said seriously. "They prevent blood clots."

She laughed. "Yes, I know," she said. She rolled up one leg of her black trousers to reveal her own long, ugly compression stockings.

I smiled and started to do some heel lifts.

"Couldn't sleep?" she asked.

"No."

"Me neither," she agreed. "You ever been on an international flight before?"

"No," I admitted. "Have you?"

"Lots of times."

"Then why can't you sleep?"

"I'm thinking about a story I'm working on. I'm a reporter."

"Cool," I said. "What's going on in Vienna?"

"Lots, I'm sure," the woman said. "But I'm actually going to Sarajevo."

"Oh!" I said. "I'm visiting my dad in Vienna, and the au pair he hired is from Sarajevo."

"How nice!" the woman said. "Is she a refugee?"

"Refugee?"

"There's a war going on in former Yugoslavia. That's why I'm going to Bosnia. I'm a correspondent with CNN."

"A war reporter!" I exclaimed. "Isn't that scary?"

"Sometimes."

I stood on one leg, stretching the other while I thought that over. I had heard about the war, of course, watching the news at night with my mom. But I hadn't paid it much mind. It seemed like something very far away. "Where is Bosnia exactly?" I asked. "I mean, I'm not very good at geography. I thought Austria was the place with the koala bears."

"Well," she said as she pulled out a cocktail napkin, brushed off some peanut crumbs, and started to draw a little map. "Austria is here. And right next door is the country that used to be called Yugoslavia. It had six states: Serbia, Bosnia-Herzegovina, Croatia, Slovenia, Macedonia, and Montenegro. Sarajevo is the capital of Bosnia-Herzegovina."

"I've never heard of any of those places."

"I bet you have," the woman replied. "In school, didn't you learn about the beginning of World War I?"

"Oh yeah!" I remembered. "That archduke guy was assassinated."

"Franz Ferdinand," she reminded me. "And he was killed in Sarajevo."

"Oh." I hadn't made that connection. "And you're going there?"

"Yes."

"Then why are you on a plane to Vienna?" I asked.

"The airport in Sarajevo is closed to all commercial flights. Only a few humanitarian flights are getting in. It's easier to get there by land. It's only about a day's drive from Vienna."

My dad was living "only about a day's drive" from a war zone?! I hadn't made *that* connection either. I reached up in the air, stretching as if I were trying to touch the roof of the plane. "What are they fighting about?" I asked.

She sighed. "The short version is that about two years ago, the country began to break apart, with many of the states declaring their independence. Bosnia-Herzegovina was one of the most diverse, containing Bosnian Muslims, Serbs, and Croats. Even though they had lived together in peace for many years, they had different ideas for the future of their country. Fighting broke out when the Serbs tried to take control of the region."

"So it's a civil war?" I asked.

She nodded. "Your au pair is lucky she got out when she did. There are reports of . . . horrible things happening to young women in Bosnia now."

"Then why are you going?" I asked.

"Sometimes you have to do scary things. Because they are important to you. I want the world to know the truth about the war, so I have to go."

I stared, my stretches forgotten. She was clearly much, much braver than me.

"Getting tired?" she asked.

"A little," I admitted.

"Me too. I'm going to try to get some rest. They'll serve coffee in a couple of hours. And croissants with butter and jam. They're delicious."

"I'm too young for coffee."

"Hmm," she said. "You're old enough to ask real questions about the world. I think that makes you old enough for coffee too."

She handed me the napkin map, and I went back to my seat. I must have dozed a little, because the next thing I remember was Little Red Riding Hood coming by and asking, "Coffee or tea?"

Hot chocolate, please was right on the tip of my tongue; I knew they had it, because I had read in the in-flight magazine that was one of the beverage options. But Mom was still asleep, and the flight was almost over, and when I opened my mouth, what came out was, "Coffee, please."

I froze, surprised at my own daring. But the flight attendant didn't bat an eyelash, just picked up a ceramic mug and asked, "Milk and sugar?"

"Yes, thank you."

Mom was still snoring softly as I raised the cup to my lips. It smelled bitter and sweet. I took a sip. It tasted like confidence.

CHAPTER 5

The Welcoming Committee

M OM FINALLY WOKE up as the flight attendant was collecting my breakfast dishes. The croissant *had* been delicious. Mom got up to go to the bathroom near the kitchen and came back with a croissant and a cup of coffee. "Becca!" she whispered excitedly, still standing in the aisle. "Hester Madden is on this plane!"

"Who's that?"

"She's a CNN reporter."

"Oh yeah! I met her last night."

"What?"

"I couldn't sleep, and . . . we had a whole conversation about Bosnia."

"That's so exciting!" Mom said.

"Yeah, she's really nice." I paused. "Mom, do you think it's safe in Vienna?"

"What?"

"I mean, Ms. Madden said it's only a day's drive to where the fighting is in Sarajevo."

Mom sat down next to me and looked straight in my eyes. "Becca, there is nothing for you to worry about. You're completely safe in Austria. The war in Bosnia will not affect you at all."

I wasn't so sure. Still, I had more immediate things to worry about—like getting off the plane.

Landing wasn't quite as scary as taking off, even though technically it's just as dangerous. (See DJ #1, p. 5.) I think it was easier because even with the coffee, I was so tired it was hard to think about anything except sleep. My mother held my hand from the time we started our descent until we touched down.

Mom was so excited she was practically bouncing up and down as we picked up our bags and waited to go through customs. "Your father said he would give me a ride to the train station. Once I get to Salzburg, I'll find my hostel and take a little walk around to get oriented. Then tomorrow I'm going to do the *Sound of Music* tour and then the salt mines the day after that, and then I'm going to rent a car and go see the castles in Bavaria."

I tried to catch her excitement. Here I was in a real foreign airport! But it looked pretty much like the airport I had just left, except the signs were in English *and* German. Mom and I handed the man at customs our passports. "I'm visiting my dad," I volunteered. He stamped my booklet and waved us through.

The airport was fairly small. I saw an old man being greeted by a group of smiling children. I watched a young woman run up to her boyfriend and kiss him. But I didn't see my father. *Did we miss him? Did we get the day wrong? Did*—

"Becca!"

I turned around, and there he was.

His brown hair was longer, but I liked his short beard. Instead of jeans, he wore khaki pants and a button-down shirt. He'd traded in his sneakers for expensive-looking leather shoes. I waved, and a grin spread across his face.

Dad ran toward me and gave me a big hug. He smelled the same. He sounded the same. He was still my good old dad.

"Was the plane okay?" he asked.

I nodded and squeezed harder.

"She did great," Mom said. "I was so proud of her."

"Thanks for bringing her over," Dad said.

"Of course," Mom said. "This turned out to be a win-win for all of us."

I wasn't so sure about that, but before I could protest, Dad turned to introduce a woman standing just behind him. She was dressed in a black skirt and a pink blouse, her hair was curled around her shoulders, and she was wearing a full face of makeup. She looked as if she were going to a party, even though it was barely seven in the morning local time.

"Becca," Dad said. "I'd like you to meet my girlfriend, Katarina." He grinned like a dorky teenager who had just won one of those stupid giant stuffed animals at the county fair.

Katarina grabbed my hand and began pumping it up and down. "It is so lovely to meet you! We are going to have *such* a wonderful summer." She spoke near-perfect English with a slight British accent.

"Hi," I managed to choke out.

My mom smiled and shook Katarina's hand pleasantly, and they exchanged "Nice to meet yous."

When they were done, Katarina pushed forward a skinny boy with curly blond hair. "Becca, I want you to meet my son, Felix."

Felix barely looked up from the book he was reading. In fact, he didn't move his head at all, just flicked his eyes up to get the briefest glimpse of me, then went back to his reading.

"Hallo," he whispered to the words in his book.

His hair fell over his eyes and ears as if he had missed a haircut. Dad had said Felix was my age, but he must have misunderstood, because Felix looked about nine years old.

"Hey, Felix," I said, as friendly as I could.

He kept reading.

Katarina beamed as if she thought our introduction had gone extremely well. "I'm sure the two of you are going to be *best* friends!"

Oh yeah. At home I always hung out with nine-year-olds.

"And this is Sara," Dad said, pointing to a young woman behind him. "She's going to be your and Felix's au pair!"

I'd imagined Sara as a plain, smiling girl, like Fräulein Maria, except with a headscarf instead of a wimple. This Sara looked nothing like that. She had light-brown hair with a streak in the front dyed neon green. Her lipstick was way too red, and she had caked on a bunch of green eye shadow. She was wearing a black dress and black sandals and had a silver necklace with a small star and crescent moon around her neck.

"Nice to meet you," Sara said shyly. Her green eye shadow matched her hair, and she had a stronger accent than Katarina.

"Sara also speaks Bosnian, Latin, a little Russian, French, and German," Katarina said.

"I don't speak any of those," I said.

"No problem!" Katarina said. "Felix attends the International School, where all the classes are in English. So if there are any words Sara doesn't know, he can translate."

Felix actually glanced up from his book at that. He looked about as pleased as I felt.

Yeah, kid, I felt like saying. *It's going to be a long summer.*

"What a great experience for the children!" Mom exclaimed.

"That's exactly what I said!" Katarina agreed.

Dad picked up our bags and led the way to his car, followed by Katarina and Mom, who were chatting away like old friends. Sara, Felix, and I walked behind them; we didn't say a word. Right before we went outside to the parking lot, Sara put a hand on Katarina's shoulder. "Wait one moment, please?" she asked.

"Of course," said Katarina.

We all stood and waited while Sara intently studied a small bulletin board hung on a wall between car-rental signs. I wasn't sure what it was. It looked like a bunch of handwritten notes pinned with old thumbtacks. She took a piece of paper from her pocket and pinned it to the board.

"Any luck?" Katarina asked when Sara returned to our group.

Sara shook her head.

Before I could ask any questions, Dad shooed us out the door. His car wasn't far, and we dumped our bags in the trunk. Dad, Katarina, and Mom squeezed into the front seat; Felix, Sara, and I climbed into the back.

Mom and Katarina kept up a light, chattery conversation, Mom telling us all the places she wanted to visit, and Katarina offering suggestions. From time to time, Dad would chime in. Felix pretended to read, but I could tell he was listening to their conversation.

"They're divorced?" he whispered to me finally.

"Yeah."

"But . . . they get along so well," he said.

I shrugged. "Doesn't your mom talk to your dad sometimes?"

Felix turned his attention back to his book. By the time I realized he wasn't going to answer, we were already on the highway. It seemed too weird to repeat myself, so instead I turned to Sara and asked, "What were you doing at the airport?"

"My family stayed behind in Sarajevo," she answered. "I hope they come to Vienna. I think, maybe they left a note."

"But if your family comes to Vienna, wouldn't they just call you?"

"I sent them a letter with my number." Sara sighed. "But I not sure they got it. I only received one letter from them. So I posted this." She handed me a copy of a piece of notebook paper. In neat block letters she had written, *Ich suche Petra Tahirović, 44, und Eldin Tahirović, 6*. There was a phone number at the bottom.

"That's my mom and little brother," she explained.

"Oh." I tried to give the paper back to her, but she shook her head.

"Keep it. I have many copies."

Dad was already pulling up to the train station, so I folded up the paper and stuffed it into my pocket. I climbed out of the back seat, and Mom and I waited on the curb while Dad got her bag out of the trunk.

"They all seem nice," Mom said.

"Yeah," I agreed.

I could feel Felix and Sara watching me from the inside of the car. I was determined not to cry.

Mom gave me a long hug, but it felt awkward, as if I were a fish, already slipping out of her grasp.

"You have the list of all the places I'm staying," Mom said. "You can always give me a call."

I nodded.

Then Mom kissed her fingers and pressed them to my forehead.

That's when I cried.

"Becca," Mom said. "You can do it. You're going to have a wonderful summer."

She hoisted her backpack onto her shoulder, pulled up the handle of her roller bag (*Purple! So no one will mistake it for theirs*), and walked off toward her own adventure.

Leaving me to deal with mine.

CHAPTER 6

The Happy Chicken

N O ONE MENTIONED my tears when I got back into the car. Katarina chattered on about the lovely garden in front of my father's town house. I imagined rows of beans, corn, and tomatoes, but there was no garden—it was only a little patch of grass, barely enough to mow. There were five town houses in a row, each with a small yard out front. The one next to my father's was filled with dozens of ceramic gnomes: one with a dog by the front gate, one with an umbrella, one with a tiny watering can, one wearing sunglasses, one on skis, a baby in a diaper, a grandpa with a beard and a cane, and so on. In between the gnomes were flowers. *Lots* of flowers. There were boxes; there were baskets; there were pots. It looked like a flower shop run by Smurfs.

"That's Frau Gamperl's house," Katarina explained. "Felix, Sara, and I live on the other side."

At my father's front door, Katarina gave me a hug and told me she would see us later. Sara waved, but Felix just kept reading as they walked away. I sighed with relief as they left. Finally, it was just me and my father.

Dad smiled as if he were thinking the same thing. "Welcome home," he said as he unlocked the door. "I know it might seem a little weird at first, but I really do want you to feel like this is your house too."

Inside, there was a big room with a dining table, a large L-shaped couch, a TV, and a stereo. To the left was a galley kitchen with a tiny table, only big enough for two. Everything looked new and clean, and there was a lot of light. Upstairs, there were three bedrooms—a large one with a balcony for my father, my dad's study, and a bedroom for me.

My room had a double bed, a desk by the window, and a couple of empty bookshelves. There was a small dresser in the corner. Everything was sleek and modern. It was also really hot. We dumped my bags in the room and went back downstairs.

"Is there something wrong with the air-conditioning?" I asked. "It feels kind of warm in my room."

"Hmm?" Dad asked as he started to make some oatmeal on the stove. "Oh, no one has air-conditioning here."

"What?"

"Well, it doesn't usually get this hot," he said. "I think I have a fan in the basement."

We sat down for breakfast at the little table. Dad had

made the oatmeal just the way he did at home, with a little honey and brown sugar. I was starting to feel a bit better, when I heard Katarina call "Hello, you two!" through the open window.

She barged inside without even knocking. Sara followed, carrying a laundry basket full of wet clothes. Felix trailed them both, holding a bag of clothespins in one hand and a book in the other.

"My laundry line is already full, and we have *so* much wash. Do you mind if we use yours?" She didn't even wait for my father to answer, just strode through his living room and out onto his back patio. Katarina and Sara hung up pants and T-shirts; Felix handed them neon-pink clothespins without looking at them.

"Go right ahead!" Dad called.

"Don't they have a dryer?" I grumbled.

"No one has a dryer," Dad explained. "It's bad for the environment. That's how Katarina and I met. The washer is in the community room across the way. I was looking for the dryer and asked Katarina where it was. She laughed and laughed at me!"

The oatmeal, which a minute before had been delicious, suddenly felt lumpy in my mouth. "So how long have you two been . . . going out?" I asked.

"About three months now," Dad said. "I thought it was so sweet that she wanted to come to the airport with me to pick you up."

"Yeah," I said. I stirred my oatmeal, even though it was already cool. Through the glass patio door, I noticed Sara watching us. When I caught her eye, she quickly looked away.

"What happened to Sara's family?" I asked.

"I'm not entirely sure," Dad said. "For some reason, they weren't able to leave the country with her."

"Is there really fighting in her city?"

"Yes."

"Mom's not traveling to . . ."

"Of course not," Dad said. "Your mother is only visiting Western Europe. It's perfectly safe."

That's what Mom had said. I thought about Sara coming here all alone, leaving her family behind. "Is there anything we can do to help her find them?" I asked.

"I've inquired at the US embassy, but since they aren't American citizens . . ."

At that moment, Katarina walked back into the kitchen and kissed my father on the cheek. "You are the best!" She glanced at my bowl of oatmeal. "What?! That's all you're having for breakfast?"

"I like oatmeal," I said.

"No, no, no." She grabbed my father's arm. "You *must* come over to our place. We will have a *real* breakfast, a Sunday brunch, to welcome your daughter."

Suddenly, I was being shoved out the door when I

just wanted to have a quiet talk with my father. We were marched two doors down to Katarina's house.

The table in their great room was large, big enough for eight, so the five of us had plenty of room. My father and I were instructed to sit while Katarina, Sara, and Felix got things ready. I watched Sara intently. I would be a mess if I didn't know where my mom was, but Sara's hands were steady as she brought food to the table: pastries with apricots and cherries; a plate of cold cuts with salamis and hams; a basket of round rolls, some with poppy seeds and some without; a cheese spread; a container of honey; and two carafes, one with coffee and one with hot chocolate. And finally, in front of each plate, a hard-boiled egg in a little eggcup.

Well, I did like eggs. So after everyone sat down, I tried to peel mine. I tapped it on the table until it cracked. Bright-yellow yolk oozed out. "Oh," I said, "it's not fully cooked!"

I looked up and everyone was staring, even Felix. I thought Katarina would be embarrassed, but she was looking at me as if I were the one who was crazy.

"Um, I don't think you cooked them long enough," I said.

Katarina laughed. "Oh, Schatzi," she said, "they're *soft*-boiled eggs."

I glanced at Dad.

"We didn't eat soft-boiled eggs at home in Virginia, did we, Becca?" Dad said kindly. "But they're actually pretty good. Look. You slice off the top." He used his knife to cut the shell, removing the top curve of the egg like a little hat. He pushed his egg over toward me and handed me a tiny spoon. "Put some salt and pepper on it, and you just scoop it out of the shell."

The yolk oozed over the side. "It's raw!"

"It's not raw," Dad insisted. "It's just not as fully cooked as you're used to."

"But, Dad!" I lowered my voice. "What about salmonella?"

"Try it, try it!" urged Katarina.

"Raw eggs can make you sick," I said. It was in Doomsday Journal #3, somewhere near the end. Consuming raw or undercooked eggs is a major risk factor for contracting salmonellosis.

"Oh no, no, no," Katarina trilled. "These are eggs from happy chickens!"

"What the heck are happy chickens?" I said.

"Becca doesn't like to eat foods that aren't completely cooked," Dad explained. He sounded a little embarrassed. Or maybe he thought I was being rude, but I didn't care. I was *not* going to end up with food poisoning on my first day in a new country.

Katarina didn't seem offended. "Happy chickens," she explained, "are from happy farms. Where the animals get to run around and eat freely and aren't cooped up in cages like they are in *some* places. Because we have happy chickens, we don't have the same problems with salmonella like you do in the United States."

That sounded pretty weird to me. I glanced at Dad.

He shrugged.

"I think I'll have a pastry instead," I said, reaching for an apricot thingy.

Dad took the egg back and scooped out a spoonful of yolk.

"Dad!"

"They're good," he said. "Katarina writes about economics with a specialty in food production. She knows what she's talking about. See, her article is right here on the front page." He handed me a tabloid-style newspaper. It was all in German, of course. I couldn't read the headline, but underneath in bold letters was *Katarina Müller.*

"Very impressive," I said. To be extra polite, I decided to flip through the pages, pretending I was actually interested. Page 3 had a picture of a smiling woman. There was only one thing odd. The woman wasn't wearing a shirt. Or a bra.

"What kind of paper is this?!" I pushed it back toward my dad.

"Oh yeah. I forgot about that." He looked embarrassed.

"What is it, Ben?" Katarina asked.

He held the paper out to her.

She looked at him blankly.

He pointed to the naked woman.

"Oh." She turned to me and smiled. "You Americans are so funny about nudity."

"What kind of paper do you write for?" I asked.

"A normal one. I mean, it's not the *New York Times*, but . . ."

"There's a topless woman in the newspaper!" I exclaimed.

"That's just the Girl of the Day," Katarina explained.

"Okay," Dad said, folding up the paper. "Let's put the paper away and enjoy our breakfast."

I caught a glimpse of Sara looking up for just a second over the edge of her coffee cup. And I swear she was smiling.

AFTER BREAKFAST, I was exhausted. Though it was eleven o'clock in Vienna, it was five in the morning back home. I'd barely slept on the plane, so I wanted to take a nap, but Katarina insisted I go outside in the sunshine to "reset my internal clock."

"Let's all take a bike ride!" she suggested.

"No," I said firmly. "I don't feel like riding a bike."

The truth was I didn't feel like riding a bike because I *couldn't* ride a bike. Sure, it's a little unusual for a twelve-year-old not to be able to ride a bike. But the statistics on bike accidents? They are just scary. (See DJ #1, pp. 22–23.)

"Okay, a walk, then," Katarina replied. "Come along, Schatzi."

"Why does she keep calling me that?" I asked my father as Katarina led us up a dirt path through a vineyard. "Doesn't she know my name?"

"Of course she does," Dad whispered back. "*Schatzi* is a term of endearment, like *sugar* or *sweetie*."

"Well, tell her to just call me Becca."

"Okay," Dad said. "Will do."

I didn't want to like the vineyards, but they were pretty. There were rows and rows of grapevines on stakes and a dirt path that ran between them, up and down rolling hills. It would have been picturesque—if I hadn't been so tired. I could barely put one foot in front of the other.

Finally, Katarina agreed I'd had enough sunshine, and I was allowed to go back to my room. I collapsed on the strange bed and was instantly asleep.

When I woke up, it was dark, and the house was quiet. I looked at the clock on the dresser, and it was just past midnight. I guessed Dad was asleep, but I felt wide awake. And I was hungry.

I crept downstairs to the kitchen. There was a note on the kitchen table:

Guess you were more tired than you thought!
No worries, sweetie. I'm going to bed now, but
if you wake up and are hungry, feel free to help
yourself to anything in the kitchen. Mom called
earlier—she said not to wake you. She'll try you
again tomorrow. Afraid I have to go to work in
the morning, but Sara and Felix will be over
at 9 a.m. They're planning to show you around
the city. I'll be home by 5 p.m. and we'll have
dinner. Love you!

Dad had told me to make myself at home, but it still felt odd, prowling around a kitchen that wasn't mine in the middle of the night. I opened every single cabinet, looking for a jar of Skippy or Jif, but I couldn't find any kind of peanut butter. I felt ridiculously disappointed. I sat down at the kitchen table and felt something uncomfortable in my pocket. When I pulled it out, I realized it was the flyer about Sara's family.

I suddenly had a lump in my throat. I wanted to go upstairs and get my Doomsday Journal. Write down all my worries. How Dad might get food poisoning and die. How Katarina thought I was a prude just because I didn't like my news with a side helping of naked lady. How Sara was separated from her family. I got a glass of water and took a big sip, but I couldn't get rid of the feeling that there was something stuck. Finally, I remembered Mom had given me the number of the youth hostel where she was staying. Maybe she was awake with jet lag too. And if not, she wouldn't mind me waking her up.

I ran upstairs to get her number. It didn't seem right to throw away Sara's paper, so I tucked it in my Dooms-day Journal. Then I returned to the kitchen and studied the phone on the counter. It was big and red and squat. It had a rotary dial. I picked up the handset, which had a cord. Even the dial tone sounded strange. I dialed the country code. It beeped twice. And then a recording came on in English, prompting me to enter my number and my account code. After what seemed like *forever*, the line began to ring.

It rang and rang and rang, but no one answered. After a few minutes, I hung up and started to cry.

There was a creak on the stairs.

I jumped.

"Becca?" my dad called out.

I wiped my eyes as Dad came padding down the stairs in a navy bathrobe and pajamas. "Why are you up?" Dad asked. "Is everything okay?"

"No," I said. "I tried to call Mom, but she didn't pick up the phone." I thought about how Sara was unable to call her mother. "I think something must have happened to her!"

"Sweetie," my dad said kindly. "A youth hostel isn't like a hotel. They don't have phones in the room. And no one's at the front desk to answer the phone at night."

I looked at the clock on the stove: 12:27 a.m.

"Mom is fine," Dad reassured me. "You're worrying for no reason."

I didn't answer.

"Are you hungry?" he asked. "You slept through lunch and dinner."

"Yes," I said. "And you promised to have some peanut butter!"

"I do." He rummaged in the cabinet and pulled out a tiny jar, about half the size of the smallest jar of peanut butter you could buy at home. Still, when Dad opened it, a familiar nutty smell wafted out. He grabbed a leftover roll from breakfast, sliced it in half, and spread peanut butter thickly onto each side.

The peanut butter tasted so good, it almost made me start crying again.

"I know things seem strange," Dad said. "But—"

"I liked my life as it was!" I whispered. "Why did it have to change?"

Dad was silent for a long time. His hair was plastered to the side of his face from sleeping. *And why is he wearing a robe and pajamas anyway?* Sweats and a T-shirt had always been good enough for him at home.

Finally, he cleared his throat. "Becca, things always

48

change. You need to give yourself some time to adjust. Spending the summer in Vienna is a good challenge for you. It might even be fun. But you need to give it a real try."

I finished my sandwich, gave my dad a hug, and trekked back upstairs to bed. I'd promised Dad I would try to have an open mind. And I would try. But let's be honest: I wasn't a happy chicken.

CHAPTER 7

The Honor System

I PUT ON SOME pajamas and brushed my teeth and tried to go to sleep the proper way this time. But I tossed and turned for what seemed like forever. My room was hot and stuffy, the bed lumpy in unfamiliar ways. *What if there are bedbugs? What if I get a heat rash?* I wanted to write down my worries, but my limbs felt heavy, as if I'd been lifting weights. I must have drifted off again at some point, because the next time I opened my eyes, light was pouring in through the open curtains. I felt groggy and disoriented, as if something had woken me up out of a dream I couldn't quite remember. Then I heard it again—someone was pounding on the front door.

I jumped out of bed, my heart thumping in time with the knocking. I was terrified. *What are you supposed to do in Austria if someone tries to break into your house? Call*

911? I didn't know. *Why don't I have a page about this in my journal?!*

The pounding continued, so I crept down the stairs. I gathered my courage and then tiptoed my way to the front door to peek out the window. The person pounding on Dad's front door was . . . Felix.

Honestly, I was surprised that such a small, skinny boy could make such a racket. In any case, I pulled open the front door and demanded, "What do you want?"

Felix cringed under my gaze. "Ich . . . I . . . Wir . . ."

I felt a little bad then. He had a book tucked under one arm, and he was wearing leather sandals, as well as khaki shorts and a red T-shirt with a pocket on the front. And that's when I remembered I was still in my pajamas.

I hoped I was wearing the striped ones or even the polka dots. But from Felix's expression, I had a sinking feeling they were the ones with frogs wearing leis and grass skirts. I was too scared to glance down and find out.

"Hallo!" Sara said, walking up the front steps. Her stripe of hair was a brilliant emerald in the sunlight; she wore black jeans and a black T-shirt. She still had on the silver necklace. "Time to go." She stopped short when she saw me. "Why you wearing underwear? And why is it covered with . . . Frösche?"

"Frogs," Felix whispered.

Oh yeah. I was *so* glad he was there to translate. "It's not underwear," I stated. "They're pajamas."

"Ah," Sara said. "But it is hour nine."

That's when I remembered what Dad had told me in his note. I was supposed to go sightseeing with the two of them today. "Oh, I'm sorry," I said. "I overslept. You'll have to go without me."

I moved to close the door, but Sara stuck her foot inside. "No," she said.

"No?" I asked.

"I show you city." She held up an envelope with my father's handwriting on it. "Your father left money. He said have fun."

I stared at her. She sounded like a bossy grandmother. "It's okay," I said. "I can stay home."

She shook her head. "Your father said you do not like to be left alone. Get rid of Frosch underwear. Find real clothes!" Her face suddenly softened a little. "You have real clothes?"

I was mid eye roll when I remembered *she* had fled her home. I wondered what she had been able to bring with her. "Okay," I said. "Give me five minutes."

I found myself running up to my room and tearing through my suitcase, not quite sure *why* I was rushing to please this teenage babysitter. I pulled out jean shorts and a T-shirt, ran a comb through my hair, brushed my teeth, and put on my sneakers. Four minutes and thirty-three seconds later, I was back on the front porch.

Sara was staring at her watch. It had a large gold face and seemed too big for her wrist. She grunted in approval. "Good. Time to go."

I grabbed my purse and locked the door.

"Where are we going?" I asked.

"The city," she said.

An older woman gardening in the yard next to us stood up and called out to Sara. They had a short exchange in German, then Sara said in English, "This is Becca, Ben's daughter. She's visiting for the summer."

The woman took off one gardening glove and stuck it into a pocket in her dress. She looked like she had stepped out of *The Sound of Music*, wearing a blue dirndl with a red apron, a white blouse, and clunky black shoes. "Nice to meet you," she said pleasantly, holding out her hand. "You may call me Frau Gamperl."

I shook her hand.

"Make sure you sort your trash properly," Frau Gamperl told me. "Americans always have trouble with that. You can't just throw all the glass in the same bin! *Grün* means *green*, and *braun* means . . ."

"Sorry," Sara said. "We need to catch bus." She led Felix and me down the block.

"Don't forget to bring me your Biomüll for my flowers!" Frau Gamperl called after us.

"What's Biomüll?" I asked Felix.

"Compost," he whispered to his book.

We followed Sara to a bench with a red-and-white sign on a pole that said, "Autobus Haltestelle." Felix sat down on the bench, but when I tried to do the same, Sara took my arm and marched me over to a little open-air shop on the side of the road. It said "Tabak" in big letters at the top. There was a man standing beside a row of newspapers. Behind him I could see a postcard display and a carton of cigarettes.

"Tabak?" I asked. "Is this a tobacco shop?" *Did my father leave me with a babysitter who smokes?* Secondhand smoke could kill. I had the statistics. In either Doomsday Journal #2 or #3.

Sara rolled her eyes. "No. You need a Monatskarte." She said something to the man in German, then pulled out a bill from the envelope and handed it to him. He handed her back a square of thin cardboard. "Danke," she said, then led me back to the bench where Felix was waiting.

Out of the envelope, Sara pulled a small square photograph. She rummaged in the green purse she carried, found a role of tape, and stuck the picture to the cardboard. Then she handed it to me.

I recognized the picture she had taped to the card. I had taken it with my dad at the airport, right before he had left for Vienna. Someone had cut it down, so it looked almost like a headshot of me, except I could still see part of Dad's arm in one corner. "What's this?" I asked.

"Bus ticket," said Sara. "For month July."

I studied it. At the top it said, *1. Juli bis 31. Juli, Monatskarte, 1993.*

Before I could ask how it worked, the bus pulled up. There was a group of people waiting, so we all scrambled to get in line.

When I trudged up the steps, I held out the card for the driver to see. He didn't even glance at me. "Excuse me, sir," I said, holding up my card.

A young man pushed past me, not even waiting to show his ticket.

The driver finally turned to look at me. "Ja?"

I held up my ticket. But he just gave me a funny look and waved me on.

Felix and Sara had already sat down.

"Why didn't he check my ticket?" I asked.

"Ehrensystem," Sara said.

I gave her a look.

"I don't know the English word," Sara admitted.

We both turned to look at Felix.

"Honor system," he whispered.

"What are you talking about?" I exclaimed. "You mean they just trust everyone to buy a ticket?"

Sara and Felix both nodded.

"Then why would anyone ever buy a ticket?"

"There are random ticket inspections," Felix whispered. "If they catch you without a ticket, there's a big fine."

"Schwarzfahren," Sara said.

"That's what we call riding without a ticket," Felix explained. "It's bad."

"You mean to tell me," I said, "the whole bus line works on the honor system?"

"No, of course not," Felix said. "The streetcars, subways, and local trains also run on the honor system."

I stared at them.

"America is different?" Sara asked.

"Yeah," I said. "Very different."

Felix put his nose back into his book, and I looked out the window. At my school, they didn't trust you to buy lunch without checking your ID; it didn't make sense that a whole city would trust its citizens to buy a bus ticket.

And yet the bus was very clean and seemed new. There were businessmen in suits and old women clutching baskets, actual wicker baskets, full of food. I stared out the window. This part of Vienna didn't really look like a city, more like the suburbs. Some of the houses were in new developments, like where my father lived, but others were crumbling, as if they were hundreds of years old. Which, I realized, maybe they were.

I was about to ask Sara when she stood up suddenly and pushed a button on a pole in the middle of the bus. A moment later the bus swerved to a stop, and she motioned for us to get off.

"Are we in the city already?" I asked as I walked down the bus steps.

"No," she said. "Time for breakfast."

CHAPTER 8

Aïda

T HE BUS HAD stopped outside an old building with a
bunch of different stores on its bottom level. There
was a Drogerie (which looked like a drugstore), a store
that seemed to sell only paper, and a café with the words
"Aïda—Café Konditorei" in pink neon over the front door.
Under each window was a basket of flowers, the blossoms
overflowing the sides, the red, yellow, and orange petals
spilling like crayons out of a box.

Sara caught me looking at the plants. "Pretty, no?" she
asked.

"Yeah," I agreed. Practically every house in Austria
seemed to have window boxes.

"My mama loves flowers," Sara said as Felix pushed
open the door and led us into the coffeeshop. There
were small tables everywhere, but every single one was
occupied.

"We'll have to go somewhere else," I said.

Sara gave me a funny look, marched over to an old lady with two needles and a ball of yarn, and said a few words in German. The woman nodded without smiling, and Sara gestured for us to sit down.

I elbowed Felix. "Do you know that lady?"

"No."

"Then why are we sitting with . . ."

Sara took my arm and pushed me down into a plastic chair. The knitting lady didn't glance at me. Before I could decide if I should say hello to her or not, a young woman in a pink uniform came over to take our order.

Sara started to rattle off what she wanted, then stopped. "Melange oder heiße Schokolade?" she asked.

Felix whispered, "Eine Melange, bitte."

I had been planning to order the hot chocolate, but since the nine-year-old wasn't ordering it, I said, "I'll have the same."

"Apfel- oder Topfenstrudel?" Sara asked.

"Topfen," said Felix.

"Apple," I said, since at least I knew what that was.

Once the waitress left, I whispered to Felix, "What did I order?"

"Coffee with milk."

"Oh, okay."

Felix opened his book as I glanced around. The place appeared to have been modeled on a 1950s diner, complete with checkerboard tiles on the floor, stainless steel, and pink plastic booths.

"I come right back," Sara said. She stood up, walked to the back of the store, and started talking to a woman behind the counter.

"What's she doing?" I asked. "Did she forget to order something?"

Felix shook his head. "That lady is also from Bosnia. Sara stops here once a week to see if she's heard anything about . . ."

Her family, I finished in my head. I didn't know what I would do without my mom. My heart started to beat faster. *No,* I thought. *I will* not *freak out on my very first day. Dad would be so disappointed.*

Sara came back to our table and sat down. Felix raised an eyebrow in question, but Sara just shook her head. I wanted to say something nice to her, but it took all my energy to force the air in and out of my lungs. So I stayed silent.

Finally, the waitress returned with our food. The coffee smelled delicious, with foamy milk swirls on the top. It was served in a real ceramic cup atop a saucer, on a silver tray with a tiny glass of water on the side. The waitress also put a square, flaky pastry sprinkled with powdered sugar down in front of me. "Oh, I didn't order this!" I said.

The waitress looked at me in surprise.

"Yes, you did," Felix whispered.

"No, I ordered an apple and . . ."

Felix jabbed me in the ribs, and I shut up.

"Alles in Ordnung," Sara said. The waitress gave me one last nasty look and walked away.

"It's an apple pastry," Felix said. He had a similar pastry in front of him. "Go on, try it."

I picked up my fork and sliced off a piece. A sweet-smelling apple pie filling oozed out. I cautiously took a bite.

"It's yummy!" I took another bite, then turned to Felix and asked, "What kind of pastry did you get?"

"Topfen," he said.

I made a face.

"Quark," he translated.

"Still don't know what that is."

He pointed to his plate. A cheesy filling oozed out of his pastry.

"Cream cheese?" I asked.

He shrugged. "You can try it." He cut me off a small piece, and I popped it in my mouth.

"Okay," I admitted. "That's good too."

We chewed in silence for a moment. I don't like silence. That's when my worries start to creep in. I had to figure out something safe to talk about. "So," I said, "why is this place called Aïda? Is that like the owner or something?"

Sara smiled. "No. *Aïda* is a Verdi opera."

"Never heard of it," I said.

"Very famous opera. Aïda is a beautiful captive princess

who falls in love with a handsome Egyptian commander, Radamès. Except the Egyptian princess, Amneris, is in love with Radamès too. But he not love her. He loves beautiful Aïda!"

"And they all die at the end," Felix added.

"So romantic," sighed Sara.

It sounded a bit like a plot last summer on *Love on the Evening Tide*, which was my mom's and my favorite soap opera. We only watched it in the summer. Remembering that made me tear up, so I stuffed another bit of apple strudel into my mouth.

"If you ask me," continued Felix, "there's nothing very romantic about getting sealed inside a temple and buried alive!"

It was exactly like *Love on the Evening Tide*! Aidy and Raymon had gotten locked in a crypt in New Orleans and . . . Wait a second. Were the TV writers opera fans?

"Their love lasts forever!" said Sara.

"Oh, please," said Felix.

"You're awfully cynical for a nine-year-old," I said.

Felix suddenly turned bright red.

"I'm not nine," he whispered.

"What?"

"I'm. Not. Nine!" He was speaking in a normal voice, which for Felix was almost like yelling. "I'm twelve, just like you. In fact, I'll be thirteen in three weeks, so I'm older than you. I'm just short, okay? You don't need to point it out. My dad got his growth spurt really late, so my doctor thinks I will too. Not that it's any of your business. Now please don't ever say another word about me being small!"

Felix drained his coffee and slammed the cup down on the table. It made the glass of water on the little silver tray jump. "I'll wait for you outside." He stood up and marched out the door.

I felt awful. Dad hadn't gotten his age wrong! I picked at the rest of my strudel, but it didn't taste as good anymore. Felix had been so helpful translating everything. He hadn't even laughed at my frog pajamas.

Sara patted my arm. "Not your fault," she said. "He is very sensitive. I made the same mistake."

I looked up at her. Some of her bright-red lipstick had rubbed off on her coffee cup, and she didn't look quite as grown-up. We finished our food, and Sara gestured to the waitress. When she came over to our table, Sara said, "Zahlen, bitte."

The waitress took out her pad of paper and waited expectantly.

"Ich hatte einen kleinen Braunen und einen Apfelstrudel," said Sara. "Der Junge hatte eine Melange und einen Topfenstrudel."

The waitress turned to look at me.

"Are you ordering more?" I asked. "I mean, it was tasty, but I'm kinda full."

"No," Sara said. "Tell her what you eat . . . ate."

"Why?"

Sara looked at me as if I were crazy. "So she knows what to charge!"

"But we already ordered!"

Sara rolled her eyes. "Sie hatte eine Melange und einen Apfelstrudel."

The waitress finished her calculating and put the bill on the table.

"You mean, you have to tell them what you ordered?" I asked.

"Yes," Sara said. "How else they know?"

"But what if you said you only ordered one coffee?"

"You lie?" Sara asked, her eyes wide.

"I wouldn't!" I protested. "But someone could! Wait, is this the honor-system thing again?"

Sara nodded. "Different in America?"

"Yeah," I said again. "A lot."

We went outside and found Felix waiting by the bus stop. "Hey," I said.

He wouldn't look at me, just kept his nose buried in his book. For the first time, I looked at the cover: *The Federalist Papers.*

Wait. I knew that book. We'd read excerpts in history class at school. It was the collection of essays that Hamilton and those other guys had written to encourage the states to ratify the constitution. "Why are you reading *that*?!" I blurted out.

Felix shrugged. "I like history. And when my mom started dating your dad, I figured I should learn more about your country."

That was actually . . . really nice. Except for that one old movie Dad had made me watch, I'd done nothing to learn about Austria. "Oh," I said. "That's cool."

Felix turned back to his book.

Suddenly, I remembered something Dr. Teresa had said. She'd told me I *shouldn't* think so much before I spoke. If I had something I wanted to say, I should say it. So I took a deep breath.

"Felix, I'm sorry. And I'm not just saying that—I'm *actually* sorry. I shouldn't have assumed you were nine. I should have asked. I mean . . . I know things can look one way but be another."

"It's okay," he said. "You're not the first one to make that mistake."

He nudged Sara.

"Hey," she said good-naturedly. "I apologized too."

And then they both smiled.

Before I could say anything else, the bus arrived to pick us up. Except it wasn't a bus this time. It was a streetcar.

CHAPTER 9

The Streetcar, the Cathedral, and the Royal Hamburger

THE STREETCAR, OR Straßenbahn (as Felix informed me it was called in German), looked like a skinny bus with rounded edges, white on the top, red on the bottom. It was connected to an electrical line overhead and ran on rails embedded in the street. On the top of the curved white roof was a round black-and-white sign with the number 38. Underneath that was the word "Schottentor."

The doors slid open, and I followed Felix and Sara up the stairs. Again, no one checked our tickets as we sat down. The seats were wooden, with two seats on one side of the aisle and single seats on the other. Felix and Sara took a double, and I took the single one across from them. The doors closed and we started off.

The streetcar moved faster than the bus, zooming along in its own lane, ringing a bell to warn cars to get out of its way. I didn't usually get nervous on public transportation, but the jerking and clanking made it seem like our compartment might break apart at any moment. At the end of the block, a car was stopped squarely across the streetcar tracks in the intersection. The driver rang the bell and proceeded full speed ahead. I gripped my seat, wondering what the safety statistics were on streetcars. The bell rang again, a car honked, and the driver slammed on the brakes so hard, I bumped into the seat in front of me.

The streetcar driver cursed in German and gestured at the car. He rang the bell again, and the car finally moved out of the intersection. I sighed with relief, even though no one else seemed to think we were in any danger. Felix read his book calmly. Sara stared out the window.

"Freud's house." She pointed when I caught her eye. "Museum."

"Sigmund Freud?" I asked, still clinging to my seat. "Founder of psychotherapy?"

"Yes," Sara said.

I could use some therapy after this ride! "Can we see his couch?" I asked.

A huge cathedral came into view then, with two tall, skinny towers that pointed like fangs into the sky. Between them was a massive stained-glass window shaped like a rose. And just as suddenly as it had appeared, it was gone, as the streetcar dipped underground as if it had turned into a subway. It made my stomach lurch. I swear, the

Straßenbahn was as bad as a roller coaster. Which, by the way, I do *not* enjoy.

"Where are we now?" I asked.

"Schottentor," Sara said. "Come. We go see Stephansdom. It is a very old, very big cathedral."

"I think I just saw it."

"That's the Votivkirche," said Felix. "It's barely a hundred years old. St. Stephen's has been functioning as a church since 1160."

Over eight hundred years?!

I followed the two of them off the Straßenbahn and up an escalator, where we jumped onto another streetcar, this one with a large number 1 on the top.

"Ringstraße," said Sara.

"What does that mean?" I asked.

"Literally, it's Ring Street," said Felix.

"Why?" I asked. "Are there lots of jewelry shops?"

Felix sighed, as if I were incredibly stupid. "You do know there used to be walls around cities in Europe, right?"

"Of course," I lied.

"Well, there used to be a wall in Vienna too, forming a ring around the city to defend its citizens against invaders. By the mid-1800s, the Austrian Empire was strong and powerful; they didn't need the wall anymore, so they tore it down and built a wide, majestic street around the inner city instead. Streetcar number one takes you around it, past all the buildings they constructed on the reclaimed land."

"What kind of buildings?" I asked.

Sara pointed out the window. "Universität. Where I study German. Next is Rathaus."

"Rat house?" I asked. "Like a zoo for rodents?"

Felix rolled his eyes. "*Rathaus* means *city hall*."

"Your local government meets in a *rat house*?"

"*Rat* means *advice* in German. The animal *rat* is *Ratte*."

"Oh," I said.

"*Rat* is a false cognate," Felix added.

"What's that?"

"A word that sounds the same but has a different meaning in another language."

"Oh." German sounded confusing.

"Like *Gift*," he said.

"Like a present?" I asked.

"Nope," said Felix. "In German it means *poison*."

Yup, it was definitely confusing. I was about to say so when I got a glimpse of the Rathaus. The building had five towers: a big one in the middle and two smaller ones on either side. There was a park in front of it, complete with food stands, as if there were a festival going on. And next to the building itself stood a giant movie screen.

"They show movies?" I asked. "Like a drive-in theater?"

"Opera movies," Sara explained.

Okay, this town was weird.

Next to the Rathaus was the parliament, a Greek-style building with a statue of Athena, the goddess of wisdom, standing guard out front. The streetcar kept moving, zipping along, but there was so much to look at that it was hard to feel scared.

"Museums," Sara said. "Natural history. Art history." She pointed to the other side of the street. "The Hofburg."

"What's that?" I asked.

"A castle," she said. "And Heldenplatz."

"Where Hitler gave his speech after marching into Vienna during the Anschluss," explained Felix.

I barely got a glimpse of Heldenplatz, only enough to see it was a vast, open space with a statue of a man on a rearing horse, before the streetcar moved on.

Finally, we reached a large building with a green roof, multiple archways, and two statues of winged horses on either side of the roof. "The opera," said Sara, and then she jumped up and pushed a button. The doors on the streetcar swung open. I hurried after her as she and Felix starting walking down a large street.

And when I say they were walking down the street, I mean they were *literally* walking down the middle of the street. I gave them a horrified look. "You're going to get hit by a car!"

"Kärntner Straße is a pedestrian zone," Felix explained.

It took me a moment to realize what he meant. The road

was made of cobblestones. There were fancy boutique-style shops on either side of us, lots of people, and a few delivery trucks, but no cars. I guessed it was safe and reluctantly stepped off the sidewalk.

We window-shopped as we walked. Palmers appeared to be a fancy underwear store, like Victoria's Secret on steroids. Embarrassed, I kept my eyes averted so I wouldn't accidentally glance at their mannequins. Next to that was a Swarovski shop with crystal vases and bowls in the window. I lingered by that one, gazing at a shelf of tiny crystal animals: sparkling elephants, lions, and giraffes. There were multiple cafés, their chairs and tables spilling out onto the cobblestones. A souvenir shop hawked Mozartkugeln, which seemed to be some sort of round candy wrapped in foil and plastered with Mozart's face.

"Unlike the ring," Felix told me, "Kärntner Straße has been a road for hundreds of years."

There was something about walking on the paving stones, where people had walked for generations, that felt . . . well, interesting at the very least.

"Where's this cathedral?" I asked. "I still don't see . . . Oh!"

A huge tower suddenly loomed over the sky, attached to a gigantic, bulky base. The roof of the church was covered with multicolored tiles, which made a zigzag pattern that looked like a bunch of Ws. I didn't have to be told this was Stephansdom. I could feel how old it was.

A deep rumbling started, and I jumped. Birds streamed

out of the clock tower, circling overhead. The bells were ringing, so loud and powerfully, I could feel the vibrations in my bones.

"Legend has it that Beethoven realized he was deaf when he saw the birds fly out of the clock tower, but he couldn't hear a thing." Felix's face was shining. He was clearly in his element. "The tower used to be the main lookout for the defense of the walled city. There's even an apartment for the watchman who used to ring the bells if he spotted a fire."

"Really?" I asked.

"Well, most of the bells are automatic now. The largest was originally cast from cannons captured from Turkish invaders in 1711. But there was a fire in 1945 at the end of the war, causing it to crash to the ground. It was recast using some of the original metal. They only ring that one on New Year's Day."

"Wow." I wondered what it sounded like. Deep and rich or high and shrill or—

"The smaller bells have names from their old uses. *Feuerin* means *fire alarm*. *Kantnerin* called the cantors or musicians to Mass. *Bierringerin* . . ."

"There's a bell called Beer Ringer?" I asked.

"Yeah." Felix shrugged. "It was to tell the men drinking at nearby taverns that it was time to go home. Come on! You have to see the Christ with a toothache statue." Felix led us around a corner and stopped in front of a statue of

Jesus. "People pray in front of this statue when they have dental problems."

"Very funny," I said.

"Is true!" Sara insisted.

I studied the statue. Jesus had his hands folded, one over the other. His head was tilted to one side, his mouth half-open, his cheeks swollen and his eyelids heavy.

"When the statue was put up, people thought Jesus's expression made him look like he had a cavity," Felix explained.

It *did* look like Jesus had a toothache.

"And come over here," Felix urged. He led us to the front entrance and pointed to the wall just to the right of the door. "This is my favorite thing about the church." There was nothing to see except for a letter and a number carved into the stone.

"O5?" I asked. "What does that mean?"

"It was the symbol of the Austrian resistance during World War II," Felix explained. "Not *all* Austrians were Nazis, and some were outraged when Hitler marched into Vienna. In German, Austria is Österreich. The first letter is Ö, which is an *O* with two little dots over it."

"Called umlaut," Sara said.

"Ö can also be written *OE*," Felix continued. "And *E* is the fifth letter of the alphabet, so *O5* stands for Austria."

"Cool," I said. "How do you know all this stuff?"

"I like to read about Austrian history too."

We finally went inside the grand entryway. It was cool inside the church, as if we were entering a cave. I was already overwhelmed by so many new things. Everything seemed so ancient. Even the *bell* was older than the United States. I sat down in a pew, my head spinning.

The *O5* reminded me that fifty years ago there had been Nazis in Vienna. My grandparents on my dad's side were Jewish, but they had emigrated from Poland in the 1920s, before the war. *What if they hadn't left then? Would they have been sent to a concentration camp? Would they have been killed? What might have happened to Sara if she hadn't left Bosnia?*

It suddenly felt even colder, and I shivered. I was glad when Sara said it was time to go.

"You okay?" she asked as we walked out into the bright sunlight.

"Yeah." It felt too complicated to explain my thoughts. "I think I just need to eat something."

"Okay," Sara said, pulling out the envelope from my father. "Where?"

I looked around. There were so many bustling cafés. My throat got tight. Every place had a menu I couldn't read. Food I wouldn't recognize. Customs I didn't understand. And she wanted me to choose!

Then I saw it. A little piece of home. A golden *M*. "McDonald's!"

"McDonald's?" asked Felix.

"Yeah." I was as surprised as he was. I didn't even *like* McDonald's very much. But my mom and I had eaten there at the airport and . . . "I know it's not very fancy, but I just need something familiar."

"No, no," said Felix. "I'm excited. 'Cause my mother never lets me go!"

We pushed open the door to McDonald's, and I immediately felt more at home. The booths were red-and-yellow plastic; the air smelled of fries and grease. It took me a minute to realize a Quarter Pounder was called a Hamburger Royal in Austria. Even the burgers were fancy here!

Sara doled out the money from my father's envelope, and we sat down at a table with our food. Felix pulled out his book, and I finally started to relax. Sure, we had to pay for ketchup, and my Coke was only eight ounces with no ice. But the burger tasted exactly the same as the ones at home. There were even enough seats, so we didn't have to share a table with some stranger.

Except there was a guy at another table who kept glancing over at us. He looked about Sara's age, with a short scruffy beard and dark hair, gelled as if he were auditioning for a boy band. He wore jeans and a soccer jersey. "Sara," I asked, poking her with my elbow. "Do you know that guy?"

She turned to look, and the guy immediately grinned. "Hallo, Sara!" he called out.

Sara waved back and blushed. "Yes," she whispered as

he walked over to us. Felix peered suspiciously over the top of his book.

"Ich habe die grüne Haare gesehen," he said happily. "Wie geht's?"

"Gut," Sara answered. "Can we speak English, please? Becca not speak German."

"Sure," he said. "You're au pair, right?" he asked Sara.

"Yes. This is Becca. She arrived yesterday. This is Felix. This is my friend Marco. We take German lessons together."

He slid into the booth next to Sara. "Nice to meet you," he said. "Where you from?"

"United States," I said.

"Ooh!" he said. "I learn English watching *Fresh Prince of Bel-Air*."

I laughed. "Where are you from?"

"Firenze."

I looked at Felix. "Florence," he translated. "It's a city in Italy."

"My parents came to Austria five years ago to open a gelato shop," Marco explained.

"What's gelato?" I asked.

"Italian ice cream," Marco said. "Best in the world."

"Mmm," I said. "I love ice cream."

"Me too," Marco agreed. "Until I start working in an ice cream shop."

We all laughed.

"So." He turned to Sara. "In class you say you like to dance, right?"

"Yes, in Sarajevo I took ballroom lessons."

Marco pulled a postcard out of his pocket. "I dance too. My neighbor owns a dance studio. She's Hungarian." He handed Sara the postcard. "I help with teen ballroom class. We need a new female assistant."

"Ich soll unterrichten?" Sara asked. I guess she was so surprised she lapsed into German.

"You be great teacher," Marco coaxed. "No pay, but you get free dance lessons. And I take you out for ice cream."

Sara smiled. "Sounds fun."

"Great." He glanced at his watch. "Lunch break is over. I must go back to my father's shop. Serve more ice cream to tourists. I call you to work out details."

Sara nodded.

"Ciao!" he said as he walked off.

"He's kind of cute," I said once he had gone out the door.

Sara blushed. She tucked the postcard into her purse.

Oh yeah. She liked him.

"I'd like to learn to ballroom dance," I teased.

"I would not," said Felix.

"But this class comes with free ice cream!" I pointed out.

They both laughed.

I was done eating by then, but when I looked around

for a trash can, I couldn't find one. "Where do I put my trash?" I asked.

"Leave on table," said Sara.

"That's rude," I said. "And it makes more work for the cleaning crew."

Felix closed his book. "You can't throw away your own trash."

"Why not?" I asked.

"You might recycle it wrong!"

"So . . . in Austria they trust people to pay for a bus ticket but not to throw away their own trash correctly?"

Felix and Sara nodded.

This was clearly an odd country.

After lunch, Sara asked if I wanted to go to the Prater. I shrugged and said okay. But I should have followed my rule about visiting new places (DJ #3, p. 12), which is to always ask lots of questions. Because the Prater wasn't another church or museum or historic building. Oh no! It turned out to be something truly horrible and terrifying.

The Prater was an amusement park.

CHAPTER 10

The Riesenrad

I AM *NOT* A fan of amusement parks, not even the pretty, heavily regulated ones like Disney World. Which this wasn't. No, this reminded me of one of those traveling carnivals, with old rides that looked like they had not been inspected in about one hundred years. There was a rickety roller coaster and a decrepit merry-go-round with peeling painted horses and lots of carnival games with cheap prizes like giant stuffed tigers and neon-pink hats. And towering over everything was an enormous Ferris wheel.

"No," I said, stopping outside the entrance. "I don't want to go."

Sara looked confused. "I pay," she coaxed. "Money from father."

I shook my head.

"Come on," Felix urged. "We're already here! Let's at least go on a roller coaster."

I shook my head again. Maybe they had a death wish, but I didn't. Do you know how many fatalities and/or maimings can be attributed to subpar safety inspections of traveling carnival equipment? Well, I do. At least, I did. It was written down at home in Doomsday Journal #2. And I wasn't going to risk my life for a few thrills on some stupid roller coaster that looked like a fake rocket ship.

"No, thank you," I said. "I don't like roller coasters."

Sara looked confused. "You said . . ."

"Look, I didn't know what the Prater was," I explained. "I thought it was a museum or an old bridge or something."

"Ach du meine Güte!" exclaimed Felix. "We're here, I'm going on some rides. If you don't want to come, you can just wait for me."

He stormed off. Sara looked at me for a long moment, not saying anything. Finally, I shrugged and trudged after him. Sara and I waited on a bench as Felix went into the fun house, with its mirrors and dead ends. But I saw her looking longingly at the rocket-ship roller coaster. "Do you like roller coasters?" I asked.

"Yes. And my little brother loves them."

"What's his name again?" I asked.

"Eldin," she said. "He's six."

Six. And he was already braver than me. I sighed.

Felix came out then. "All right!" he said. "The rocket ship is next. Who's coming?"

"Sara," I said.

"No, no," she protested.

"It's okay," I said. "I'll just sit here and wait for you."

Felix grabbed her hand. "Come on."

"No," Sara said seriously. "Becca's father said she gets nervous sometimes. I not leave her alone."

I was suddenly furiously, irrationally angry. Of course my father would have told Sara about my anxiety, but I wasn't a baby.

"My dad exaggerates sometimes," I said, my heart pounding. "I can sit on a bench by myself for five minutes."

Sara still looked doubtful. "You sure, Becca?"

"Go!" I ordered. "Enjoy it for your little brother."

"Okay," she said. "We come right back."

I waved, they ran off, and as soon as they were gone, I thought, *Oh my goodness, what have I done?* I was alone. In a strange country where I didn't speak the language. This was why Dad had gotten me a nanny in the first place! *What if something happens? What if I get sick? What if I get kidnapped?!*

I tried to take a deep breath. I'd looked up the safety statistics on Austria when Dad had first moved here. It had one of the lowest homicide rates in the world! *So why am I so worried about sitting on a bench by myself?* Other people did normal things, like riding a bike or going waterskiing. Lots of kids flew on planes without their mother. Some even went on roller coasters. Felix might look young, but I was the one acting like a little kid.

Glumly, I watched the rocket-ship roller coaster dip and turn in front of the towering Ferris wheel. Like the streetcars (and the Austrian flag), the Ferris wheel was red and white. It didn't have open-air seating; instead, each of the compartments was the size of a passenger van. And something about it looked familiar. I couldn't help staring and wondering, *What's the view like at the top? What would it feel like to go up in the air? To go around and around and around?*

I looked over at the booth selling Ferris wheel tickets and noticed a movie poster: *The Third Man*. I knew that movie! It was the one Dad had made me watch a couple of days after our pancake brunch. The one that was set in Vienna and starred Orson Welles. In the film, there was a big scene on a Ferris wheel. This Ferris wheel!

I wanted to prove that I wasn't a scaredy-cat—to Sara and Felix, to my dad, and most of all, to myself. So when Felix and Sara returned smiling from the roller coaster, I forced myself to stand up and say, "Hey, why don't we go on the Ferris wheel?"

They both stopped short. "The Riesenrad?" Sara asked.

"What's that?"

"The name of the Ferris wheel," said Felix. "It literally means *giant wheel*."

My heart started to beat like crazy. My hands were clammy, but I forced them into fists and said, "Cool. Let's go."

Sara looked doubtful. "You said you scared of roller coasters."

"Yeah," I agreed. "But the Riesenrad isn't a roller coaster. I've been watching it. It moves nice and slow."

"But your father said . . ."

"My dad wants me to try new things," I argued. My voice only shook a little. "It's why I came to Vienna."

"Okay, okay," Sara said. "We go buy tickets."

I was fine—excited even—as we stood in line to buy our tickets. It wasn't until we took our place in the line to get into one of the cars that it started to feel like the metal detector at the airport.

I tried to take deep breaths like Dr. Teresa had taught me. I drummed on the railing, tapping my fingers to a chant in my head: *It's perfectly safe. It's perfectly safe.*

Sara looked at me. "You okay, Becca?" she asked.

This was my chance to be brave. "Yeah," I said.

Sara didn't look like she believed me, but she didn't say anything. There were seven of us waiting in line: Felix, Sara, and me; a mother with a toddler sleeping in a stroller; and two teenagers, a boy and a girl about Sara's age, who kept their hands in each other's back pockets. The attendant opened the door to one of the compartments, and the previous riders got off. It was almost our turn to board.

That's when I noticed the sign that stated the Riesenrad had been built in 1897. Which meant it was nearly a hundred years old. One hundred years old! Plenty of time for parts to wear out. Or rust. Or . . . My neck started to sweat. I breathed even faster.

I forced myself to think about something else. I caught sight of *The Third Man* poster again. Which made me think of the part of the movie where Orson Welles (who plays the bad guy in the film) is up on the Ferris wheel and talking about how the people below look like dots and how no one would care if they stopped moving. But my parents would care if our car detached and fell to the ground. I would care. There'd be a funeral and . . . and . . . they probably wouldn't be able to have an open casket because my body would be so mangled and . . .

That was when I realized I had made a horrible mistake. My heart was racing; I felt like I was going to throw up. My hands felt numb, my fingers tingling as if I had been sitting on them and they had fallen asleep. My chest hurt, and I gasped for breath.

I heard one of the teenagers ask "Was ist los mit ihr?" and even though I couldn't understand the words, I knew he was talking about me.

Sara put her hand on my shoulder. "No worries," she said. "Just loading passengers."

"I feel sick," I managed to choke out, jerking away from Sara and running to the bathroom.

I made it into a stall before I burst into tears. I was shaking, hot one second and cold the next; I dry heaved a couple of times but didn't throw up. I was exhausted and embarrassed, but mainly, I was disappointed. I had actually wanted to go on the Riesenrad. I'd wanted to see the view. I'd wanted to prove I could be brave. And I had failed. I sobbed and sobbed, leaning against the side of the stall.

And then, as if that weren't bad enough, someone knocked on the stall door.

"It's occupied," I called out, confused. It was a big bathroom; there were plenty of empty stalls.

"Ist alles in Ordnung?" I heard a strange woman ask. "Kann ich irgendwie helfen?"

I peeked through the stall doors and saw an older woman with gray hair wearing a white apron and clutching a roll of paper towels. Another woman was at the sink, washing her hands. When she finished, the gray-haired woman handed her a paper towel, and the other woman placed a coin into an ashtray on the counter.

She was a bathroom attendant! My dad had warned me about this. Some bathrooms in Austria weren't free—you had to pay to use them. And I didn't have any money!

My panic, which had almost started to subside, soared again. Even bathrooms in Austria weren't safe! I waited until the gray-haired woman was busy giving another girl a paper towel, and then I burst out of the stall. I tore out of the park, past the fun house and the roller coaster, running without purpose or direction, just trying to get away.

Finally, the stitch in my side got too strong, and I collapsed onto a bench. I sobbed in relief. Great big hysterical sobs. The kind that felt like they would never stop.

"Becca?" I heard a voice ask.

I looked up. Sara waited on the sidewalk, a good ten feet away. Felix hovered behind her.

"Go away," I muttered.

I was so utterly embarrassed. Except for Mom and Dad, no one had ever seen me like this, not even my best friend, Chrissy.

But Sara didn't go away. Instead, she approached slowly, as if I were a wild animal that might bolt. Sara sat down on one side of the bench; Felix perched on the other end and pulled out his book. I was grateful that he was at least going to pretend he wasn't listening.

I tensed and waited for the lecture. *It's okay. You're safe. Don't cry.* But it didn't come. Sara just sat there. Felix read on. A couple of kids walked by, but they didn't even glance at me. It was hot, and a nearby trash can smelled bad. Eventually, I gave one last little gasp/hiccup and stopped crying.

Still nothing.

"I'm sorry," I said when I couldn't stand the silence anymore.

Sara shrugged. "Worse things have happened."

"It's embarrassing."

"Why?" Sara asked. "Your father warned me you might get nervous."

"But you bought the tickets, and we didn't even get to go!" My father would be upset about that too. It was just like when I'd wanted to see *Les Mis* on my birthday.

"You tried be brave," Sara said. "That's worth a little money."

"But I failed."

Sara shrugged again. "Maybe next time you won't."

Felix sat still as a statue.

"I wanted to see the view," I admitted. "My dad and I watched the movie . . ."

"*The Third Man*," Felix finished, whispering to the pages in his book.

"You've seen it too?"

Felix nodded. "My father likes old American movies. Sometimes he takes me to the English-language theater. It has all the movies in their original language with German subtitles. Most movies here are dubbed into German. Subtitles are so much better."

"Why?" I asked.

Felix gave me a look. "Sara made me go see *The Body-guard* at a regular theater. Imagine Whitney Houston and Kevin Costner speaking in German!"

I snorted.

"And then, as if that wasn't awkward enough, Whitney's

character randomly starts singing in *English*. Because they don't bother to dub the songs."

"Beautiful movie," Sara put in. "So romantic!"

"It's awful," Felix insisted. "But good for a laugh."

I gave a weak smile. "Where does your dad live?"

"He's an actor, so he moves around a lot," Felix said.

"Cool," I said. "What's he been in?"

"Nothing you'd know," Felix said. "I think he's in Graz right now."

"When do you see him?" I asked. "I mean, what's your custody schedule? Week on, week off? Or weekends? Or do you . . ."

Felix stared at the Ferris wheel. "He sees me when he can."

"Oh," I said.

"He's not like *your* dad," he added, so quietly I almost couldn't hear.

"Oh," I said again.

Felix shrugged. "I'm sorry I pressured you to go on the rides. Mama told me you sometimes get anxious, but I thought she was just . . ."

"It's okay." I was still embarrassed, but I was also thinking about what he had said about his father. My dad had moved to Vienna, but he had never once missed our Sunday phone call. *What would it feel like not to be exactly sure where your father lived? And what did Sara mean when she said worse things have happened?*

It was such a pretty day. It must have been an amazing view from the top of the Riesenrad. I felt another pang of regret deep in my stomach, but I didn't think I was going to throw up anymore.

"We leave now?" Sara asked.

"Sure," I said.

We stood up and walked back to the subway. I was quiet as we took it partway across town and then switched back to streetcar 38. I felt sick again as the jerky motion of the streetcar rocked me back and forth. It was crowded, and I had to stand, holding on to an orange strap hanging from the ceiling. It was too high for me and made my arm ache. Every time I lost my balance, the woman standing next to me glared. "Aufpassen!" she yelled.

I would have done what she wanted, but I didn't understand.

Then Sara ushered us off the streetcar and onto the bus. "You okay?" Sara asked.

"Yes," I said. Parts of the day had been really fun, but now I just felt like I was a wet towel and someone had tried to squeeze all the water out of me. I couldn't wait to get home, eat a nice quiet dinner with my father, and watch some TV. Dad said he sometimes watched *Full House* dubbed into German to practice his language skills. I wanted to see that.

My feet ached as we walked up Dad's front steps. It was after five, and I pictured my father sitting on the couch, reading a book. Maybe we'd have grilled cheese sandwiches and tomato soup for dinner. That was what Dad always cooked for me when I was feeling down. I could almost taste the melted cheese in my mouth as I put the key in the lock.

But as I opened the door, it wasn't the smell of toasted bread that wafted out. Instead, it smelled like meat and spices. And on the stereo, blasting at full volume, was an opera.

CHAPTER 11

Sitting with Fear

M Y DAD WAS in the kitchen with Katarina, both of them wearing matching aprons. My father, who only cooked grilled cheese and frozen pizza at home, was chopping an onion with a knife that looked big enough to decapitate Bambi. Katarina was stirring something thick and meaty in a big pot on the stove. A new song started on the CD player, and they sang together, *"La donna è mobile qual piuma al vento!"* They looked like something out of a pasta ad.

I wasn't sure if I wanted to laugh or cry. I was so exhausted, I just stood there for a moment, staring. The music was loud, and they hadn't heard us come in. Finally, Dad turned and noticed me standing there. "Oh, Becca!" he called. "Good! You're home."

"Schatzi!" Katarina ran over and tried to give me a big hug. I jerked away.

I saw her flinch and felt a little bad. I didn't want to hurt her feelings, but . . . "What's going on?" I sounded angrier than I meant to, but I just wanted to flop down on the couch.

Dad didn't notice. "Katarina and I are cooking dinner to celebrate your first full day in Austria. We're making goulash!"

I could see my dreams of *Full House* and grilled cheese going up in smoke as surely as if someone had tossed a cast-iron frying pan into the TV. So while Felix said "Yum" and Sara licked her lips, I stormed up the stairs to my room.

Okay, so maybe it wasn't my finest hour.

I threw myself down onto my bed, not sure if I was angry or sad. I wanted to talk to my mom, but when I stood up to get the phone, I remembered I was in Austria. And unlike at my Virginia home, here I didn't have a phone line in my room. (Dad had given me some long explanation about a statewide monopoly and the expense of phone lines and blah blah blah.) There was only one phone in the house—and it was in the kitchen.

I burst out crying again.

There was a knock on my door.

"Go away," I cried.

"Becca," I heard Dad ask, "what's going on?"

"Nothing," I blubbered.

"Sara said there was an . . . incident at the Prater today and . . ."

"I don't want to talk about it."

"Okay." He paused. "Could you please come downstairs? Dinner is almost ready."

"No."

"Rebecca, we have guests."

"I don't care."

"Young lady, I do not . . ."

"Just leave me alone!"

I could hear him lurking outside the door, standing on a squeaky floorboard and shifting his weight from one foot to the other. "Fine," he said finally.

I listened to him walk back down the stairs. "I don't understand," he said, loud enough for me to hear. "She was doing so much better."

My heart sank. He *was* frustrated with me. But I *had* been doing better. Until he'd gone and moved to Austria! I was picking up my Doomsday Journal when there was another knock at the door.

It was Katarina. "Becca," she cooed, "are you feeling okay?"

I didn't bother to answer.

"I bet you're tired from a long day of sightseeing. I've got some tomato and mozzarella on the table for you to eat while the goulash is finishing up."

"I'm not hungry," I lied. I was starving. McDonald's seemed like a long, long time ago in a galaxy far, far away.

"All right." Through the door I could hear her start to leave, then pause. "Do you not like Verdi? I could put on some Mozart."

"Just go away!" I snapped.

She did.

They left me alone for about twenty minutes. I sat at the small desk, writing down all the horrible things that had happened that day. There were some good things too—like the Apfelstrudel and toothache Jesus and even McDonald's—but I didn't know where to put those. It was a Doomsday Journal, not a Rainbows and Butterflies Journal. I was mulling it over when there was another knock at my door. "I don't want to talk!"

But this time the door opened, and Sara walked in. I was too surprised to protest when she sat down on my bed. "Good," she said. "Because I want you to listen to my story."

Okay, so that was *not* what I'd expected. I studied her for a moment. Her green-streaked hair was limp from the heat. She had washed her face, and without the eyeliner and lipstick, she looked much younger. But she didn't look pitying, like Katarina and Dad had sounded. She looked serious, and suddenly I was curious.

"I grew up in Sarajevo," she started. "You know where that is?"

"In Bosnia. It used to be part of Yugoslavia."

"Yes, Sarajevo is a beautiful city. There is a river that runs through the middle—the Miljacka. We can see the bridge across the river from our apartment. In summer, I like to sit on the riverbank with my friends. In the evening, Mama buys us ice cream, and the three of us walk across the bridge."

"What about your father?" I asked.

"He died in a car accident when Eldin was a baby. It was very sad, but still . . . we were happy. Mama was math teacher at the elementary school. She loves flowers so much our whole apartment was full of them. I like music and dancing, and I planned to be a language teacher like my father. Everyone said I had his gift.

"Sarajevo was a very diverse and exciting place. The city was mainly Muslim, but Serbs and Croats lived there too. They were Orthodox Christians or Roman Catholic, but for years, it did not matter. We all went to the same school and lived in the same apartment buildings and ate the same ice cream."

"Wasn't Yugoslavia a communist country?" I asked.

"Yes, it became communist after World War II."

"I thought communism didn't allow religion."

Sara shrugged. "We had no official religion. But everyone knew their own religion and celebrated with family and friends. Catholic kids get Christmas presents in December, Serbs in January, and we have Ramadan. The dates change every year, but our neighbors always came over to eat Eid cake."

"So what happened?" I asked.

"How to explain?" She sighed. "There were lots of boring referendums and talk of independent states. The leader of Serbian Republic—Slobodan Milošević—wanted get rid of Muslims and Catholics in other republics. Wanted to have a 'pure' Yugoslavia. I thought that was nonsense, just politicians talking. It had nothing to do with me.

"Until my violin teacher sent Mama a note saying she would not give me lessons anymore. Because she was a good Serb and we are Muslim. Then my dance partner not show up at the studio the next week. At least he stopped by our apartment to say it not personal. They were Croats and had nothing against Muslims, but his father did not want to upset his neighbors, so he not allowed to associate with me anymore."

"That's awful!"

Sara nodded. "Snipers moved into the hills around the city. There was no more swimming or ice cream or even school. We had to close all the blinds in our apartment so snipers not target us. Sometimes we ate dinner in the bathroom. It was the only room with no windows, which made it the safest. But without sunlight, all of Mama's flowers died.

"And then the shelling started. I remember the first night bombs fell. We went down to the cellar. I not sleep at all."

I thought about Sara and her mother and brother trying to sleep in a cellar with bombs falling overhead. And I had gotten terrified about going on a Ferris wheel? "I'm sorry," I said. "That sounds awful. You must think I'm an idiot for freaking out about a ride!"

"No." Sara looked surprised. "That not point of story. I only try to tell you, I understand fear. I cry all that first night. I not brave at all. So you not need to be embarrassed."

"But you were actually in danger!" I said. "You had a reason to feel afraid."

"Fear is strange. I think sometimes our bodies get confused. Scared is good if you can do something. If you can leave. It is why I got on the bus and left Sarajevo. But when I was stuck there in the cellar, fear did no good. I learned if you sit with fear long enough, it goes away."

"I don't understand."

"My first night in bomb shelter, I not sleep at all. Third night, I sleep one hour. And by sixth, I take blanket and curl up to sleep. I learn to deal with fear. And you will too."

I shook my head.

"You will," she insisted. "But now, time for dinner."

I wasn't sure that she was right about me learning to sit with fear, but I was hungry. So when she stood up and left my room, I followed her.

CHAPTER 12

Käfer

Felix and Dad were already seated at the table when Sara and I came down the stairs. Katarina was serving big ladlefuls of a thick reddish stew into bowls. "Oh, hello, Schatzi," she said brightly to me, as if my freak-out had never happened.

Dad looked a bit warier but patted my arm kindly. "You feeling better?" he asked.

"Yeah," I said awkwardly. "Sorry. I was just tired."

I sat down. No one spoke. Sara passed me a round roll. I noticed how she tore the bread and then dipped a piece into the stew. I did the same.

Okay, I gotta admit, it was delicious. The beef was tender, and the sauce was a rich tomatoey gravy. I took another bite. "It's really good."

The tension in the room relaxed a bit. I was about to take another bite when Felix started screaming.

"Käfer!"

I didn't know what that meant.

But he said it again. "Käfer!" And with such intensity, I started to get concerned.

"In der Suppe!" he screamed. He pointed at his bowl of goulash.

Whatever it was, it seemed bad. I looked down at my bowl. There was meat and the tomato sauce. Onions. Tiny black sesame seeds. It tasted good. One of my favorite things I'd eaten since arriving in . . . Wait a second.

The sesame seeds were moving.

I looked closer. Maybe I had just hit them with my spoon. Nope. Definitely moving. I had a sinking feeling. Maybe they weren't toasted sesame seeds. Maybe they were . . .

"Bugs!" Dad exclaimed and jumped up from his chair so fast, he knocked his water glass over.

Everything seemed to happen at once then. Dad ran for a towel to mop up the water. Katarina started crying. Felix kept yelling, "Käfer! Käfer!" I stared at my bowl. There were hundreds of little black beetles swimming happily around. And I had just eaten this. There wasn't even a page in my Doomsday Journal for something this gross.

Then Sara started laughing. Big belly laughs. Gasping so hard, she could barely breathe. "So funny!" She choked. "Katarina added more and more paprika."

Dad guffawed as he mopped up the water. "Yeah. She kept saying, 'It's not red enough.'"

Katarina continued to sob.

Felix poked at his bowl with a sour expression on his face. "Did anyone look at the jar?"

"No!" Dad was laughing now. "We just kept adding more."

Katarina looked absolutely stricken. "I just wanted a nice traditional meal for Rebecca! Oh Gott, everything goes wrong for me." Her mascara ran down her face. Dad went over and put an arm around her shoulders.

"There, there, sweetie," Dad said calmly. "It was just an accident. We know you didn't mean to . . ."

"Serve us bugs?" Felix added.

Then he began to laugh too.

I wasn't sure what to do. Then I remembered I actually *did* have a page in Doomsday Journal #1 about eating bugs. "My friend Chrissy and I once found a study that said people accidentally eat a lot of bugs each year."

Katarina stopped crying. "Really?" she asked.

I nodded. "Like two pounds or something."

"Gross!" said Felix.

"Yeah," I agreed. "But it's not dangerous."

Dad smiled at me. "Good to know."

Sara walked into the kitchen and came back with the jar of paprika. She held it up, tried to say something, and burst into laughter. Felix grabbed the jar from her and shook it.

Even from across the table, I could see all the insects crawling around inside. I started laughing then, so hard I was clutching my stomach and tears were streaming from my eyes.

Finally, Katarina started to giggle too. We threw the jar from person to person so we could all inspect the uninvited guests at our dinner.

"Oh no," Katarina sighed when she finally got control of herself again. "We'll have to throw it all out."

"You know what?" I admitted. "I really felt like grilled cheese anyway."

"What is grilled cheese?" asked Sara.

"Gegrillter Käsetoast," translated Felix.

"Oh yeah," said Dad. "I make a mean grilled cheese."

Katarina looked in the fridge. "We have raclette and emmentaler. But no toast bread."

Felix jumped up. "I'll go to the store."

"Becca and I clean up," said Sara.

"Okay," I said.

"You rest," Dad said to Katarina.

We all got to work. Sara helped me scrape all the meat from the bowls into the small trash can in the kitchen. "It's a shame," I said, pouring the rest of the meat from the pot into the trash. "The goulash really tasted good."

"We'll make it again sometime," Dad said.

Sara made Katarina a cup of tea, and they sat on the

couch, chatting, while Dad and I worked in the kitchen, cutting more tomatoes for the sandwiches, frying up a bit of bacon. It felt nice to work next to my dad, side by side.

"You know," Dad said as he removed the bacon from the pan. "I was thinking."

"About what?" I asked.

"About how I was pretty tired when I first arrived here. All the new stuff. New foods and language." He paused. "Maybe it wasn't the best idea to go along with Katarina's plan for a big dinner on your first night here. Maybe I should have told her no. Maybe you would rather have had a quiet dinner with your dad."

My eyes teared up again.

"Yeah," I whispered.

"What do you say we do that tomorrow night? We'll have spaghetti with sauce from a jar. Or peanut-butter-and-jelly sandwiches!"

"Peanut butter and jelly," I said.

"The jam here is scrumptious."

"Thanks." I concentrated carefully on the tomato I was slicing, but it still made my eyes water as if it were an onion.

Dad put his arm around me and gave me a little hug. "I'm looking forward to it."

"Me too."

Felix came back with the "toast bread," which turned out to be a regular loaf of sliced bread. Dad heated up a big frying pan and made the best grilled cheese sandwiches

I'd ever had, with tomatoes and bacon and strange cheeses that tasted so much better than the fake orange American stuff.

When Katarina and Felix and Sara finally went home, Dad and I did the dishes together. I couldn't help thinking about *The Sound of Music* and that awful first dinner Maria has with the kids, when they put a pine cone on her seat. Everyone ends up crying in that scene. But it works out okay for them in the end. Maybe it would for me too.

CHAPTER 13

Produce, Pizza, and Peppermint

OVER THE NEXT few weeks, we fell into a routine. In the mornings, Felix and I would run errands or go sightseeing with Sara; we'd spend afternoons reading or playing board games. (Dr. Teresa firmly believed that being tired increased anxiety, and I'd overheard Dad telling Sara to build in more downtime so I wouldn't get quite so exhausted.) In the evenings, Dad and I would alternate between eating dinner with just each other and having a bigger meal with Felix, Katarina, and Sara.

Mom and I chatted about twice each week. It was hard to get in touch with her at the youth hostels ("which aren't only open to *youth*," Mom told me on the phone, "although I've been told I look much younger than forty-five"), but she sounded so excited. She'd danced around the fountain at Mirabell Gardens while singing "Do-Re-Mi" and jumped from bench to bench while humming "Sixteen Going on

Seventeen" at Schloss Hellbrunn. The connection wasn't always the greatest—and Mom needed to feed money into the pay phone to connect to the local country number. You had to pay for *local* calls by the minute too. But it was nice to hear her voice, even if just for a little while.

Dad and I did get to have those peanut-butter sandwiches. He went a little overboard, buying three kinds of bread: "toast bread," Semmeln (traditional Austrian round rolls), and a small dark loaf so thick and nutty, I could practically taste all the fiber. He also got three types of jam: apricot, raspberry, and blueberry. We had our own taste test, mixing and matching all the flavors. We used up a whole jar of peanut butter, not because we ate so much, but because the jars were so incredibly small.

But that wasn't a problem, because people in Austria seemed to go grocery shopping every single day. If you felt like eating a peach, you just went to the store and picked one up. It was sure to be juicy, sweet, and ready to eat—no need to let it sit for a few days and ripen on the counter. You had to bring your own bag with you—or pay money for a reusable one. They didn't pack your bags for you either, so Sara liked having me and Felix along to do that for her.

No one smiled either, not at the grocery store or at any other shop. "Why would they smile?" Sara asked. "Their job is to sell you stuff," Felix pointed out, "not to pretend to be your friend." Only Dad understood. "I know!" he exclaimed. "I spent the first month thinking I had accidentally done something to offend everyone. They all seemed so grumpy! But it's just a different custom. No one has the expectation that someone working in retail will be friendly and cheerful. It's actually kind of nice once you get used to it. I mean, sometimes I just want to buy a liter of milk without engaging in small talk."

Speaking of milk, that was odd too. It came in brown glass bottles, which you returned to the store once you were done with them. The milk was so thick that the first time Dad poured me a glass, I thought he had accidentally given me cream. Sara gamely helped me search for skim or 2 percent, but the only reduced-fat milk we could find came in boxes, didn't need to be refrigerated, and tasted awful. Katarina found it amusing that I still drank milk— "It's only for little children!" I tried to explain that everyone drank milk at home, even Dad sometimes, but I don't think she believed me.

About two weeks into my trip, Dad had a special event at work. There was a conference with a dinner and a party after, and he said, "I'm afraid I won't be home until really, really late." It was decided that I would spend the evening at Katarina's, and then Sara would come home with me and sleep on our couch.

Katarina took Sara, Felix, and me out for pizza at an Italian place nearby. It was a warm evening, but we sat outside because there was so much smoke in the restaurant—

and it wasn't air-conditioned anyway. But it wasn't too bad under the trees. We ordered large bottles of sparkling water, and it was almost as refreshing as soda. The pizza was paper thin, and instead of sharing one, like we always did at home, we each ordered our own. I asked for pepperoni and was disappointed to discover *Peperoni* means *peppers* in German. (Felix said I should have ordered "salami" instead.) Luckily, Katarina liked peppers, so she switched plates with me. Her pizza was plain, topped only with sauce, blobs of mozzarella cheese, and fresh basil. It looked a little funny, but it tasted oh so good.

"Felix," Katarina said between bites of pizza, "I thought we should start planning your birthday."

"No."

"But it's next week!"

"Yes, it is," said Felix.

"Don't you want to have a party?"

"No," said Felix. "I want to have cake at home and then go to the movies. Like we do every year."

Katarina made a face. "That was fine for last year. You were turning twelve. But this is thirteen! You'll be a teenager."

It was Felix's turn to make a face. "Don't remind me." He took another bite of his ham-topped pizza.

"But being a teenager is wonderful!" Katarina exclaimed. "All the new freedom! The excitement! It's a fabulous time in your life."

That was not how I heard most people describe being a teenager, but hey, I was only twelve, so what did I know?

"Maybe for you, Mama," Felix said, "but I'm different."

"We could have it at a Heuriger," Katarina continued. "Right up the road."

"What's a Heuriger?" I asked.

"It's like a little tavern," Katarina explained. "Very Austrian. They serve new wine and bread, cheese, and salami on a cutting board. It's casual. Fun. There's even music!"

"Wine?" I asked. "For thirteen-year-olds?!"

"No, no, no." Katarina laughed. "The wine is for the grown-ups. There's sparkling grape juice for the kids."

"If we have to go out, I'd rather just come here again," Felix said. "Then we can just jump on the bus to the movie theater."

"But we come here all the time!" Katarina said.

"That's because I like it," Felix said.

"Becca has already been here," Katarina insisted. "A Heuriger would be something new."

"But I like *not* new things," Felix said.

"Don't make a big deal about this, Schatzi," Katarina said. "Just invite a few friends from school and have a party. It can be a little one."

"Ich will aber nicht."

I could tell he was upset. Felix rarely lapsed into German when I was around.

"Okay, okay," Katarina said. "We'll discuss it later."

Luckily, they did not discuss it later. Instead, after dinner we sat around their living room playing a silly board game called Mensch Ärgere Dich Nicht. Each person had four colored pegs; you threw dice to move them around the board, trying to get them all Home. If you landed on an opponent's piece, you could send them back to Start. Basically, it was the German version of Sorry! It was pretty fun!

When it was time to go to bed, Sara and I walked back to my dad's house. She brought a bag of overnight supplies with her: toothbrush, pajamas, etc. I got out a blanket and an extra pillow and helped her make up a little bed on the big L-shaped couch, since we didn't have a guest room. Then I brushed my teeth and crawled into bed, pretty sure I was going to dream about pepperoni and peppers and parties and moving little colored pegs around a board.

I was woken by a scream. At first, I thought I might have imagined it. It was raining hard, and as I lay in bed, lightning lit up the window, followed a moment later by a boom of thunder. Then I heard it again—a loud, short shriek.

I jumped out of bed and ran, panicked, down the stairs. The lightning flashed again, and for a moment I could see Sara thrashing about on the couch. She screamed again, but I breathed a sigh of relief. She was just dreaming.

I turned on the lamp on the side table next to the couch.

Sara was sweating, the green lock of hair sticking to her forehead like a piece of overcooked spinach. I put my hand on her shoulder and shook her gently.

"Sara," I said. "Wake up! You're having a nightmare."

She moaned and tried to pull away from me. Then the living room lit up from the lightning again, and the room shook with thunder. Sara opened her eyes with a shriek.

"It's me, Becca!" I said. "It's just a thunderstorm."

Sara blinked once or twice, and then something clicked and she recognized me again. "Oh, Becca!" she said. "I had such a bad dream!"

"It's okay," I said.

Sara huddled in the corner of the couch, her blanket wrapped around her. She looked terrible, with big dark shadows under her eyes. It scared me a little.

"Can I get you something?" I asked.

Sara took a deep breath in, held it for a long moment, and then exhaled slowly. "Could you make a pot of tea?"

"Sure." I was glad to have something concrete to do. Dad had an electric kettle. All you had to do was fill it with water and plug it in, and in a couple of minutes, you'd have boiling water. It was so fast! Something to do with the different current in Europe.

Sara got up from the couch and went to the bathroom. She looked a little better when she came out. She'd splashed some water on her face, though her eyes were still puffy.

"Do you want peppermint or chamomile?" I asked.

"Pfefferminze," she said.

"Okay."

The tea was loose—another thing my dad had had to show me how to use—but I scooped some out of the tin and put it into a cloth bag on a little metal ring that sat on the lip of the teapot. Then I poured the hot water over it. The smell of peppermint drifted into the living room. It smelled like candy canes and Christmas.

"Okay if I put on some music?" Sara asked.

"Of course," I said.

She took a CD out of her bag and went to the stereo. Mournful violins began to play.

"What's that?" I asked.

"*La Traviata*," she said. "My favorite opera."

Okay. So it wasn't what I listened to when I couldn't sleep at night, but if it made her feel better, I didn't mind. The clock in the kitchen chimed midnight.

"Becca," Sara asked shyly. "Will you sit with me?"

"Sure." I ran upstairs and grabbed a blanket off my bed. I poured each of us a mug of tea, and we settled in on the couch, each of us curled up on one end of the sectional, our feet meeting in the corner, our hands warmed by clutching the mugs. I felt cozy and safe, listening to the rain outside.

Sara was staring at her tea as if she expected to find a prize at the bottom of the cup.

"Want to tell me about your dream?" I asked.

She looked up in surprise.

"You don't have to," I added quickly. "But if I have a nightmare, it always makes me feel better to tell someone."

"I not want to scare you."

I shrugged. "I'm not scared of dreams."

"You scared of eggs," she pointed out.

"Raw eggs are scary!" I insisted. "But a bad dream can't hurt you."

"Okay," she said finally. "I will tell."

CHAPTER 14

The Bridge

Sara sipped her peppermint tea. "I mention the bridge near my house, yes?"

"Yeah," I said. "The one you'd walk across with your mom and little brother and eat ice cream."

She nodded. "When Serbian snipers first moved into the hills, they started targeting that bridge. People were already leaving the city, and sometimes they could not take their pets with them. One day, I watched a little dog walk back and forth across the bridge. All day long he walked, looking for his owner. Poor little sad dog. Finally, he started to howl. Then a sniper shot him."

"What a terrible nightmare!" I said.

"That not my dream," Sara said. "I saw that happen."

"A man shot a dog for barking?"

"Yes."

"That's awful!" I shivered and tucked the blanket in closer around me.

"My dream," Sara continued, "was about my little brother's birthday. He was turning six. We were in our apartment in Sarajevo. Mama scrambled eggs for breakfast. The war was still going on—I knew because I could see the bullet hole above the stove. The first week of fighting, a sniper missed my mother by only a few inches. There was blue paint on the wall, and it left a big white crater where the bullet lodged in the plaster. That's when we started closing the blinds.

"In my dream, my mother put out yellow crocheted place mats. They looked bright and cheerful, even with only strips of light coming in through the blinds. As we ate, she showed us some German marks she had saved."

"German marks?" I asked. "Don't you have your own money?"

"Of course. But when the war started, there was lots of inflation. Pretty soon, our money not worth much anymore. Mama had saved this money for a special occasion. 'I go to the market and buy flour, sugar, eggs, and butter, so I can make Eldin a real cake for his birthday!' she announced in my dream.

"Eldin clapped his hands for joy and went to play in his room with his toy trucks. I begged Mama not to go. Too dangerous. But she insisted: 'War or no war, my son will have a cake for his birthday.' She put on a white sweater, very fluffy, like a rabbit, something you wear to a party, not the market. I knew it was a dream, because Mama would never buy something so impractical. She picked up my purse, the little green one, said, 'Keep an eye on Eldin while I am gone,' and marched out the door.

"She was gone all day. Much too long for a trip to the market. Eldin and I looked out the window, saw boats float by, people by the river. It was like everyone had forgotten there was a war. Finally, I spotted Mama coming back from the market. She was walking across the bridge, with the white sweater and my bright-green purse, carrying a bag of groceries. She waved at us, as if to say *I got everything!*, and we waved back. I told Eldin, 'Put on your shoes; let's go meet her.' But before we could walk out the door, there was a loud bang.

"I ran to the window; I could see Mama lying on the ground. Right where the dog had fallen. And her white sweater was slowly turning red. I screamed and ran from the building, forgetting all about Eldin. I got to the bridge, and I found the green purse and the groceries, the bags of flour and sugar smeared with blood. But she was not there. I not find her anywhere. I screamed again and again and . . . and then you woke me up."

We sat there on the couch for a long time. The music played on in the background; the rain fell hard on the roof. I took a sip of my tea, but the minty water tasted wrong in my mouth. That was a terrible nightmare, and the worst part was, Sara couldn't walk to the next room and see her mother peacefully sleeping. She couldn't give her a call in the morning and laugh about her overactive imagination. She couldn't reassure herself it was just a dream. Because she didn't know where her mother was.

"I'm sorry," I mumbled finally.

"Maybe I heard the thunder in my sleep," Sara mused. "Maybe that is why I dreamed about hearing shots."

"Yeah."

"Eldin had no cake on his real birthday," Sara said. "He was so sad."

"Tell me another story about your mom," I said. "A happy one. Maybe that will get the . . . bad taste of the dream out of your head."

Sara took a sip of her tea and thought for a moment. She ran her fingers through her messy hair.

"Before I left Sarajevo, a friend came over one day. Her aunt was hairdresser, but she had left for Holland the week before. My friend brought over all her hair dyes. We looked through the colors.

"I wanted to dye my hair green. The color of grass. Leaves. My favorite color. But Mama got so upset! She screamed. She yelled. She said a good girl never has green hair. I said I was eighteen. No one saw me anyway, so why did my hair color matter? I ran to my room and slammed the door.

"I forget about the argument. But a few weeks later, I

was on the bus, alone, on my way to Croatia, and I looked in my bag for dry socks. At the very bottom, I found a small box with a note: *For Sara. I love you.* It was the green hair dye."

"She changed her mind!" I exclaimed.

"No." Sara said. "She still hate green hair. But she loves me more. When I got to Austria, first thing I did was dye my hair. It will stay green until I see Mama again."

We smiled at each other. I'd assumed Sara's green hair was some sort of teenage-rebellion thing. I'd never expected it to be a reminder of her mother. I had more questions—lots, in fact—but the front door opened then, and we both jumped.

"Oh!" my father said, walking in the door and shaking off his umbrella. "You're still up."

"The thunder woke me," I said. "Sara and I were just chatting."

"Nice," Dad said.

"Did your evening go well?" I asked.

"Great!" Dad said. "Such wonderful colleagues. I'm exhausted, though. You heading back to bed?"

I glanced at Sara. She had gone back to staring into her mug. "No, I think I'll sleep here tonight. Have a girls' sleepover."

"Okay," Dad said. "Don't stay up too late!"

He gave Sara a wave, blew me a kiss, and turned off the table lamp. I heard him carefully make his way up the stairs, and once his door closed, Sara whispered in the dark, "Thank you for staying, Becca."

"Of course," I said. "I know what it's like to feel afraid."

We didn't talk anymore after that. The music ended, but the rain pattered on. My toes were warm under the blanket; the pillow was cool under my cheek. I listened to Sara's breathing turn slow and even. And as I drifted off myself, I thought, *It feels really nice to have a new friend.*

CHAPTER 15

The Police Station

A COUPLE OF DAYS after her nightmare, Sara, Felix, and I stopped at the Julius Meinl grocery store on the corner by the bus stop to buy a picnic lunch. We picked out salami and fresh bread, a hunk of cheese, a bunch of peaches, and a big bottle of sparkling mineral water.

"We have picnic at the zoo," Sara announced once we were settled on the streetcar. "But I need to make a stop first."

"Where?" I asked.

"Polizei," Sara replied.

"Police," Felix translated without looking up from his book. He had finished *The Federalist Papers* and was now reading a book about the Revolutionary War.

"Why do we need to go there?"

"I need a new stamp in my passport," Sara said.

Sara balanced the basket of food on her lap. It rattled as

she bounced her knees up and down. I noticed that she had pinned her hair back with a barrette that morning so that the streak of green was barely visible. She had on about half as much makeup as normal, and although I could see the chain, her crescent necklace was tucked away, hidden in her shirt. For once, she wasn't even wearing all black; instead, she wore a jean skirt, a white T-shirt, and sandals.

Sara stood up suddenly, ushering us off the streetcar at an unfamiliar stop. We were on a busy street, more run-down than where Dad and Katarina lived and not as grand as the downtown. A gray stone building lurked in front of us.

Sara paused on the steps. She glanced at the door, then away, then back at the door. Suddenly, she sat down on the front step. "I rest a minute," Sara said. She put the basket down beside her, then put her elbows on her knees and cradled her head in her hands. Her breathing sounded loud—as if she were exhausted from running a race. But we'd been on the streetcar.

Felix looked confused, but I knew what was going on. She was having an anxiety attack! It was odd to see it happen to someone else. Every time it had happened to me, I'd felt so conspicuous. And yet, unless you actually knew her, it looked like Sara was just resting after a stren-uous walk.

Felix stood frozen, but I sat down next to her. "Sara," I murmured.

She didn't answer.

I put a hand on her shoulder, like Mom always did when I was upset. "I have a Benadryl in my purse," I offered. "Sometimes that helps me when . . ."

Sara shook her head. She was singing to herself, so softly it was almost a hum.

"What are you singing?" Felix asked.

"*La Traviata*," she whispered. "Italian opera by Verdi."

Oh! It was the opera we'd listened to the other night.

Sara continued singing. "*Di quell'amor ch'è palpito dell'universo intero.*"

"What does it mean?" Felix asked.

"Love is the heartbeat of universe. Or maybe breath." She spoke with her eyes closed. "Translated different ways. But to me it means, listen to the mystery and beauty in the universe."

Felix sat down on the other side of Sara, and we all stopped and listened. Honestly, I didn't hear any mystery or beauty. I heard a car honk, a streetcar rattle by, a dog bark, a baby crying in a stroller. But Sara must have heard something, because she took two long, deep breaths—Dr. Teresa would have been proud—and opened her eyes.

"Thank you for patience." She reached out and squeezed Felix's and my hands. "Police make me worry."

"Why?" I asked.

"In Sarajevo, ethnic background became more important than the law. The police came to 'talk' to our neighbor, and when they left, he had a broken arm."

Sara took another deep breath, stood up, and smoothed the wrinkles out of her skirt. "You two say nothing," Sara said. "Unless policeman ask you a question. Then say, 'Sara family friend.' Not nanny. Not au pair."

"But you are our au pair." I was confused. My parents didn't have too many rules, but "Don't lie to the police" was definitely one of them.

"No," Sara said firmly, almost to herself. "I family friend. The money Katarina and Ben give me is not salary—only so you and Felix have fun."

"But . . ."

Felix nudged me in the ribs. He leaned close and whispered in my ear. "Sara doesn't have a work permit. If they find out she has a job, they could send her back to Bosnia!"

"There's a war going on! They wouldn't do that."

Sara stared at me, her big green eyes round and serious. "Yes, they would."

I thought about the little dog on the bridge. "Family friend," I agreed.

We all turned together to walk up the front steps. The wooden door was twice our height, making the building look like a fortress. A smaller door was cut out of the larger one. Sara grasped the metal handle and pulled it open.

The temperature dropped what felt like twenty degrees as soon as we stepped inside. The big stone buildings in Austria might not have air-conditioning, but the solid rocks they were built from were so thick and dense, they kept the air inside cool and dry. Still, as we walked into the room, a cold sweat ran down my neck.

There were hard wooden benches lining the perimeter of the vestibule—and they were all filled with people. Most looked tired and disheveled; many carried suitcases or bags, as if this were an airport or a train depot instead of a police station. There were families, old people, single men, even a woman holding a whimpering baby. Sara went up to the woman and said a few words to her in a language that didn't sound like German. I looked at Felix.

"Bosnian," he whispered.

I couldn't understand what Sara was saying, of course, but I caught a few words. *Petra Tahirović? Eldin Tahirović?* The woman shook her head sadly. Sara thanked her and moved on. There was a girl a few feet on who looked about my age, staring at her old boots. Sara reached into our basket and handed her a peach. The girl bit into it immediately, the juice running down her chin.

Up ahead, a police officer in uniform was sitting behind a counter. Sara walked up to him and asked a question in her clear, crisp German. The man pointed down a long corridor, and we turned to go.

As I was following Sara, an old man grabbed onto

the strap of my purse. "American? American?!" he called desperately.

Sara exchanged a few words with him in her language, and he let go. We kept walking.

Even though we were in a police station, it had been kind of scary. I clutched my purse closer to me. There wasn't much inside, just my bus pass, some coins in case I needed to use the restroom or make a phone call, and my passport. I had a copy at home in case it was lost, but I often needed it as an ID. "Austrians like paperwork," Dad had told me. I'd already shown it twice at museums for a student discount.

"What did that man want?" I asked.

"The old man was confused," said Sara. "He thought you could help him. He has a cousin in New York."

"How did he know I was an American?" I whispered to Felix.

"Your shoes," he said.

I glanced down at my sneakers.

"Only Americans wear Turnschuhe when they aren't playing sports," Felix explained.

The hall seemed to go on forever. Sara led us up a flight of stairs and into another waiting room, which was even more crowded than the first. An old woman was weeping silently in the corner.

We got in line in front of another desk. Sara shifted the

picnic basket in her arms, as if it were getting heavy. I took it from her without a word.

The police officer handed the man in front of us a clipboard full of papers and rattled off a series of instructions in German. The man looked bewildered. The police officer repeated his words, only louder this time. The man shook his head.

"Entschuldigung," Sara said in a small but clear voice. "Darf ich übersetzen?"

The police officer nodded.

Sara pointed to the papers and explained what to do. The man clutched his hands together and thanked her (that was clear even if I didn't understand the words). He went to squeeze in on the bench, next to the weeping woman in the corner.

Then it was our turn. "Sie sprechen aber gut Deutsch," the officer said as Sara stepped up to his desk.

"Danke," she replied.

"He complimented her German," Felix whispered in my ear.

The officer and Sara spoke for a minute longer. Sara pointed to Felix and said, "Österreicher." Then to me and said, "Amerikanerin."

The officer broke into a grin then. "American, eh?" Then he added in heavily accented English, "I visit New York and Washington last year."

"I live outside Washington!" I said before I remembered I wasn't supposed to speak. "In Alexandria, Virginia."

"George Washington home!" he exclaimed. "I visit."

We smiled at each other. Then he handed Sara a thick clipboard of papers. "You go that line," he added in English, pointing to a door down the hall. "Is shorter." And he winked.

We waited in yet another room, with another line, while Sara filled out the papers. I wasn't sure quite what to think. On the one hand, the police officer had been friendly and nice. On the other, it didn't seem quite fair that we got to wait in the shorter line because he'd once visited Mount Vernon.

The actual stamp only took a minute or two, and pretty soon, we were back outside, standing on the steps of the police station. I blinked in the bright sunlight.

"Never been so quick before," Sara said, even though we'd been there over an hour. It hadn't seemed quick to me. "We had pig."

"What?" I asked. "Pig?"

Felix laughed. "Sara, you can't say that in English." He turned to me. "In German, there is an expression: *Ich habe Schwein gehabt*. It means *I was lucky*. But literally, it's *I had pig*."

"Why is having pig good luck?" I asked.

"In the old days, if you had a pig, you were considered well-off," explained Felix. "Around New Years, everyone gives out tiny plastic pigs for good luck. Or you can buy little marzipan piggies and eat them."

I smiled. "That's weird."

"Maybe," Sara said. "But today, I helped translate and I got my stamp. I say, we had pig!" She held up her passport and shook it in the air.

"Don't lose it!" I warned.

"I make a copy," Sara said.

"You two worry too much," said Felix.

"It's a sensible precaution," I argued.

"Like not eating eggs?" Felix asked.

I glared at him.

"Kinder, Kinder," Sara said. "Time for zoo!"

CHAPTER 16

The List

THE ZOO WAS part of Schloss Schönbrunn, a vast palace complete with formal gardens, a maze, and a fake Roman building on a hill. Felix said Schönbrunn had been the summer residence of the Hapsburgs, the royal family that had ruled over the Austro-Hungarian Empire. The palace was a bright, cheery yellow, longer than it was tall, with lots and lots of windows.

"Can we go inside?" I asked.

"Tour is boring," Sara said. "Let us go to Tiergarten and eat first."

"*Tiergarten*," Felix informed me, "literally means *animal garden*. But you can also just call it the Zoo." He pronounced it as if *zoo* rhymed with *toe*. "Founded in 1752, it's the oldest continuously operated zoo in the world."

We sat down on a bench and opened our picnic basket. The sun was shining, every building was the same cheery yellow, and the food was good, yet it felt like the chill of the police station had still not left me.

I tried to listen as Felix prattled on about facts and dates, but the animals looked kind of depressed to me. They were in old-fashioned cages with bars and cement floors. No carefully sculpted habitats. Not even any plants. I watched a lion pace back and forth, back and forth, trapped like my thoughts in an endless loop. His eyes were sad, his mane scraggly, and somehow, he reminded me of the old man at the police station who had grabbed my purse.

"Sara," I asked suddenly, before I could lose my nerve. "Why didn't your mother and brother leave Sarajevo with you?"

Sara froze. She had just popped a bit of cheese into her mouth, and she left it there, not even bothering to chew.

"I'm sorry," I said quickly. She clearly didn't want to talk about it. "I didn't mean to remind you of painful—"

"You cannot remind me," she interrupted. "I always thinking of them."

I understood what she meant. It was like when well-meaning people said, "Don't worry about getting nervous and it won't happen." But the worry was always there, like a hungry dog, lurking in the shadows.

"We all planned to leave on a special bus last November, organized by La Benevolencija," Sara said slowly. "That is Jewish humanitarian society."

"Wait," Felix interrupted. "A Jewish society? I thought you were Muslim."

"I am."

"But you don't wear a headscarf?" I asked.

"Not all Muslims wear headscarves."

"But why were you on a Jewish bus?" Felix asked.

"Sarajevo Muslims helped Jews hide from the Nazis in World War II. Now they help us. The head of Jewish community, Ivan Ceresnjes, organized evacuations. Jewish buses were the safest way to leave Sarajevo. The airport was closed. Many Serbian checkpoints on the roads. But Jewish organization negotiated safe passage, so their buses got out.

"Mama was lucky. She got three seats. Then, the night before we left, my little brother became very ill. High fever. He cannot walk. Too big to carry. Mama told me I must go alone. They come on the next bus, as soon as he is better." She paused for a long while. "We did not know that would be the last bus."

"Did your brother get better?" I asked.

"Yes. I get one letter. Only Grippe."

"Flu," Felix translated.

"Flu," Sara repeated. "All better. But bad timing. Very bad."

"So you took the bus to Vienna all alone?" I asked.

Sara shook her head. "The bus took me to Croatia. I have a friend there from dance class. She had a cousin in

Vienna. I took another bus here to stay with her. I applied for asylum; they said no. I received temporary protected status instead."

"What's that?" I asked.

"I allowed to stay but not work," Sara explained. "But how can you live without work? My friend's cousin cleaned offices. I worked with her for two months, at the newspaper office, where I met Katarina. I am bad at cleaning but good at languages. Katarina and I became friends. About a month ago, she invited me to come live with her."

Sara turned to look at me. "It is true what I say to the police, Becca. I not lie. Katarina explained she cannot pay me money, cannot hire me as au pair. But as friend, yes, she can help. And I can help her by watching you."

"What about your mom and brother?" I asked. "Why are you looking for them if you know they are still in Sarajevo?"

Sara got very still. "I called them once from Croatia. Phone was disconnected after that. I sent them many letters, but I only received one. I have not received any since I moved in with Katarina. Maybe they found a way to leave. Maybe they are on their way to Vienna."

Or maybe they were dead.

The beautiful day suddenly seemed wrong. Why were kids skipping by with ice cream and balloons when Sara's family was missing?

"How can you just sit there?" I yelled, suddenly irrationally angry. "How can you be so calm? I would be a mess. I would be hysterical!"

"How would that help?" Sara asked quietly.

"I couldn't do it," I say. "I couldn't stand it! All the worrying. I could never get on a bus by myself and travel across a war zone!"

The more I yelled, the calmer Sara got. "Rebecca." She was almost whispering now. "You are braver than you know."

I shook my head. "I can't even get on a Ferris wheel."

She patted my back. "I was very scared too. But I knew I must get on the bus. And to help me be brave, I made a list of the things I want to do when the war is over. When I go back to Sarajevo."

Sara reached into her green pocketbook and pulled out a piece of paper. It was a simple lined sheet of notebook paper, as if ripped out of a school binder. There were five items listed on it, written in a language I didn't understand.

"What does it say?" Felix asked.

Sara cleared her throat and translated. "Number one: Play violin recital."

"You play violin?" I asked.

"Yes. Number two: Study languages at Uni."

"University," Felix translated.

"I not sure I smart enough, but I try."

"You speak six languages!" I said. "Of course you're smart enough!"

Sara blushed. "Number three: Perform ballroom dancing."

"Aha," I said. "So that's why you're teaching that dance class with your friend!"

She ignored me and kept reading. "Number four: Bake cake for brother."

I understood that one—I remembered her dream.

"Number five: Get ice cream with family and walk across bridge."

I was quiet for a moment. It was a great list. Simple things. And yet . . . hard too.

"I like lists," I said finally. "The make me feel safe. They make me feel focused."

"Yes," Sara agreed.

"I want my own list," I said. "Things I can do here in Austria."

"Like go to concert? Go to museum?"

"No," I said. "I don't want a sightseeing list. I want a list like yours! A list of things that are important to me. What if I make a list of things I'm scared of—so I can be brave and do them?" *And then my dad won't think of me as the girl who worries too much anymore.*

"Okay," Sara said. "I help you with your list."

I got my Doomsday Journal out of my purse and pulled out a pen. *What am I most afraid of? What do I want to do?*

"I don't know," Felix said as he bit into a peach. The sun had brought out the freckles on his nose, and his hair fell into his eyes. He pushed it back. "Sounds kind of weird to me. What are you going to put on your list—*eat a soft-boiled egg* or something?"

"Yes!" I exclaimed. "That's perfect." In my careful, neat handwriting I wrote down, 1. Eat a soft-boiled egg. And I immediately started to feel nervous. I mean, salmonella.

"What?!" Felix asked. "I was joking."

But Sara smiled. "That good thing to start with. Not too hard."

Next, I wrote, 2. Learn to ride a bike.

"You don't know how to ride a bike?" Felix marveled.

"Hush, Felix," Sara said. "You make a list next."

Felix rolled his eyes.

I added 3, then stopped to think.

"What else you scared of?" Sara coaxed.

"Nuclear war," I said. "Cancer. Zombies."

Felix laughed.

"Car crashes, scorpions, large crowds."

"Crowds," Sara repeated. "You mean large groups of people?"

I nodded. "You could get trampled. You could get robbed. You could—"

"Write that down," she said.

So I did. Hang out in a large crowd. Then the next one came to me without effort: 4. Go on the Riesenrad.

"I thought you hated Ferris wheels," Felix said.

"I've never been on one," I admitted. "How do I know if I hate them or not?" I paused, chewing on the end of my pen as I thought of number five. I wanted something big. Something so large, I wasn't sure I could do it. I slowly wrote down, 5. Travel somewhere.

Felix peeked over my shoulder. "You've done that."

By myself, I added. "I mean, what if Dad stays here? Mom can't come with me every time I want to visit."

Sara looked over my shoulder. "Good list."

"You'll help me, right?"

"Of course!"

We grinned at each other.

"Okay, Felix," Sara said, turning to him. "You next."

"What? Me?" He shook his head. "I'm not scared of riding a bike or going on a plane or eating an egg."

Sara shrugged. "Everyone scared of different things."

"Well, I don't have any fears," Felix said.

"All right," Sara said, letting the matter drop. "Let us go see Gloriette."

The Gloriette was the fake Roman building on top of the hill behind the main palace. It was a long, hot walk in the sun, trudging up a switchback gravel path. But when we finally made it to the top, the view was beautiful.

Bright-yellow Schönbrunn was in the foreground, and the rest of Vienna in the back. I could see St. Stephen's and the green from all the parks, and off to one side, I even caught a glimpse of the Riesenrad.

For a moment, I was so sad that I had missed it. But now . . . I had this list. Would it really help?

Dr. Teresa had once asked my mother to come up with a few examples of things I was afraid of. Dogs were on the list. The next week, Dr. Teresa wanted me to go pet her neighbor's dog. I told her no. *It might bite me. It might not have been vaccinated properly. It might have rabies!* She said okay, then we could just look at it through the fence, but I refused to budge from her couch. She finally let it drop.

But I was older now. And last year when my friend Chrissy got a dog, I *had* eventually learned to tolerate it. I guess it made more sense to me now what Dr. Teresa was trying to do. The thing was, Sara had actually lived through something awful. She was *still* living through horrible uncertainty now. And even though I knew she was worried, she still seemed to be enjoying the ice cream we had bought at the café on top of the hill, smiling as she licked her cone and looked out at the view.

I wanted to be like her.

CHAPTER 17

Another Item for the Doomsday Journal

THAT EVENING, WHILE Dad made spaghetti for dinner, I told him about our day. "Did you know Sara doesn't have a work permit?"

"Yes," he said. "Katarina explained the situation to me before you arrived."

"Why didn't you tell me?" I asked.

"I didn't think you'd be interested in her exact legal status," Dad said, stirring the sauce.

"Dad!"

"You worry a lot, Becca," Dad said seriously. "I didn't want to give you one more thing to write down in your Doomsday Journal."

"It helps me to write things down."

"That's what you and your mother say," Dad said. "But sometimes I think focusing on all the things that could go wrong just makes you feel worse."

Well, *that* certainly made me feel worse. I guess Dad really did see me as the girl who worried too much. My eyes felt itchy as Dad plated the spaghetti and grated a block of parmesan cheese over the top. We sat down at the tiny table.

Dad sat upright, his posture perfect, as if he were meeting with a four-star general. I slouched down further in my chair.

"Becca, don't pout," Dad said. He still had his dress shirt on, his tie loosened around his neck. His eyes looked tired.

"Maybe I would worry less if you told me more."

"Fine," Dad said. "What do you want to know?"

"Why can't Sara get a work permit?"

"It's complicated."

"I've got a lot of spaghetti to eat."

Dad sighed. "During the Cold War, it was very hard for Soviet citizens to immigrate to the West. Vienna is actually further east than Prague, and so it was the closest Western city to a number of former Soviet-bloc countries. Austria could afford to be generous about granting asylum to refugees who did manage to get through, because there were very few of them.

"But after the Berlin Wall came down in 1989, things started to change, and with the end of the Soviet Union in 1991, large numbers of Eastern Europeans began to move west, looking for more political freedom and more economic opportunities. Wait, I need to back up. Do you know what asylum is?"

"An old-fashioned word for a mental hospital?"

"Yeah, but not in this context. Asylum is an official legal status granted to someone who has left their country due to persecution. It gives the seeker many benefits, including the right to work and settle in the new country permanently. That was fine when it was only a trickle of Soviet scientists or artists fleeing a repressive regime. But now that it's become a flood of refugees escaping a war zone, some leaders here have started to worry about these new immigrants overwhelming their social services: unemployment, health care, schools, et cetera.

"So in June of last year, a new immigration law went into effect. Now less than 10 percent of applicants in Austria are granted asylum, and instead, most receive TPS—temporary protected status."

"What's that?" I asked.

"It means they can stay in the country, but they are not allowed to work. They get a certain amount of money for food, shelter, and health care, but no work permit, because the goal is, once the fighting stops, for them to go back home." Dad shook his head. "It's a little confusing even to me. Apparently, there are different agencies in Austria for work and residence permits, and they have different quotas. All sorts of strange things can happen, like a foreigner having a work permit but not being officially allowed to live in Austria or vice versa."

"What do I have?" I asked.

"You have a tourist visa. It's good for three months."

"Do you have permission to live in Austria?" I asked.

"Yes."

"Do you have a work permit?" I asked.

"Of course!"

"Why did they give you one and not Sara?"

"Because I'm an American and they know I have enough money to support myself and . . ."

"If Sara could get a job, she could support herself too!"

"True." Dad sighed. "The pasta is getting cold. Let's eat."

I twirled a bunch of spaghetti around my fork, but I wasn't very hungry anymore.

"I wish Sara hadn't taken you to the police station," Dad said crossly. "I just want you to have a fun time in Austria this summer. I don't want you to worry."

I wanted to tell Dad about my list, about how Sara was going to help me face my fears. But I was afraid he wouldn't understand.

🐗

THE NEXT MORNING, after my dad left for work, Felix and Sara came over. I watched Sara as she took three eggs from the carton on the counter and placed them in a pot, then added just enough water to cover them. My stomach started to hurt. "We eat egg with you," she said. As soon as the water began to boil, she set the timer.

I began to shiver as the clock counted down. I set the table, putting out tiny spoons, little eggcups, and a knife to cut the shells off the top.

My head was throbbing. I felt like I was going to throw up. The oatmeal I'd eaten for breakfast sat like a lump in my stomach. I had no room for an egg even though I'd only eaten half my normal serving.

Felix set the eggs down on the table. Sara cut off the tops. The yellow yolk oozed down the side of the shell. Felix added salt and pepper to his egg and dug in. "Yum."

"Becca?" Sara asked. "Tastes best warm."

I picked up my spoon, feeling like a prisoner being told to walk the plank over shark-infested waters. Except I had asked to be there. *What's wrong with me? Why did I ever think I could do this? They're crazy. Raw eggs can kill you!*

"It is cooked," Sara said. "Not like you used to. But cooked. Try."

I stuck the spoon into the egg, and the yolk coated the metal spoon yellow. It dripped like pus.

"I'm sorry," I said, standing up and pushing in my chair. "I just can't!"

"Is safe egg," Sara coaxed. "From nice chicken."

"I don't know that!" I yelled, in a panic now.

I ran to my room and slammed the door, throwing

myself on the bed. This was so embarrassing. I was so disappointed. I really wanted to try it. But, but, but . . . I started to cry.

☙

TWENTY MINUTES LATER I heard a knock on my door. "Becca," Felix called out.

"What do you want?"

"Sara has an idea."

"I'm not eating an egg!"

"She doesn't want you to eat anything," he said. "She wants you to meet a chicken."

That was the stupidest thing I'd ever heard. I jumped up and opened the door. "Meet a chicken? That's the best you could come up with?"

"I'm not joking," he said.

"No joke," Sara called from downstairs. "Grab bus pass."

"Come on," Felix said. "We might as well go. I'm gonna bring a book."

I *had* asked Sara to help me with my list. And I didn't really want to spend the day crying in my room. "Fine," I snapped. "Guess we're going to meet a chicken."

CHAPTER 18

The Egg

THIS TIME WE took the bus in the opposite direction, away from the city. "Lovely day to visit a farm," Sara said. "See cows. Feed happy chickens."

I scowled. "I'm not eating—"

"No eating," Sara agreed. "Just meet animals."

The bus took us up into the hills outside of Vienna. It was a pretty ride; I'll give Sara that. Finally, we got off at an isolated house with a sign that read, "Gasthof Müller."

It was big yellow house, the same color as Schönbrunn Palace, with dark wooden balconies and window boxes overflowing with flowers. A woman with gray hair in braids pinned up on her head came out carrying a tray of drinks. She was wearing a dirndl, her dress light green with a pink apron.

Sara spoke rapidly in German to the woman for a

moment. The woman looked confused at first, then her face brightened. "Grüß Gott!" she said.

"This is Frau Müller," Sara said.

I shook her hand.

"Meine Tochter zeigt Ihnen die Tiere," the woman said.

"She said her daughter will show us the animals," Felix translated.

We followed her around the back of the house to what appeared to be a small outdoor restaurant. Long wooden tables sat in the sunlight, covered by an awning overgrown with grapevines for shade. There were two other groups there, drinking and chatting in the dappled light.

A moment later Frau Müller's daughter came out of the house. She looked about my age. Unlike her mother, she wore jeans and a T-shirt. Honestly, she wouldn't have looked out of place at my school.

"Hi," she said shyly. "I'm Tanja. You want to see animals?" she asked in English. She had a thicker accent than Felix.

"Ja, bitte," said Sara.

"Come," she said.

There was a small barn beside the house. Inside was a large white cow with brown spots, chewing some hay. "This is our milk cow, Gertrude," she said, patting the big animal on the nose. "We call her Gerti."

I was a city girl. I mean, I'd seen cows before, of course,

but usually from the car as we drove by. I hadn't realized they were quite so . . . big.

"You can pet her," Tanja said.

I looked at the stall. It was made of strong dark wood. It looked like it would hold. Cautiously, I patted the cow's nose, as Tanja had done. The cow ignored me.

In a stall next to the cow were two goats. "Max and Moritz," Tanja told us. "Even though they are girls. They make good cheese."

Outside the small barn was a pigpen. "Franz, Fritz, and Frederike." The girl turned to look at me. "But you want to meet chickens," she said.

I nodded.

Behind the barn was a small red henhouse painted neatly with white trim. In front of the house was a fenced area. Four chickens ran around, with red combs and a few black specks in their otherwise cream-colored feathers. "These are my princesses," Tanja said proudly. "Sisi, Maria Theresia, Elisabeth, und Diana."

Tanja threw some corn into the pen. The chickens eagerly ran over and pecked daintily at the grain on the ground. "Come," Tanja said. "We get eggs."

I followed her into the henhouse. It was warm and smelled of clean hay. There were little compartments, neatly labeled. In the one labeled "Diana," on a bed of hay, was a fresh spotted egg.

"Take egg!" Tanja urged.

I picked it up. It was warm. It felt safe. Or maybe I wanted to keep it safe. In any case, I cradled it carefully in my palm as I backed slowly out of the tiny house.

Tanja was holding three more eggs in her apron. They didn't look like the ones at the store. One was pure white, one tan, one brown, and mine was speckled. "I cook for you," she said, holding out her hand. Almost reluctantly, I handed over my egg.

We went to sit at the long wooden tables in the sunlight. After a few minutes, Tanja came back with thick black bread, sliced fresh butter ("From Gerti," she told us), and an egg. My egg. I could tell because of the spots.

"I don't really like eggs," I told Tanja.

"You like this one," she said.

"You said I wouldn't have to eat anything," I said to Sara.

She shrugged. "You not have to. Your choice."

Tanja was watching me expectantly. I picked up a knife. My hands were shaking, but I managed to cut off the top. I made a bit of a mess, getting the yolk on my fingers. The yellow was so deep and bright it was really more of an orange.

"It's a weird color!" I said.

"Diana's eggs always orange. Taste extra good!"

Felix passed me the salt and pepper. I picked up a spoon. How had I gotten talked into this? We'd passed a health clinic on the way. It wasn't far. Maybe two bus stops. If I got sick, I could probably walk.

I wanted to do this. Didn't I? Yes. I wanted to show myself how brave I could be. I dipped the spoon in the egg, coating the metal with orange yolk.

No, I couldn't. I wasn't brave after all.

I was about to put my spoon down when one of the chickens let out a loud call. We all turned and looked. It was Diana. She had walked to the edge of her pen and was looking at me through the wire. She tilted her head, as if to say, *Go on,* and let out another little coo.

So quickly, before I could think about it, I popped the spoon into my mouth.

Think of the lightest, fluffiest scrambled eggs you can imagine, but make them lighter, creamier. It almost didn't taste like eggs at all, but a salty, rich pudding, warm on my tongue.

Before I knew it, I was taking another bite. And then another. Finally, I was scraping fully cooked egg whites from the edge of the shell.

"I did it!" I said.

Felix high-fived me. Sara smiled. Tanja and Frau Müller went about their business, serving the other customers.

I sat there, waiting for the stomach pains to begin. Waiting to feel sick. Waiting for my anxiety to come back. I could feel it starting. *You did something so foolish! Even if it tasted good, why take the chance?!* I started to feel hot, then cold, then hot again. Then a cool, wet nose came to snuffle my arm.

It was a dog. "He wants to play." Sara laughed.

I threw the ball for the dog for a while. And I didn't feel sick.

I petted the cow again and watched Tanja milk her. And I didn't feel sick.

Before we left, Tanja gave me a handful of corn, and I threw it to the chickens. They all came running to me, and this time all I thought was, *Thank you for the delicious egg.*

I MADE FELIX and Sara stick close to home the rest of the day. I wanted to be near the phone in case anything went wrong. I felt a little dizzy if I thought too much about what I had done. But I'd taken my temperature three times, and it had remained a steady 98.6 (or 37 degrees, according to Felix's Celsius thermometer).

To keep my mind off the rod-shaped bacteria that were possibly at this very moment invading my intestinal track (although probably not—I mean, Diana did seem like a very nice chicken), Sara and I helped Felix decide who to invite to his birthday party. Turned out, he had lost that battle, and his mother had already scheduled it for the following weekend.

"There's nobody I like at school!" Felix argued.

"No one?" Sara asked.

Felix ignored her and crossed his arms.

"Maybe you need a list too," I said.

Felix glared at me. "I'm not afraid of having a birthday party!"

Sara and I glanced at each other.

"I'm not!" Felix protested.

"Okay," I said.

"Just because you're scared of stupid things like riding a bike or eating an egg doesn't mean I . . ." He paused, and when I looked over at him, he was blinking frantically, as if a grain of sand had blown into his eye. "They don't like me."

"Why not?" Sara asked. "You very nice."

"It's hard talking to people I don't know. It's easier to just read a book."

"We all fear different things," Sara said.

"I ate the egg," I pointed out.

"Fine," Felix sighed.

I pulled my Doomsday Journal out of my bag and ripped out a page from the back. I only spent a moment worrying if I had weakened the binding of the book, before I handed the paper to Felix. Sara found a pen and gave it to him.

Felix wrote swiftly, reading his words aloud: "Nummer eins: Geburtstagsfeier beim Heurigen. I'll have a party. Satisfied?"

Sara and I nodded.

"Now we just need to figure out who to invite," I said. "Do you have a yearbook or something?"

There was no yearbook, but he did have a school directory. Sara and I studied tiny black-and-white photos as Felix described his classmates. Rasheed's father was from India and his mother was Austrian, and according to Felix, he was the least annoying person in chess club.

"Chess club?" I asked.

"I only go because Mama said I *had* to join one club."

"Hey," I said. "I like chess."

Daisy was English, a short girl with glasses and a blond ponytail. They'd worked on a science-fair project together once.

Peter was born in Nigeria but had lived in Austria since he was two. "He doesn't say much," Felix said, "but when he does, he's funny."

And then there was Mai. All Felix would say about her was that her family was from China. All I could tell from her picture was her hair was cut into a short black bob. "So you think she's cute?"

Felix blushed so fiercely, I knew I was right. "She's never spoken to me," he said. "Mama said I had to pick four people. It's not like any of them are going to come."

Still, it had been fun picking them out. I was sort of looking forward to the party. That evening, as I was getting ready for bed, I realized I still didn't have a fever or cramps or vomiting. I'd done it! I'd eaten a soft-boiled egg. And it felt really good to cross that first item off my list.

CHAPTER 19

At the Heuriger

FELIX'S PARTY WAS scheduled for Sunday afternoon. The Heuriger reminded me a bit of a log cabin, with a bundle of twigs tied to the front door, wooden paneling, and long tables for people to share. Katarina had reserved a spot on the back patio. She fluttered around like a monarch butterfly in her orange-and-black dress, calling out instructions to my dad, who arranged and rearranged the pitchers of new wine and sparkling juice until Katarina was satisfied. There were plates of cheeses and meats, and baskets of fresh bread on our table. Although I wouldn't have said it to Felix, it seemed like a pretty nice place to have a party.

All the kids we'd picked out had actually agreed to come. Katarina had called the families, told them it was Felix's birthday, explained that I was visiting, and then invited their parents too. With my dad and me, Sara, a couple of

Katarina's friends, and our neighbor Frau Gamperl, it was going to be quite the little group. As we waited for them all to arrive, Felix paced from one side of the patio to the other. His mom had made him get a haircut, and he wore a new button-down shirt.

Seeing him so anxious made me sad. I mean, I'd never met these kids before, but from their pictures, they seemed okay. And they'd agreed to come, so they obviously didn't hate him. How bad could it be? But as I watched Felix fidget and twist his napkin, I realized he felt exactly like I had when I was facing down that happy egg.

Daisy and Mai arrived first, their families walking in together. Daisy wore a jean skirt, a T-shirt, and sandals; Mai had on a dress covered in big sunflowers. Dad and Katarina welcomed them and pointed in our direction, but before they could move, Peter and his parents walked in.

The grown-ups started chatting, and I turned to Felix. "Why aren't any of your friends Austrian?" I asked.

"I go to the International School," he said. "It's for the kids of diplomats and such. And they aren't my friends anyway."

"But your mom's not a diplomat."

"No, but she wanted me to be fluent in English."

The kids were all bunched up by the entrance to the patio. Rasheed had joined them. He was as short as Felix but talked a whole lot more. Both he and Peter were wearing soccer jerseys.

Sara was taking the presents as people arrived and placing them on a table with the cake Katarina had baked the night before. (She'd had to do it twice. The first time she'd accidentally put in salt instead of sugar.) I caught Sara's eye. She mouthed *Help him* and pointed to Felix.

He had pulled out his Revolutionary War book and was huddled over it, as if it were a fire on a cold night. I realized if I didn't do something, he'd probably leave his own party even more convinced that no one liked him. I couldn't let that happen to him on his birthday.

So I plucked the book from his hand and threw it under the table. "Come on," I said, pulling him up. "I need you to introduce me to the other kids."

"You already know their names," he said.

I dragged him across the room. Daisy and Mai were chattering loudly in a language that definitely wasn't German. "That sounds like French," I said.

"That's because it is French," Felix mumbled.

"I thought you spoke German and English at school?" I asked.

"Yeah," he said. "But Daisy's grandmother lives in Paris, and Mai has an aunt in Switzerland."

"They each speak three languages?"

"No," Felix said. "Mai and Peter speak four."

We didn't even *start* a language until eighth grade. Guess I was a little behind. I kept waiting to freak out myself. I mean, social situations don't usually upset me, but it's happened before. (There was that time at the fifth-grade Halloween party of which we will not speak.) But there was something about helping Felix that kept me calm. Like I had a bigger purpose. Besides, who cared if the others didn't like me—I'd probably never see them again. But Felix would.

The four kids were clumped together in a corner as we approached. "Hi," I said loudly. "I'm Becca."

The conversation stopped, and they all turned to look at me. Okay, so my heart *did* start beating faster then. Beside me, Felix was staring at the floor and trembling, so I knew he felt even worse.

"My dad is dating Felix's mom, so that makes him and me, like . . . friends." *Okay, so that was probably the stupidest thing I could say.*

"You're the American," Peter said doubtfully, in a thick British accent.

"Yup," I admitted. "How'd you know? I didn't even bring my horse and cowboy hat." *Nope, that was even stupider.*

But Daisy burst out laughing. "Becca, you are so funny! And you have the cutest accent."

Me? They were the ones who all spoke English like they were on *Masterpiece Theatre.*

"I'm Daisy," she continued. "This is Peter, Mai, and Rasheed."

"Nice to meet you," I said. "I'm Becca and this is Felix."

They all laughed again, even Felix.

"Hi," Felix whispered to the ground.

"Come on," I said. "Let's go get some food."

We sat down at the table Katarina had reserved. Peter poured everyone a glass of the grape juice. We talked about movies. And the Statue of Liberty. Rasheed and Mai had been; I had not. Daisy wanted to go see the Hollywood Walk of Fame. I told them about how last summer, my mom had taken me on a covered-wagon trip where we pretended to be cowgirls. "Wow," Peter said. "I thought you were kidding about the horse."

I laughed. When the girls went to the bathroom and the boys went to get some more food, I nudged Felix. "They're nice!" I said.

"I can never think of anything to say," Felix grumbled.

"But you're a good listener!" I pointed out. "That's an undervalued skill."

Felix didn't look convinced.

By the time the others returned, it was time for cake. Dad and I sneaked off to a side room to light the candles. We had bought Felix some frog candles, since he still teased me about those pajamas. I couldn't believe I'd already been in Austria for three weeks. Sara got out her violin and played along as everybody sang "Happy Birthday."

Felix smiled when he saw the candles on the cake.

"Make a wish!" Katarina cried out.

Felix closed his eyes and made his wish. He blew, we clapped, and while Katarina cut the cake, Sara played songs on the violin. She was really good. Frau Gamperl tapped her foot in approval, and the owner of the Heuriger actually came over to listen. He disappeared for a moment and then returned carrying an accordion. He said something to Sara, she nodded, and then they launched into a folk song, which apparently everyone knew (except for me and my father), because they all started singing along in German.

It was super weird.

And kind of cool too.

I sat and ate my cake. Felix didn't reach for his book again, but he still stayed close by my side. Daisy tried to get the other boys to do some traditional dance with her. Mai started laughing hysterically as Daisy spun Peter around and around in circles. Rasheed told a long, boring story about his favorite football team, and Felix listed so intently and politely, for a minute I thought he was actually interested. When Sara and the owner started playing the chicken-dance song, we all stood up and flapped our "wings," as if we were, well, some of those happy chickens.

After the song, I threw myself down into a chair and

poured myself another glass of juice. Katarina was standing behind me and talking to a woman who sounded familiar, though I couldn't quite place her. Grown-up conversation isn't usually that interesting, so I pretty much ignored them, until I felt a tap on my shoulder and turned around.

It was the journalist I'd talked to on the plane.

CHAPTER 20

The Present

Ms. Madden still had her gold hoop earrings, but she looked more casual this time, in jeans, a pea-green shirt, and a leather jacket. "I thought it was you!" she exclaimed.

"Do you two know each other?" Katarina asked.

"Yes." Ms. Madden said. "We met on the plane. Wait, you said you were going to visit your father. Is he that nice American man Katarina has been dating?" She pointed to my father.

"Yeah, that's him."

"Ha!" She laughed. "As I say, Vienna is really just a big small town."

"How do *you* two know each other?" I asked.

Katarina linked her arm with Ms. Madden's. "We were roommates in journalism school."

Dad walked over then. "Your daughter has quite the

sense of curiosity," Ms. Madden said to my father. "She made me give her a lecture on the geography of Yugoslavia in the middle of the night on an airplane!"

Everyone laughed.

"I didn't make you," I protested. "All I did was ask a couple of questions."

"Spoken like a true journalist!" said Katarina approvingly.

"I did save the map you drew me," I admitted. I'd taped it into my Doomsday Journal.

"That settles it. Mr. Greenberg, you *must* bring your amazing daughter to the candlelight vigil Katarina's friends are organizing next month."

"What's that?" I asked.

"We're protesting Haider's Österreich Zuerst petition," Katarina explained. "Literally, it means *Austria First*. Jörg Haider is a former governor of Kärnten."

"That's one of Austria's states," Ms. Madden added.

"Haider and his party are hoping to get more-restrictive immigration policies in place," Katarina went on, "to prevent more refugees from coming. He's trying to get one million people to sign his petition outlining his twelve-step plan to keep Austria 'pure.'"

Ms. Madden rolled her eyes. "Some people forget that the Austrian Empire included many different peoples: Germans, Hungarians, Czechs, Slovaks, Poles, Slovenes, Croatians, Serbians, Romanians, Italians, Ukrainians.

Austria has always been a multicultural society. What is this idea of a pure Austrian?! It doesn't exist."

"We want to make sure the petition fails," Katarina said. "So some friends of mine are organizing a protest in *support* of foreigners and refugees. Hester's agreed to cover it. And I was actually just talking to Rasheed's mother about it. She's an immigration lawyer. We should all go together!"

"What do you say, Becca?" Ms. Madden asked.

"I'd love to come." I remembered all the people I'd seen waiting at the police station.

"Becca," Dad said gently. "There are going to be lots of people there. I know you don't like—"

"I want to go," I insisted. I *had* to go. It was on my list.

"Fine," Dad said. "We can talk about it later."

Our exchange hung awkwardly in the air like a bad smell. Sara and the accordion player launched into another song.

"Who is this fabulous violin player?" Ms. Madden asked.

I was grateful to her for changing the subject. "It's Sara, our au pair."

"Ah, the famous au pair." Ms. Madden said. "Well, she is very good."

Dad and Katarina excused themselves to go mingle with the other guests, but Ms. Madden and I sat and listened. "Did you make it to Sarajevo?" I asked.

"Yes, I just returned. I'll go back in a day or two, but I'll return to Vienna in time for the protest."

"How are things there?"

"Bad. The Serbs' policy of 'ethnic cleansing' involves shelling towns until most of the population flees. Then they send in small squads to clear out whoever remains."

"Sara's mom and brother are missing," I confessed. "They had to stay behind when she left. Do you think you could find them?"

"Becca," Ms. Madden said kindly. "Sarajevo is a city of half a million people. I have a TV camera, not a magic wand."

"Can I give you their names? You could keep an eye out. Just in case."

"Sure," she said. She passed me a paper coaster with the Heuriger's name on it and handed me a pen. I still had Sara's flyer in my Doomsday Journal, so I remembered how to spell their names. I carefully printed *Petra Tahirović, age 44*, and *Eldin Tahirović, age 6*, and handed the coaster back to her.

Ms. Madden stuck it in the pocket of her blazer. "I'll see what I can do." She glanced at her watch. "I'm afraid I have to go. But it was lovely to see you again."

Felix was in the middle of opening presents when I rejoined the other kids.

Frau Gamperl gave Felix a tomato plant ("Never too early to start gardening!"), Dad and I gave Felix a book of

Lincoln's speeches, Katarina got him a bunch of sweaters, and one of the boys gave him a board game. He got a card with money from his father, a couple of more books, and then Mai handed him another card.

"Happy birthday, Felix," she said. "You mentioned once in history class that you liked old movies, so . . ."

Felix ripped the card open. "Frau Kovács Tanzschule?" He sounded uncertain. "You gave me dance lessons?"

"No!" Mai gasped. "Mom, I told you to get him a gift certificate to the English-language movie theater. Not a dance class!"

Her mom looked confused. "But . . . but . . . you and Daisy signed up for the teen ballroom dancing class. I thought it would be fun."

"Why didn't you tell me?" Mai wailed.

"I did! In the car. You were listening to your Walkman."

Mai burst into tears and ran out of the room.

An awkward silence fell over the table. "I'm so sorry," Mai's mother said. "I guess we got our wires crossed."

"It was a lovely idea," Katarina agreed.

"Wait," I said. "Frau Kovács—is that a Hungarian name?"

"Yeah," Daisy said. "The dance studio is right next to this café that serves the *best* gelato."

"Hey!" Sara said. "That's where my friend works. I'm the teaching assistant for that class."

"Oh yeah!" Felix remembered. "The guy from McDonald's."

"You went to McDonald's?" Katarina scolded. "Felix, they do not use happy eggs."

"Can I sign up?" I asked. I liked classes. I was good at classes. There were rules and instructions to follow. Policies to keep everyone safe. And the chicken dance *had* been pretty fun.

Rasheed's mother jumped in next. "I've been trying to get Rasheed to take a dance class for years. This would be the perfect opportunity."

Rasheed sighed. "I'll do it if Peter signs up too."

"I'll do it if Felix does it."

Everyone turned to look at the birthday boy. Felix's face took on a greenish hue. "Okay, I guess."

"Wonderful!" Katarina looked delighted.

I grabbed Felix's arm. "Let's go find Mai."

"How could you let this happen?!" Felix snapped at me as we searched through the rooms of the Heuriger.

"Mai was so embarrassed. We had to do something!"

"My father is the one who likes to dance, not me!"

"Maybe you will like it. And you can add it to your list." Felix glared.

We found Mai sitting on a bench in front of the Heuriger. "I'm so sorry!" she cried when she saw Felix. "I wanted to give you something . . . different. I thought maybe we could go to the movies together and . . . this is so embarrassing!"

"Aww, it's not that bad," I said, sitting down next to her. Felix hovered nearby. "We actually all decided to sign up."

"What?" Mai wiped her eyes with a napkin.

"Tell her, Felix."

He swallowed hard. "Yeah. Peter and Rasheed and Becca and I are gonna sign up too. Might be fun?"

"Felix," she said with a little smile. "You're even nicer than I thought."

We went back to the others, but it was time to go.

"Great party!" Daisy said as her family was leaving.

"Thanks for the invite," said Rasheed.

Peter clapped Felix on the back and cried, "I'll see you in dance class!"

Mai just waved and blushed.

Katarina fluttered around, packing up all the gifts. "Mai's mother gave me all the details. The class meets Fridays at two p.m. We'll sign you both up. I'm so proud of you, Felix! And you can ride your bikes there."

Wait. What?

"Bikes?" I asked.

"It's a short ride," said Katarina. "Lovely. Through the park, with only a short section on the street. And no worries, Becca. We have an extra bike for you."

"I'd rather take the bus," I said.

"Oh, no, no, no," said Katarina. "There's no direct route.

You'd have to change three times. It would take forever. Bikes are the way to go."

"Oh dear," Dad said sadly. "Becca can't ride a bike."

I glanced over at Felix. He was trying so hard not to laugh. *On your list,* he mouthed at me.

"Actually, Dad," I sighed. "Maybe it's time to give bike riding another try."

"The class starts Friday," Dad pointed out. "That doesn't give you much time."

"Oh, Schatzi," Katarina said to Dad. "Sometimes you worry too much. She'll learn!"

"I don't want to pay for the class and have her not be able to go," Dad said.

"I teach her," Sara said. "My little brother learned, and he only six."

Finally, Dad nodded. "Okay. We'll sign you both up for the class."

"Great!" I said, but all I could think was, *Now I have five days to learn to ride a bike.*

CHAPTER 21

Erdbeerkopf

FIRST THING THE next morning, we had to go buy me a bike helmet; I absolutely insisted on it. Even though no one wore them in Austria. Even though we had to take a subway all the way across town to find a bike store.

Just walking in made me nervous. The first salesman who came up to us had his arm in a sling. "What do you think happened?" I whispered to Felix.

"He probably fell off his bike," Felix whispered back.

I gave Felix a shove.

"What?" he asked. "You know I'm right."

"Just wait till we get to that dance class. All those girls you'll have to dance with."

"Yeah," he said with a grin, "but you have to get there first."

Sara did all the talking. There weren't that many choices. The only helmet that fit me was huge and red.

"Erdbeerkopf," I heard the salesman say.

Sara giggled.

"What's Erdbeerkopf?" I asked Felix.

"Strawberry head."

I looked in the mirror. It *did* look like I had a humongous strawberry on my head. I laughed too. "As long as my head doesn't get squished like one, Erdbeerkopf is okay with me!"

When we got home that afternoon, Felix, Sara, and I went to the storage unit where everyone in the community kept their bikes. It was a small room just off the communal laundry. Felix and Sara had their own bikes; Katarina had said I could borrow hers. Felix lowered the seat until I could sit on the bike and keep my toes on the ground. He put air in the tires and oil on the chain.

"How did you learn to do all that?" I asked.

He shrugged. "Just did."

It seemed pretty impressive to me.

Felix had to show me how to walk the bike, holding one hand on the handlebars and one hand on the seat to keep it steady. Sara thought I should practice by the local school. There was a blacktop there, but when we went over to take a look, it was already filled with little kids on bikes, riding around in circles. Kids who were much younger than me.

"No," I said. "It would be *way* too embarrassing to practice here."

Sara bit her lip. "I have an idea."

She led us away from the main road, toward the vineyards, back to the path where Katarina had made me go walking on my very first morning in Austria. The uphill slope was slight, but now that I was pushing this death machine of metal and rubber, I felt every step.

"Good spot," Sara said finally. "Soft dirt if you fall off. No one to watch."

Doubtfully, I positioned the bike in the middle of the path and sat down on the seat. They were both full of advice.

"Walk the bike first, using the brakes if you want to stop," Felix suggested.

"Look ahead, not at your feet," Sara instructed.

"Coast down a gentle slope."

"Walk and then pick up your feet."

I tried. Walking was okay, if a little awkward. But when I lifted up my feet and tried to coast, I panicked. The bike wobbled, and I overcorrected and promptly crashed into a grapevine. Unripe grapes fell onto my forehead. I felt like an idiot. And my elbow hurt. I'd probably broken it. *Can you bend your arm if it's broken?*

"Get up," Sara said.

"Try again," Felix urged. "Start with the pedals in the two o'clock position."

"Push down with right foot."

"Find your balance."

"Use brakes."

"Don't forget to steer!"

I tried to listen—I really did! But my heart was beating so loudly, it was hard to hear them. Again, I ended up in the soft dirt.

The next time it was harder to get back on the bike. To swing my leg over, grip the handlebars. Every time I coasted forward, I thought, *When am I going to fall?* And instead of balancing, I'd drag my feet to stop the bike.

Finally, I'd had enough. Felix rode the bike home; Sara and I walked slowly back to the house. "We try again," she said.

"No."

"We try again," she insisted. "You get it all at once."

I did not believe her.

On top of everything else, I was covered in dirt. I decided to take a bath before Dad got home. The hot water felt good on my sore bones, except I didn't like seeing the bruises springing up on my arms and legs, big purple blotches on my pale skin. Bruises were a sign of internal bleeding, which I had detailed notes on in Doomsday Journal #3, page 27. Bleeding was bad. I hated bleeding. Just the idea of blood made me feel light-headed.

I quickly got out of the bath and put on jeans and a long-sleeve shirt so I wouldn't have to look at my bruises. I still had half an hour before my father got home. My thoughts were spinning. Deciding to ride a bike was a terrible idea. I was going to get really badly hurt. I mean, look at the bike salesman. He'd broken his arm, and he was a professional!

The phone rang, and I jumped. I'd never been so happy to hear my mom's voice.

"I'm in Venice," she told me. "I went to the glass factory in Murano this morning and bought these beautiful red wineglasses. I'm going to a concert tonight, but I wanted to give you a quick call before I left. How are you, Becca?"

I told her about the bike and the dance lessons, and I even explained about the list. Mom listened without interrupting.

"I'm just going to forget about the whole thing," I said. "The list thing was probably stupid. I mean, better safe than sorry, right?"

Mom was quiet.

"Mom, did you hear what I said?" I asked. "Katarina wants me to go bike riding. On the street! How dangerous is that?!"

"I don't know," Mom said. "Wouldn't it be nice to ride a bike?"

"Yes, but . . ."

"And your father agreed that it was safe."

"Dad doesn't really think I can do it."

Mom tsked. "Becca, I don't think that's true. Of course your father believes in you!"

I didn't say anything.

"I need to go now," Mom said. "I'm having dinner with

a new friend I met on the train before the concert. But, Becca?"

"What?"

"*I have confidence in confidence alone!*" Mom sang.

I groaned. *The Sound of Music* was not going to help. "Bye, Mom. I love you."

"Bye, sweetie. Love you too."

Once she hung up, I went back to my room and looked at my list:

1. ~~Eat a soft-boiled egg.~~
2. Learn to ride a bike.
3. Hang out in a large crowd.
4. Go on the Riesenrad.
5. Travel somewhere by myself.

The egg hadn't been so bad. But the rest? I was afraid they were impossible.

CHAPTER 22

The Man from Barcelona

S ARA WANTED ME to try bike riding again the next morning, but I refused. My bruises were too fresh—I needed a day to recover. At least that's what I said. The truth was I needed the rest of the year to recover. Every time I thought about getting on that bike again, I felt nauseous and jittery.

We hung around the house in the morning. After lunch, my father called to say he would be home late, then Katarina called to say she would also be working late.

Felix and I were watching TV on his couch when Sara said, "I have idea."

"What?" I asked.

"Surprise," she said. "Put on a dress."

"Dress?" Felix teased.

"Du—eine lange Hose," she instructed him.

"A long hose?" I asked. "Are you going to fight a fire?"

"It means *pants*," Felix said.

As much as we nudged her, Sara wouldn't tell us her plan. I went back to my dad's house to change. I'm not really a dress person, but Mom had made me pack one—a Laura Ashley blue floral-print dress with a sweetheart neck, a full skirt, and little cap sleeves. I thought it made me look like I was an extra on *Little House on the Prairie*, but Mom thought it was cute.

"Okay," I called, letting myself back into Katarina's house. "I'm ready."

Sara had changed into a high-necked party dress. It was black, white, and hot pink, with rhinestones along the neckline, and a puffy tulle skirt. "Cool dress!"

Sara blushed. "I bought for senior dance in Sarajevo. I not get to go. Not practical thing to pack, but—"

"I love it."

Felix came down next. He had on khaki pants and a red polo shirt. He'd even brushed his hair.

"You look nice," I said.

He grunted. "So where are we going?"

"I tell you on the way."

Sara ushered us out the door and onto the bus. Once we were settled in our seats, we turned to look at her. "I have a very exciting plan," she said, pausing dramatically. "Tonight, we see . . . José Carreras!"

Um. Yeah. Okay. I had no idea who that was. I glanced at Felix. He shrugged.

"Who's that?" I asked.

"José Carreras!" Sara exclaimed, even more emphatically. "The famous tenor. From Barcelona."

"Never heard of him," I said.

Sara looked like she was going to freak out.

"Wait," Felix said slowly. "Is he one of those Three Tenors dudes? The guys who sang at the World Cup?"

"Yes!" Sara grinned triumphantly.

"Cool!" Felix exclaimed. "We're going to a football game!"

"Soccer?" I asked.

"No." Sara sighed, exasperated. "We go to opera."

"Opera?" I asked.

"Yes." Sara seemed thrilled just thinking about it. "We see the opening night of *La Traviata*. My favorite. José Carreras sings Alfredo."

Felix crossed his arms. "You tricked us. I could have just stayed home."

"Alone? No."

"I'm thirteen!" he argued.

"Good for you to go."

"What's it about?" I asked. I mean, I'd only listened to it once, but Sara seemed pretty excited about it.

"Well," Sara started, "*La Traviata* tells the story of a Parisian courtesan, Violetta. She has a party. Alfredo, handsome young man, declares love, but she says no. Must be free!"

"Free to do what?" Felix asked.

Sara ignored him. "A few months later, Violetta is in love with Alfredo. They move to the country. Very happy, until Alfredo's father tells Violetta she must leave his son."

"Why?" I asked.

"Violetta has a bad reputation."

"That doesn't make sense," Felix said.

"No. It is an opera," Sara said, as if that explained everything.

"So do Alfredo and Violetta break up?" I asked.

"Yes. Then get back together. Then she dies of tuberculosis!"

Felix rolled his eyes.

"Death sad," Sara admitted. "But music—beautiful and romantic!"

"Hmm." The plot sounded a bit like the time on *Love on the Evening Tide* when Georgio met a cocktail waitress and brought her home to his family. He'd wanted to marry her, but his family threatened to disown him and give his portion of the casino on the family steamboat to his third cousin. So he'd broken up with her. But then she'd come down with cancer, and he'd rushed to her side and . . . Okay, it sounded exactly like *Love on the Evening Tide*. (I hoped Grandma was remembering to tape it.) "I'll give it a chance," I said cautiously.

"Thank you, Becca," Sara said.

We got off the bus and onto the streetcar and were

almost to Schottentor before I realized I had forgotten to ask the most important question of all. "Wait—where is this opera?"

"At the opera house," said Sara.

"That's like a theater, right?"

"Yes."

No. No, no, no. "I don't like crowds," I said, my voice wavering. *Doesn't she remember? It's number three on my list!*

"I know. It number three on your list."

Okay, so she did remember. "I'm not ready to do this tonight," I said, beginning to sweat. Occasionally, I could go to the movies, like on weekday afternoons when they're mostly empty. But never on opening night. You could get trampled. Or robbed. Or what if someone yelled, *Fire?* There'd been a whole Supreme Court case about that (DJ #2, p. 17, *Schenck v. United States, 1919*).

"You are," Sara said. "You need to build confidence. Then you ride bike."

"You tricked me!" I complained.

"She tricked both of us," Felix grumbled.

Sara nodded. "I very tricky."

"You're sly. Deceptive. Devious. Sneaky!" Felix went on.

Sara nodded again. "English has many good words."

My heart was pounding by the time I followed Sara and Felix onto Straßenbahn 1. I'd gone to the symphony at the Kennedy Center once, on a field trip in fourth grade.

I'd ended up spending most of the visit in the bathroom, throwing up. My teacher had not been pleased.

"No," I said. "I don't want to go."

"It's on your list," Felix pointed out.

Okay, so I did want to go. But not now. Sometime . . . later. In the future. When I didn't feel so scared. "I'm too afraid when I can't easily leave a place. Like in a theater."

Sara looked at me kindly then, her lock of green hair sparkling in the late-afternoon sun. "Rebecca," she said slowly, breaking my name down into its full three syllables. "You were afraid to eat egg."

"I did that," I admitted.

"Felix was afraid to have a party," she continued.

"He did that," I said.

"Feeling afraid is part of being brave."

"No, it's not," I said.

"Yes," Sara said. "Most important part."

It was time to get off the streetcar then. The opera house didn't look pretty to me anymore. It looked like a big, squat jail.

"You have choice," Sara said. "You get back on Straßenbahn, go home alone. Or you go to opera."

"I don't like those choices."

Sara shrugged. "Choosing is part of being brave too."

She waited for me to make my decision. I said nothing. I couldn't choose. I *did* want to be brave. I wanted my father to buy me tickets to the latest musical. And do you think I enjoyed always waiting for a movie to come out on video? Heck, I even kind of wanted to see the opera. But I didn't want to die! And being trapped in a room full of strangers in the dark, well, it sounded like a nightmare. My thoughts went around and around in a loop, like that ancient Greek snake that eats its own tail. I was scared of snakes too and—

"Can I go home?" Felix asked.

"No," Sara said.

"Why not?" Felix asked.

A snake eating its own tail made a big circle, and that made me think about the Riesenrad and how awful I'd felt when I hadn't gone on the ride. What made me think the opera would be any different?

Except . . . I had eaten that egg.

"Felix, please stay," I said, "because I want to see the opera. And if I'm going to sit there with all those hundreds of strange people, I'd like to have a friend on both sides."

"Fine," Felix said. "You can sit in the middle."

And just like that, the snake gobbled up the last bit of itself and disappeared.

CHAPTER 23

Standing Room

I N THE MOVIES, when someone does something brave, the soundtrack swells with inspiring music. Or the people around them burst into spontaneous applause. But when I agreed to go to the opera, all that happened in real life was Sara said, "Good. Becca made a decision. But no sitting."

She led us to an escalator that would take us under the busy street. I was still worried, but I felt better. Deciding, I remembered, was another one of Dr. Teresa's techniques. "Don't worry about making the *perfect* decision," she'd told me. "The important thing is just to do *something*." Maybe she was right.

"Wait a second," Felix said. "What do you mean, 'no sitting'?"

"You have the tickets, right?" I asked. Forgetting tickets was another fear of mine. I'd made Mom check our boarding passes fifteen times on the way to the airport.

"No," Sara said. "We get standing room."

"What's that?" I asked.

"Standing room," Sara said impatiently. "Where you stand and listen to the opera."

"We don't get a seat?" I asked.

"No, that why it called standing room!"

"How long is this opera?" Felix asked.

"Short one. Only a bit over two hours," Sara said.

"We're going to stand for two hours?!" Felix asked.

"Little railing to lean on." She turned to look at us. "Now we buy scarves."

"Scarves?" I was confused. Sara was changing topics every other second.

She ignored me as we stepped off the escalator into an underground shopping mall. There were shops and stands around the sides and a restaurant in the middle. Tunnels led off in different directions toward the subway station.

Sara dragged us over to one of the little stands. A short man with black hair and a thick mustache stood proudly in front of a number of different scarves displayed on a rack.

"Nur hundert Schilling," he said to Sara.

"Well, go on," she told us. "Pick one out."

"What's it for?" I asked.

"To mark our place at the opera."

I didn't know exactly what she meant, but the scarves were pretty, all super thin and soft, like silk. There was a bright-red one, one with purple swirls, and every color of the rainbow in between. I picked out a blue one to match my dress; Felix got black. Sara already had a scarf stuffed into her purse.

Sara handed the man a couple of bills and hurried us off. I did a quick calculation in my head—Dad had told me one dollar was equal to ten Austrian schillings. *Hundert* meant *one hundred*, so each scarf had cost ten dollars. We stepped onto another escalator, and when we got off, we found ourselves right at the foot of the opera. I stared up at the big doors, my heart starting to beat faster.

"No, no," Sara said. "Side door. Hurry!"

"Why?" Felix said, glancing at his watch. "It's barely five! The opera doesn't start until seven thirty. We still have over two hours."

"People already in line."

She led us around the side of the grand building to a nondescript door. This felt much better. It was just a normal door. Like to a library or an office building. Sara held it open and gestured for us to go inside.

The corridor looked like a hallway at school. Boring beige tile. Fluorescent lighting. It wasn't intimidating at all. Except for the two hundred people ahead of us, already waiting in line.

Sara bustled us inside and gave a huge sigh. "We made it," she said.

"Is the line sometimes longer?" Felix asked.

"Sometimes it goes around the building."

"People wait in line for the privilege of standing at the opera?" I asked.

"Standing room in Galerie offers the best acoustics," Sara said firmly.

An old woman who had followed us inside nodded in agreement, then looked back at her newspaper as soon as we glanced at her, as if she hadn't been listening to our conversation.

I looked around the corridor. The room was so mundane and drab, it reminded me of my school cafeteria. There was no reason to feel nervous. Right? The line snaked around, back and forth, organized by a red velvet rope. Near the front of the line was a couple. They looked like they had been there awhile, because they had brought their own folding chairs and were sitting patiently, holding hands, each reading their own book. Two old men sat on the floor with a chess game set up between them. In front of us was a young man, maybe a college student, studying a musical score clutched in his hands. In front of him was a young woman with headphones on, her eyes closed, her hands moving as if she were conducting her own private orchestra.

"Opera seems to be popular here," I observed.

The woman behind us snorted. "Once," she said in English with a thick German accent, "I was in line to get tickets to see José Carreras in *Carmen*, and when the tickets went on sale, people started pushing and shoving. I nearly got trampled!"

I felt dizzy.

"Did you get a ticket?" Sara asked.

"Of course!" the old woman said. "I pushed right back! And Carreras was amazing. Worth every bruise."

The room was spinning now. It was like when I was trying to get on the Ferris wheel.

"Becca, are you okay?" Felix asked.

I couldn't reply. Couldn't even shake my head. *Trampled.* That was what the woman had said. *And bruises! I already have as many bruises as I . . .*

"Sit down," Sara instructed, pushing me to the floor.

I sat right where I was in line, cross-legged on the tile, and put my head down in my lap. I waited for the murmurs to start, for people to come over and ask if I was okay. I knew they meant well, but it always made it worse, my embarrassment making me even *more* anxious. I squeezed my eyes shut and waited. And waited. I felt so dizzy I was sure I was going to faint or throw up or . . . The feeling got worse and worse. I wanted to run away, but I didn't know where the bathroom was. My heart was beating so quickly, I was sure I was going to die.

But I didn't. In fact, nothing happened. I just sat there on the cold, hard, uncomfortable floor, feeling sick.

And then, for no reason at all, I started to feel a little

better. It was like a dog had had its teeth in me, and it just decided to leave and chase a squirrel instead. My heartbeat slowed. Not a lot. But a little. I waited a while longer.

Finally, I opened my eyes. There was a speck of lint on the floor. Bright-pink fuzz, as if it had fallen off someone's sweater. I looked around.

No one was staring at me. In fact, a number of people were sitting down on the cold tile floor themselves, including a man in a tuxedo. Next to him, two women in jeans and sweaters were doing a crossword puzzle. The old men still played chess. The young woman conducted to herself. No one paid the slightest bit of attention to me.

I looked up. Felix's face was pale, but Sara was smiling. "You are brave, Becca."

I nodded, almost too scared to move. I took one deep breath and then another. Dr. Teresa had told me this might happen. If I could ride out the anxiety long enough, the spell would pass. It would simply go away. I thought about Sara on the steps of the police station.

I felt as if I had run a race—exhausted but a little exhilarated too. Sara pulled a couple of magazines out of her bag. She offered me one. It was in German, but I took it, flipping through the pictures but barely seeing them. *I didn't run. I didn't die. In fact, nothing happened!* Boredom started to creep in, slowly, slowly, but welcome, like an old friend. I realized we still hadn't gotten any closer to the box office. "Why isn't the line moving?"

Sara glanced at her watch. "Tickets go on sale eighty minutes before showtime. Still have a while."

Once I was done with the magazine, I played with my new scarf, weaving it in and out of my fingers. It was so soft! Like flowing water. Maybe it really was silk. Maybe it was a good-luck charm that had washed my anxiety away.

At precisely 6:10 p.m. the window at the box office opened, and everyone jumped to their feet. Sara clutched a couple of coins in her hand. "How much are the tickets?" I asked. The opera sounded expensive. *What if I get nervous again and can't stay for the whole thing? How much money did Dad put in that little envelope?*

"Fifteen," she said.

She must mean fifteen hundred, I thought. Fifteen hundred schillings was $150, and $150 times three was $450. That was a lot of money! "Did my dad give you that much?" I asked.

Sara gave me a strange look. "Each ticket costs fifteen schillings." She held up one fifty-schilling coin.

"But, but . . . ," I sputtered. It didn't make sense. "Fifteen schillings is only a dollar fifty. That's cheaper than a Big Mac. That's cheaper than the scarf!"

"Of course," Felix said. "There's a large government subsidy. How else could poor people go to the opera?"

Apparently, Austrians believed poor people *needed* to go to the opera! But I didn't have time to wonder about that, because once the line started moving, it moved very quickly. When it was our turn at the ticket counter, Sara said, "Drei Galeriestehplätze, bitte," slid across her coin, and received three white tickets and five schillings in return.

She led us through another set of doors, and as soon as she reached the stairs, she began to run. "Come on!" she called.

In fact, everyone was running up the stairs. Felix and I ran too, struggling to keep up with Sara. "Why are we running?" I asked. "Didn't we just get our tickets?"

"We have to mark our spots!" she huffed as we turned at a landing and hurried up another flight of stairs. Finally, we were at the top. There was a crowd of people waiting in another line in front of a closed door.

Once again, we stopped to catch our breath. It looked like a normal stairwell, not at all what I had pictured for the opera. After a moment, a sour-faced usher threw open the door, and the crowd poured out of the stairwell into a lobby. I started to get nervous again, my hands cold, my breath shallow. I wanted to find a nice quiet corner, but Sara rushed forward with the crowd into the auditorium. I didn't want to be left alone, so I followed her.

The theater was amazing! It was a cavern filled with red velvet seats. Far below were the orchestra seats. Next, I could see three levels of boxes. Not cardboard boxes, but little rooms where people could sit in armchairs and watch the show. Just below us was another balcony filled with seats. We were at the very top. A giant round chandelier hung overhead, with sconce lighting on every box. There were people bustling around me, but I didn't notice. My anxiety melted away, like an ice cube in a cup of hot chocolate.

"Becca!" Sara called. "Felix!"

She was standing in front of a railing, waving at us. We pushed past another woman and walked over to her. "Look!" she exclaimed. "I got a nice spot!"

"It's a railing," said Felix glumly.

It was behind the last row of seats, on the very top balcony. But actually, as I glanced at the stage, I could see pretty well. The seats were staggered, like at a stadium. All of them were empty.

Sara rummaged in her purse and pulled out a delicate purple scarf. She tied it in a neat bow around the railing. "Now tie yours."

I took out my new blue scarf and tied it too, around a section of railing right next to hers. Felix tied his black one on the other side of mine.

Sara bounced excitedly on her toes. "We made it. Got good spot! Now go get snack."

"But . . . ," I protested.

She turned to look at me. "You hungry?"

"Yes, but if I leave my new scarf here, someone might take it," I said.

Sara gave me a look as if I had suggested that a dolphin

might swim up to watch the final act. "Why they do that? It marks your spot!"

I glanced around. There were scarves tied all over the railings. But strangely, almost no people, as if they had run up the stairs, marked their spots with pieces of cloth, and then disappeared. Okay, so maybe that was exactly what had happened.

Then I realized. "Is this another honor-system thing?"

"What?"

"Never mind. Let's go."

CHAPTER 24

The Opera

WE TREKKED ALL the way down the stairs and back toward the subway. I sat on a bench while Sara and Felix went to one of the food stands lining the Ringstraße and came back with three plates. Each one had a round roll, a long sausage that looked like a skinny hot dog, and a big dollop of mustard. The mustard was much spicier than I was used to, but it tasted good. I watched how Felix tore off chunks of the bread and combined all three ingredients.

"I've never actually been to the opera," Felix mused, his mouth full of mustard and sausage. "Does the Staatsoper have supertitles?"

"You mean subtitles," I said.

"No," Felix said. "Subtitles are at the *bottom* of the screen, like in a movie. Supertitles are projected onto a little screen *above* the stage."

Sara shook her head. "No. But I told you the plot. You will *feel* the music."

I was a little doubtful about that. "How did you learn all this?" I asked. "Where to go and what to do?"

Sara blushed. "I love music. First time I went to the opera, I did everything wrong! Stood in wrong spot. Man yelled at me. I not know to bring scarf. But a nice lady saw me, and she had an extra ticket. She gave it to me. I got a seat! Listened to beautiful music. In country that makes opera so cheap, everyone can go. And it made me feel like maybe everything would be okay."

When we were done eating, we went back to the opera, walking in the front doors this time. The main entrance looked more like a concert hall and less like the corridor behind the school gym. There was a massive marble staircase with a red runner. We spent a while admiring the paintings and gilded statues, the clothes on the other people, the ornate gold chandeliers. We took the marble staircase this time, walking slowly up the carpet, which was so plush, my sandals seemed to sink into it. It didn't feel quite real—had I paid $1.50 and suddenly been transported to a castle? I kept waiting for the anxious feeling to return, but there were so many new and interesting things to look at.

We finally made it back to the top floor. I saw an usher handing out programs and went to get one, but when I held out my hand, she said something to me I didn't understand.

"You have to pay for the program," Felix translated.

"Oh," I said. "Can I buy one?"

Sara rummaged in her purse and handed over a few coins.

"How much did it cost?" I asked.

"Twenty-five schillings," Felix said.

"The program costs more than the ticket?!"

Sara laughed. "Yes. That is odd!"

The program was nice, though. It was really almost a thin book instead of a program. There was even a page that had a summary of the plot in English. I read it quickly. We found our spots on the railing, and I breathed a sigh of relief that my scarf was still there.

The theater was filling up now. I scanned the rows, looking for empty seats, places to run and hide. There were none. "Is it sold out?" I asked.

"Yes," Sara said.

My heart started to beat faster again. I looked down. We were so high, it made me dizzy. *No, not again!* My hands started to sweat, and I wiped them on my new blue scarf, leaving stains.

Suddenly, the lights went down. A hush washed over the theater. I was going to faint. I was going to throw up. I was about to run out.

And then the music started.

The music was gentle, shimmering at first. I shivered. I couldn't see the orchestra, but I could hear it, as if the music were just appearing out of the darkness. Then a waltz started—one, two, three, one, two, three—slow and sweet and longing.

The curtain rose on a party scene. The stage was filled with people in ball gowns. Who cared about exit rows and possible stampedes when there was a ball to watch!

A man with dark hair walked onto the stage, and the audience roared, cheering and applauding, even though he hadn't opened his mouth yet. I figured it must be the José guy. He didn't have a microphone, and yet when he did start to sing, I could literally feel my head vibrating. I'd never heard anything like it—pure, clear, unamplified music that sounded as up close and personal as if I were wearing headphones. It was like a plug was pulled on my fears, draining them all away with the music.

I couldn't understand exactly what was going on most of the time, despite Sara's description and the summary in the program, but it didn't really matter. I understood what the characters were feeling. And I loved it. When the curtain came down and the lights came up, I was disappointed it was over, until I realized this must be intermission. Alfredo and Violetta hadn't gotten back together. And no one had died.

Sara led us to a mirror-lined salon filled with couches to sit on and a counter where a waitress was selling champagne and chocolate-covered strawberries. Sara bought us each a small bottle of sparkling water. Next, we picked up a Plakat—this was a poster, printed on thin newspaper, advertising that night's opera, complete with the times and the cast. The saleslady wrapped a rubber band around it as she handed it to me. The water and the poster each cost more than my ticket.

I started to feel nervous again in the crowded hall. It was hot. Without music, my throat felt dry, even though I'd just drunk all that water. Sara glanced over at me, and I must have looked a little green or something, because she took my hand and led Felix and me up another set of stairs. We went out a door, and suddenly we were on a rooftop balcony.

I immediately felt better. There were only a few people on the roof, and the air was cooler too. I let out a great sigh. The green copper statues of horses rearing were now at eye level, with the stores of Kärntner Straße visible below.

"What do you think?" Sara asked. "Of opera?"

"Well," Felix said sheepishly. "I have to admit, it's not half bad."

"I love it," I gushed. "I thought the José guy would be lame, but when he sings, it feels like that 'Crisscross Applesauce' game kids play to give each other goose bumps. It gives me shivers!"

Sara smiled. "I so happy!" We stared at the lights below, twinkling in the summer evening. I took deep breaths of the cool air until it was time to go back to our seats. I mean, our *non*-seats. I just had the slightest brush of nerves this time as I walked into the enormous hall. It felt like instead of careening around in my stomach, the butterflies were fluttering around me, caressing my cheeks. My feet were starting to feel a little sore, but as the lights went down again, I forgot all about them, and the butterflies were chased off by the music. I leaned on the railing, closing my eyes sometimes when the music was just too pretty to bear any other way.

Okay, so maybe I cried a little at the end too.

I looked over at Sara as the lights came up. She was dabbing at her eyes with her purple scarf. I did the same with my blue one. The audience cheered and stomped their feet and yelled "Bravo" as the singers took their bows, and even Felix joined in. People threw flowers. Mr. Carreras gathered a few of them up and presented them to the soprano singing with him. The crowd screamed even louder. This went on for a good ten minutes. Every time I thought the audience was done, José came out to take another bow, and it started all over again.

Sara grinned. It made me happy to see her looking so happy.

When the singers were finally done, I carefully collected my program, my poster, and my ticket. As we walked down the plush stairs, I could see the crystals in the chandelier shift a little, almost as if someone were still singing, as if a high note from an aria were making the glass vibrate.

We came out of the big doors onto Kärntner Straße.

It seemed like a different, magical place in the darkness, all lit up. People walked toward the Straßenbahn stop, humming to themselves. I was part of something; we had all had the same amazing experience together. The rattle of the streetcars was the percussion; the murmurs of the people were the violins. And for the first time, I understood what Sara meant when she told me to listen to the universe.

CHAPTER 25

The Letter

THE MAGICAL MOOD lasted until we got home. The door opened before I could even pull out my key. "Finally!" Dad called out. He sounded worried.

"I left a note," Sara said, glancing at her watch. "We back right on time."

"No, no," Dad said, ushering us all inside. "It's just . . ."

Katarina stood up from where she'd been sitting on the couch. She was clutching something small and rectangular in her hands. "Sara, you got a letter!"

"Einen Brief?" Felix asked in German.

Katarina nodded. She handed the letter to Sara. It was bent and wrinkled, as if someone had crumpled it up and flattened it out again. Small cursive letters formed Sara's name. "From Bosnia. But not Mama's handwriting."

"Hester and her team found some bags of mail that had

never been delivered in a bombed-out post office. They sent them to the newspaper. We were going to try to get them to the right people, maybe write a story about the missing letters. An assistant sorting through them noticed this one was addressed to my office. Where you used to work as a housekeeper. She thought it was odd and brought it to me."

"I sent Mama that address when I first arrived," Sara said. "That was months ago. She not get my other letters?"

"I don't know," Katarina said simply.

Sara started to shake. "Why she not write herself? Did something happen?"

"I don't know," Katarina repeated. "Do you want us to leave you alone while you open the letter?"

Sara shook her head. "No. Please stay."

She ripped open the letter. A single piece of paper fell to the floor. Trembling, she bent over and picked it up. The rest of us—Dad, me, Felix, and Katarina—stood in a hushed circle around her as she read.

Sara started to cry.

"Is it . . . bad news?" I asked.

"No, it's from Mama. She asked a neighbor to post the letter."

"Oh, thank goodness," said Katarina.

Sara read the rest of the letter quickly and silently. When she was done, she sat down slowly on the couch.

The tulle of her skirt flipped up; the hot pink, so flattering before, washed out her face now. The rhinestones twinkled annoyingly. "May I have a cup of tea?" Sara asked.

I ran to get the water.

A few minutes later, we were all gathered around the couch, mugs of tea in our hands, listening intently as Sara paraphrased the letter.

"Mama says since Jewish humanitarian society stopped their evacuations, she paid a woman to help them sneak across the no-man's-land of the Sarajevo airport."

"What?!" Dad exclaimed. "There was a report on the news about that last week. If they get picked up by the United Nations peacekeeper forces, they'll simply be brought back to Sarajevo. However, if the Serb forces find them—"

"Dad," I interrupted. "This isn't a news report. It's Sara's family." She didn't need to be reminded that they could be raped or tortured or killed. We'd all watched that news report together.

"I'm sorry," Dad said. "Keep going."

Sara took another sip of her tea and continued, "Mama says she knows it's dangerous, but things are worse. There's no electricity, little food, and they moved in with a neighbor because our apartment was damaged by shelling. This is a way to literally walk out of war zone. If it works, if she and Eldin make it to the Bosnian-held territory on the other side of airport, they'll go to the village Butmir, where they can take a bus to Croatia. Just like I did. From there, they hope to find a way to Austria."

"That's good news," Katarina said. "You know they're alive and they are coming here."

I took Sara's hand and squeezed it.

"Mama left a phone number. A friend of a friend in Croatia."

"Call!" Katarina insisted. "Now."

Sara walked over to the big red phone on the kitchen countertop. We all stayed on the couch and pretended we weren't watching her. Sara carefully laid the letter on the counter and dialed, slow and deliberate. She turned away so we couldn't see her face as the phone began to ring. I watched her fingers play with a bit of netting from her skirt, bunching it into a ball and then smoothing it out again.

The phone rang. And rang. And rang.

"No one . . . Ah, halo!"

We all gasped as Sara started speaking quickly in a language none of us understood. She spoke for a minute or two. I realized I was holding my breath and forced myself to breathe in and out. *Will she get to talk to her mother? Did she find them?*

Suddenly, she hung up the phone. She still had her back to us, and her shoulders started to shake. "They not there," she managed finally. I couldn't hear her cry, but when she turned to face us, her mascara was running down her face. "She expected them three weeks ago. But they never showed up."

"Oh, Schatzi," Katarina sighed.

I ran to give Sara a hug.

"Where could they be?" Sara wailed. "What happened?!"

"There was probably just a problem finding a bus," I said. "Or maybe they decided to come directly to Austria?"

"Maybe." Sara clung to me tighter as she cried. "Eldin is only six. His best friend was a little Serbian boy. He had curly brown hair. And then they . . . they wouldn't let him come over anymore. They wouldn't hurt him, would they?"

I looked to Dad or Katarina to say something to fix this, to make the situation better. But they just stood there, frozen. I realized they didn't know what to say either. There was no answer I could write down in my Doomsday Journal. My head spun, as if I were back in line at the opera, except this time, Sara wasn't looking calmly on. This time, I had to be the calm one.

"Sit down," I told Sara, leading her back to the couch. She followed me like a lost puppy. I picked up her mug; it was cold. "Could someone get her some fresh tea?"

Everyone sprang into motion then: Felix ran to refill the cup, Katarina draped a blanket over Sara's shoulders, Dad picked up the envelope and studied the postmark. We didn't really do or say anything; we just sat there. It felt weird. And uncomfortable. But eventually, Sara stopped crying, and she and Felix and Katarina walked home.

Dad hugged me as soon as they left. "I'm so grateful that you are here and not . . ."

He didn't finish his sentence, but I knew what he meant. "Me too."

"I'm exhausted now, but I have one question before you go to bed. Did you really go to the opera?"

I nodded.

"With all those people?"

"Yeah."

"And you stayed the whole time? Without getting upset?"

"I was nervous at first," I admitted. "And I did freak out when we were waiting in line. But Sara was super patient, and I just sat there and eventually the fear went away. Like Dr. Teresa said it would. And the opera!" I grinned, remembering. "It was so great, Dad! It felt really different, listening to the music with other people there. It was like we were all doing something together!"

"Becca, I am so proud of you." Dad smiled, but then he looked sad.

"What's wrong?" I asked.

"Do you remember last year, when you wanted to go see *Les Mis* for your birthday?"

"Yeah."

"I vetoed the idea because I was worried that you might get nervous. Well, I think I might have made a mistake." He gave me a bear hug, and for a moment, I felt like the bravest person in the world.

I went to bed then, but I couldn't sleep. I'd never felt such a mix of emotions—I was happy about the opera and sad Sara didn't know where her family was. My dad was proud of me! And yet I still squirmed with disappointment that my anxiety had prevented me from doing so many things in the past.

Finally, I gave up on sleeping and picked up my Doomsday Journal. I got a pen and drew a thick line through item #3 on my list.

1. ~~Eat a soft-boiled egg.~~
2. Learn to ride a bike.
3. ~~Hang out in a large crowd.~~
4. Go on the Riesenrad.
5. Travel somewhere by myself.

Two! I'd crossed two things off my list now. But now there were only a few days left before the dance class. After how proud Dad had looked tonight, I didn't want to disappoint him. And Sara. I had to do something to distract her from worrying about her family. But just thinking about getting on that bike again made me nervous.

If only I could re-create how I'd felt tonight—connected to everyone and everything. If I could feel like that, I was sure I could do it.

Then I had an idea. A good one. I turned to a blank page and began to write.

CHAPTER 26

"Do-Re-Mi" Ride

THE NEXT MORNING as I was getting dressed, I caught sight of the bruises on my thigh. They were dark-violet now—truly purple. I didn't get many bruises. I didn't take many chances. I didn't remember ever having so many bruises before. As if an invisible force were poking them, they started to ache. *What if I have internal bleeding?! What if . . .*

No. I forced myself to pull on some jeans and went to get some oatmeal.

After breakfast, Felix, Sara, and I rolled my bike up the little hill. Sara was maybe a little quieter than usual, but she seemed okay. It was a beautiful summer day. The sunshine was yellow but not too hot; the sky blue and clear; the grapevines green and winding; my helmet as red as a wild strawberry. It felt a bit like I was Dorothy, walking into a Technicolor world. I was nervous, but I forced myself to take a deep breath. The strap on my helmet cut into my chin, so I loosened it, then tightened it again. I swung my leg over the bike and sat down on the seat. And then in my head, I imagined José Carreras starting to sing:

Do, the bike, it stays upright.
Re, the pedal two o'clock.

I put the pedal in the two o'clock position, and before I could think about it too much, I pushed down with my right foot. My hands were shaking on the handlebars. I know Felix noticed, but he didn't say anything. Sara held the seat as she ran along beside me.

Mi, push off, you're balancing.
Fa, just ride, don't try to talk.

The grapevines were whipping past me. I wobbled once, and then it suddenly felt easier. As if the bike were part of me, and I could control it. Like I controlled my arms and legs.

So, you're rolling down the hill.
La, it's really quite a thrill.
Ti . . .

I realized Sara was no longer holding on, and immediately, I lost control of the bike and crashed into a grapevine. I was sure a bruise was forming on my bruise, probably as purple as the grapes. But for once I didn't care. Because I'd done it. I knew I had. Just for a second. But still. And what I kept hearing in my head was this:

Ti, get up and try again.
That will bring us back to do-oh-oh-oh.
Do, the bike, it stays upright.

As if following orders, I jumped up and put the bike back on the path.

Re, the pedal two o'clock.
Mi, push off, you're balancing.

And then it happened again. The motion. The movement. The lyrics in my head. It felt as if I were flying. *It must be a fluke,* I thought. *Beginner's luck.*

Fa, just ride, don't try to talk.
So, you're rolling down the hill.
La, it's really quite a thrill.

The words and motions flowed together as I rode far into the vineyard. I could hear everything: the wind in the grapevines, the squeak of the back wheel, a bird calling overhead, the squish of mud as I rolled through a puddle.

When I stopped, there was no one around. I was alone. In the hills somewhere in the outskirts of Vienna. All by myself. But I didn't feel alone. It was quiet, and the sky was blue, and I felt happy as I listened to the heartbeat of the universe.

Finally, I started pedaling again, heading back to Felix and Sara. I sang out loud this time. Maybe I wobbled a bit, and sure, my voice shook, but I kept riding. My parents would be so proud of me. I was so proud of me! When I got home, I could ride to the pool with Chrissy. Mom and I could go on a bike ride along the river. I could ride with Felix to dance class! On the street. On the hard street. With no soft grapevines to crash into. All at once, my fears rushed back, and I fell off the bike.

No, I told myself sternly as I picked myself up from the dirt. That was a worry for another day. Today, all I had to worry about was singing my song.

Felix and Sara didn't even wait until I'd fully stopped before running over to me.

"You did it!" Felix said.

"You see?" said Sara. "Very brave."

"Thank you," I whispered to both of them. "You gave me the idea."

"What?" Sara looked puzzled.

"With the music last night," I said. "Today, I sang a song as I rode."

"Opera?" Felix asked.

"No." I laughed. "But I did imagine José Carreras singing it. I just made up words to an old song."

"What song?" Sara asked.

"Do-Re-Mi."

I got a blank look from both of them.

"From *The Sound of Music*."

"Never seen it," said Felix.

Sara shook her head.

"What?!" I exclaimed. "Neither of you has ever seen *The Sound of Music*?"

"No," said Sara.

"I've heard of it," Felix said defensively. "But it's kind of a cliché in Austria. No one actually walks around wearing dirndls."

"Except Frau Gamperl," added Sara. "And the waitresses at the Gasthof. And—"

"Okay, so *almost* nobody wears a dirndl," Felix amended.

We flopped down in the grass on the edge of the vineyard. Sara passed out bars of Kinder Schokolade, or chocolate for kids. (Katarina insisted that they were healthy because they contained milk. I hated to tell her all milk chocolate contained milk.) Felix handed out bottles of Almdudler. That was an Austrian soda; it tasted a lot like ginger ale.

"Thank you," I whispered to both of them again. There was more I wanted to say, but that was all that came out. We lay there a long time, gazing at the sky, our shoulders touching in the grass. Listening.

THAT EVENING, AS soon as he got home from work, I asked Dad to come down to the blacktop with me. There were still a couple of five- and six-year-olds zipping around on their bikes, but I ignored them. I fastened my helmet, put my foot on my pedal, sang my little song (in my head this time), and pushed off.

I only wobbled once. And Dad grinned the rest of the evening.

CHAPTER 27

The Pig Journal

The next morning, Sara, Felix, and I were planning to ride all the way to the dance studio, just so I could get a feel for the route before class on Friday. However, when we woke up, it was raining. Like, really pouring. I mean, Austrians don't usually let a little rain stop them, but it was raining cats and dogs, and I'm pretty sure there were a couple of cows and chickens in there too.

"Sorry," Sara told me.

"You'll be fine," Felix reassured me. "There's a bike path the whole way."

I knew there was a path. I'd made him sketch me out a little map. But the last two blocks were on the street. *What if a car makes an unexpected turn? What if a bus stops suddenly? What if a truck swerves into the bike path?* Still, there was nothing we could do. I couldn't practice in a thunderstorm—we might get hit by lightning! (DJ #2, p. 12.)

Then that afternoon, Sara got a phone call from Marco. He asked her to come in early on Friday to participate in a more advanced group. Sara refused at first, not wanting to leave Felix and me to make the bike ride alone. But I kept thinking about her list, how she wanted to perform ballroom dancing, and finally told her she should call him back. Felix and I could do the bike ride alone.

She asked our parents if it was okay with them. "Of course," said Katarina. "Felix rides his bike to school every day alone!" I was worried about Dad, but he simply asked me, "Do you feel okay with that plan?"

I nodded.

"Then it's all right with me."

For once, Dad believed in me! So I couldn't back out now. But on Friday morning I found myself regretting my offer. Why hadn't we all gone early *with* Sara? Felix and I could have just sat there and read a book while she and Marco practiced. But she was already gone, so it was too late. I slowly packed my backpack: map, bottle of water, first aid kit. I was as ready as I was ever going to be.

There was a knock at the door. It was Felix, looking like his best friend had died. And he was two hours early.

"What's wrong?" I asked.

"I can't go to dance class today."

"What are you talking about? You have to go. It was Mai's present."

"Don't care."

"But it's on your list!"

"Nope. I'm taking it off."

"Why?" I asked.

"I feel like I'm going to throw up."

"You're not going to throw up." I paused. "Okay, so I *have* thrown up from nerves before. But you're *probably* not going to throw up."

"You're not helping!"

I wanted to help. "Which part are you worried about?"

"All of it!"

"The bike ride?"

"No. But the rest of it. Having to dance with girls from my class."

"But you like Daisy and Mai," I pointed out.

"That makes it worse!"

I studied Felix. I knew that feeling. Like you were out of control. Like you absolutely could not handle what was going on. I couldn't just abandon Felix to his anxiety. He'd helped me with the bike. He'd stood next to me at the opera. I had to do something to help him.

"I'm terrible at social things," Felix went on. "And what is more social than dancing?"

Then I had an idea.

We took the bus a few stops and got off when we reached Aïda. "I'm jittery enough," Felix said. "I don't need any coffee."

I ignored him and led him into the paper store next door. I'd remembered it from our first visit to the coffee shop. The shelves were filled with all kinds of items—wrapping paper, drawing paper, newspaper, computer paper, tissue paper, greeting cards, and journals. Lots and lots of journals. "Pick out a journal," I told Felix.

"Why?"

"Just do it," I said. "I'll explain when we get home."

We searched the aisles. There were flowered journals. And plain leather ones. There were diaries with pictures of puppies and cats and with geometric designs. Felix finally chose one with a pattern on the front: black and brown and gray and tan.

"Are those . . . bugs?" I asked.

"Yup."

"Why?"

"Remember the goulash?" he said.

"How could I forget?"

"That was a fun evening."

"Yeah," I agreed. "It was."

We went to the counter and got in line to pay. There was another display of journals right by the register—Vienna landmarks. Those diaries were obviously meant for tourists, but on the front of one of them was a beautiful sketch of the Riesenrad. At the last minute, I put it on top of the bug journal and bought it too.

Truthfully, I was a little surprised at myself. I mean, I still had plenty of pages left in Doomsday Journal #4. But for some reason, I knew I had to buy it.

When we got home, I told Felix to wait in the living room while I went to my room to get something. A few minutes later, I came back downstairs carrying all four of my journals: the map one, the one with polka dots, the rainbow one, and even the hot-pink one with the unicorn.

"What are those?" Felix asked.

"These," I said dramatically, plopping them down onto our coffee table, "are my Doomsday Journals."

He tried not to roll his eyes, but I knew him well enough by then to know what he was doing. It was totally an eye roll, even if he tried to pass it off as a blink. "And what in the world is a Doomsday Journal?"

"It's one way I cope with my fears," I said. "I write down all the bad things that might happen. Disasters. Catastrophes. The worst-case scenarios."

"And that helps?"

"I know it sounds crazy. But it does help. Because I also write down all the ways I could cope if the worst really *did* happen."

"It sounds stupid," Felix said.

"Hey," I said. "I've shown only a few people in the entire world these journals. Show a little respect."

"Sorry," he grumbled.

"Listen . . . This is what I wrote my first day in Austria." I flipped through the pages of Doomsday Journal #4 and read an entry aloud: "They are trying to make me eat raw eggs. What if I get salmonella?! High fever. Vomiting. Okay, so what if that happened? Dad would take me to the hospital. I'd get antibiotics. And maybe an IV (I hate needles—see DJ #1, p. 10)."

"Wow," Felix said.

"Yeah, I know," I said. "But look how much better I am now. I ate a soft-boiled egg!"

Felix gave me a look.

"And I hung out in a crowd." I flipped frantically through the pages again. "Here it is: 'How to Cope with a Stampede. Number one: Be sure to protect your head. A broken arm or leg can be fixed. A broken skull is much more difficult to repair.'"

"You are strange."

"And bike safety is in here too." I flipped some more and read, "Always be sure to wear a helmet and use hand signals. Most accidents occur when—"

"Fine, fine," he said. "I get it. Just . . . stop reading."

I held out the bug journal to him.

He took it. "So what do I have to do?"

"Go to your room and write down everything you're afraid might happen at dance class. And then once you have everything down, come up with at least one way to cope with each one."

Felix looked doubtful, but he took the journal.

Once he left, I took everything back up to my room. The thing was, even though I acted as if I were fine, I was nervous too. Not about the dance class—but about the bike ride to get there. I sat down at my desk and opened Doomsday Journal #4.

What if I fall off my bike? I wrote. What if I get hit by a car? What if I get run over by a Straßenbahn? I might break my arm. I might break my leg. I might end up a vegetable in the hospital. What if someone sees my bike helmet and calls me Strawberry Head?

I still felt a little off. Something wasn't quite right.

The red of the Riesenrad journal caught my eye, and a new idea flashed into my mind. *What if I start another journal? A different kind. One where I list everything that goes right.*

I thought about that for a moment. *What if I pay a little more attention to the good stuff? All the fun things. I mean, not all the time. But just a little bit. What if I had a place to write down some of my successes?*

My hand was shaking as I picked up a pen. I wasn't sure what to call this idea, so I just started doodling on the first page. I drew a big circle, and then I added some lines that turned into ears and feet and, finally, a little curly tail. It was a pig! I didn't know I could draw such a cute little pig. I remembered that *having pig* in German meant *having good luck*. Sara and Felix had told me that the day we visited the police station.

Then it hit me! I wrote in big block letters over the little drawing.

MY PIG JOURNAL

Instead of my Doomsday Journal, this would be my Good-Day Journal. My little piggy book, full of luck.

I started writing then, and the words just flowed. How proud I was that I had learned to ride a bike. How amazing it was that I had eaten an egg. How beautiful the opera music had been!

Yeah, on this trip I really have had a lot of pig.

CHAPTER 28

Climb Every Mountain

Felix and I met up in front of the bike-storage room about an hour later. "Okay," he said with a grimace. "Maybe it helped a little."

"You wouldn't be talking about my completely silly diary idea, would you?"

"Come on, bike rider." He smiled. "Let's go."

The first part of the journey was pretty easy. I wobbled a bit as I got on the bike but quickly found my balance. The path through the park wasn't crowded, and the wind felt nice, cooling my ears under my helmet. The trees grew together over the path, creating patterns of light and shadow on the pavement. Before I knew it, we had reached the section of the trail that went along the street. Felix turned the corner. I took a deep breath and followed him.

There was a marked bike lane, but the road was busier than I'd expected. Cars whizzed by. The traffic didn't seem to bother Felix. *Does that mean it's safe? Or is he just reckless?* My heart started to beat faster. It was only a few more blocks. I could do this. *Right? Right?!*

A Straßenbahn turned onto the street then, ringing its bell, ordering the cars out of its way. I tensed up. My elbows and knees no longer felt like joints. I was the Tin Man from *The Wizard of Oz*. Seriously, it's hard to ride a bike without joints. I began to wobble, almost running into a parked delivery van, but I recovered my balance. One more block.

A car horn sounded, loud and sharp. I squeezed on the brakes. Too late, I remembered that was exactly what Sara had told me *not* to do. It was too hard and too fast. I swerved wildly, hoping that would somehow keep me from pitching over the handlebars.

It didn't. I ended up near the curb, tangled in my bike.

Another car whizzed by, so close I could feel the wind.

There was blood on my knee. A lot of blood. This was my worst nightmare. I'd fallen off my bike in the street. *Maybe I hit my head too.* I felt my helmet. It didn't seem damaged. *But maybe I'm disoriented.*

I could feel the tears welling up, the panic rising in me, like the crowd at the opera, leaping to their feet to applaud. *Good job, Becca!* my brain was yelling at me. *You've gone and gotten yourself hurt!*

"Hey." Felix had noticed I wasn't following him, and had doubled back. "You all right?"

No! I wanted to scream. *I'm not. I knew this would hap-pen. I never should have tried. I never should have left home.*

"Oh, gosh, you're bleeding," Felix said. But the thing was, his tone was conversational. As if he were talking about the weather. He didn't really sound that upset.

Panic! My brain instructed. *You got hurt!* And yet there was Felix, acting like this wasn't a big deal. And that was when I had an amazing thought. Really unique, at least for me.

Maybe it wasn't a big deal.

I mean, sure, I had gotten hurt. But I was pretty cer-tain nothing was broken. And my helmet didn't have a scratch on it, so I hadn't hit my head. I had fallen between two parked cars, so I was safe from oncoming traffic. Sure, this wasn't great—I'd end up at dance class with a scraped and bloody knee. But maybe this was like when I'd freaked out in the line at the opera. Maybe I could handle it.

"Yeah," I said, reminding myself not to look at the blood running down my leg. "I, um . . ." I swallowed hard. "I have a first aid kit in my backpack."

Felix jumped into action, zipping open my bag and pull-ing it out. "Got it." He rummaged around until he found a roll of gauze. "Come sit on the curb," he said, "and I'll clean you up."

I untangled myself from the bike and crawled over to the curb. Felix knelt down next to me. Every time I caught a glimpse of the blood, I felt woozy. *You have a concussion!* my brain screamed at me.

Probably not! I yelled back. *Since I didn't hit my head.*

Felix cleaned my leg, using a piece of gauze to wipe up all the blood. He used an antiseptic wipe to apply pressure to the wound; it felt cold on my skin. When he was done, I forced myself to look down.

The cut was much smaller than I excepted, only about an inch long, just under my kneecap. There was a long scrape on my calf too. But that was it. No broken bone poking out of the skin. No huge gash exposing tendons and muscles.

You're going to get an infection!

Shut up, brain, I said to myself. And then to Felix, "I think there's some antibiotic ointment in there too."

He dug around in the kit, found the tube, squeezed some out onto a clean piece of gauze, and spread it gently onto the cut and the scrape. A drop of blood oozed out and then stopped.

"Plaster?" he asked.

"I don't think it's broken . . . Oh." He was holding up a Band-Aid. "Yes, please."

He pasted it on, as gentle as my mom. "There!" he said when he was done. He picked up the bloody gauze and threw it in a nearby trash can.

I sat numbly on the curb. So I hadn't died. "I don't think I can get back on the bike," I said.

Felix sighed and sat down next to me. "Did I ever tell you why I don't like to dance?"

I shook my head. I was happy to listen to any story if it meant I didn't have to get back on the bike.

"When I was really little, maybe four or five, my father took me to a dance class he was teaching. I had these tiny little tap shoes, and I remember being so excited. But when the class started, it was a disaster. The students were nine or ten, and they looked giant to me. I stood in the back row with no idea what to do. Halfway through the class, I started to cry. My father had to stop instruction and get me a drink of water. I felt so awful. I had let him down! My parents split up about a month after that class. And for years I sort of thought he left because he was embarrassed to have a son like me."

I opened my mouth to say that wasn't true. But hadn't I worried about the same thing with my father?

"I know that doesn't make sense," Felix went on. "Those kids were twice my age. My parents were already having problems—he probably took me that evening because Mama was meeting with her lawyer or something. And yet I couldn't shake the feeling that the night of the failed dance class was when everything started to go wrong."

"I've felt that way too," I admitted.

"I want to go to the dance class," Felix continued. "I don't want to disappoint Mai. But it's more than that. I want to tell my dad that I tried again. But I don't think I can do it if you're not there to help me. So please, Becca, get back on the bike."

I did.

Of course I did.

And I followed him into the traffic. Even though I was terrified. It's a lot easier to be brave when you're helping out a friend.

THE DANCE STUDIO was located in a big old building with a central courtyard. We left our bikes there and followed the signs up a rickety set of stairs to the studio. In the first room, there were little benches with cubbies underneath for your belongings.

Sara walked over to me as I was storing my backpack. "What happened to your knee?"

"Oh," I said. "I had a little . . . mishap on the bike."

"Mishap?" Sara asked.

"I fell off," I admitted.

I waited for her to worry. To say, *Are you hurt? Did you clean the cut?* Like my parents would have done. But instead she said, "You okay."

It was a statement, not a question, and somehow, that made me feel better.

"Yeah," I agreed. "I am."

The instructor, a tall, impossibly thin woman with a dance skirt and a bun, came out and clapped her hands. She said something in German I didn't understand, then repeated herself in English. "The teen dance class is beginning shortly. Please come into the studio."

We followed her into a large, open room with polished wooden floors. The walls were lined with mirrors. A barre for ballet had been shoved to the back of the room.

"Felix! Becca!"

We turned around to see Daisy and Mai.

"I'm so glad you came," Mai said to Felix.

Felix nodded. He looked a little green.

Rasheed and Peter waved to us from across the room. I waved back, and then the teacher clapped her hands again. "Gather around, please. Girls facing clockwise, boys facing counterclockwise."

Felix grabbed my arm. "Be my partner," he said desperately.

"Sure," I said. Daisy and Rasheed squeezed into the circle next to us. Mai and Peter were on the other side.

"Willkommen!" The teacher cleared her throat. "I am Frau Kovács. These are my assistants, Sara and Marco." Marco gave a little bow, and Sara curtsied. "They will be demonstrating the steps. This is a five-week class on ballroom basics. Everyone who completes the class will get an invitation to the University Ball on August 28."

"A ball?" squealed Daisy.

August 28 was a few days before I was going back home. A ball sounded like a pretty cool way to wrap up my visit.

"We start with a waltz," the teacher continued. "There are three counts. Count with me. Eins, zwei, drei. Eins, zwei, drei."

We ran through a few basic steps. Sara and Marco demonstrated and walked around the circle to help anyone who was having trouble. I listened as intently as if we were learning the safety procedures for skydiving. It turned out I was actually a pretty good dancer. "Just like following a recipe," I told Felix.

"Wunderbar!" said Frau Kovács. "Now we change partners."

"You can do it!" I whispered as Felix moved around the circle to the next girl. It was Mai. She was smiling. Felix was as pale as the powdered sugar on an Apfelstrudel.

My new partner was Peter; he was a decent dancer. Rasheed was awful but so cheerful about his mistakes, he was fun to dance with. Then there were a couple of guys I didn't know, and the next time the teacher called "Partner wechseln!" Felix was standing before me again.

"I did it!" he exclaimed as we practiced the steps. "And I only stepped on her foot once! I apologized, of course, but then she said Peter had stepped on her foot three times, and Rasheed had stepped on her five times, so I was actually doing the best of all!"

The class went faster than I'd expected. "Hmm," Frau

Kovács said when we were done. "You are not terrible. See you next week!"

AFTER CLASS, MARCO led our little group to his father's ice cream shop. Giovanni's Gelato was just around the corner, in an old building with marble floors and carved ceilings. The molding on the walls was old, but the furnishings were modern, with glass tabletops made from bits of melted glass and sleek metal chairs. Colorful masks and robes covered the walls, all feathers and flowers and beads, as if a masquerade party had hung up their costumes.

A man who had a mop of thick gray hair and was wearing an apron greeted us when we came in. "Buongiorno!" he said. "Willkommen bei Giovanni! Das beste Eis im . . ." He groaned when he saw Marco. "Mein Sohn bringt die ganze Klasse." Everyone laughed.

"What'd he say?" I asked.

"He complained about his son bringing the entire class," Felix whispered.

Marco chattered with his father in Italian for a moment. His father looked at us again, with more interest this time, and then he grinned and said something in Italian.

"My father welcomes you to our shop," Marco translated. "He says, 'Friends of my son are friends of mine.'"

Marco showed us to a big booth in the corner, surrounded by windows and padded with little blue velvet pillows. He handed each of us a menu. Instead of words, this menu had color photos of the most amazing ice cream sundaes I'd ever seen.

Felix and Peter got the Schoko-Lovers sundae; Daisy ordered the Hawaiian—pineapple gelato, vanilla sauce, and pistachios. Sara got the Klimt (apparently a famous Austrian painter who liked gold leaf), and everything was golden on her sundae—butter-pecan gelato, butterscotch, and toasted almonds. Mai ordered a Berry Bonanza, which had so much fruit, I wasn't sure it counted as a treat after all. Marco and Rasheed each got an iced coffee with vanilla ice cream, and I got the Mozart, the house specialty, which had a little bit of everything.

"Oh my gosh!" Daisy exclaimed when Marco placed the sundae down in front of me. "It's huge!"

We dug in. "You're so lucky your parents let you bike here by yourselves," Rasheed said between bites. "My mom made me carpool with Daisy."

She shoved him playfully.

His comment made me remember his mom was a lawyer. I glanced over at Sara. She and Marco and his dad were chatting in the corner of the store, out of earshot. "Rasheed, can I ask you for some advice?"

"Sure," Rasheed said. "Chess or Legos? Those are my two areas of expertise."

I laughed. "Legal advice."

"I don't know anything about the law," Rasheed said. "If you want to know about that, ask my mom."

"Yeah," I said. "That's the idea. At Felix's party, Katarina said your mom specializes in—"

"Immigration law." He sighed. "It's all she ever talks about now. She used to work for a big corporate firm, but then she quit her old job and started her own practice."

"Why do you care about immigration law?" Peter asked.

"It's not advice for me," I admitted. "It's about Sara."

"She is *such* a good dancer," Mai sighed. "I heard the teacher ask her and Marco to help open the ball."

"Open the ball?" I asked. "What does that mean? They stand at the door and hand out programs?"

Daisy laughed. "No, at the beginning of every ball, they ask a bunch of young couples to perform the first dance."

"It's a great honor," added Mai. "And they get to wear these beautiful white dresses."

Peter rolled his eyes. "Becca asked for legal advice, not fashion tips."

Rasheed leaned in close. "Is Sara here illegally?"

"No. But she only has that temporary thing."

"TPS?" asked Rasheed.

"Yeah," I said. "So she can't work."

"Oh," said Peter. "I guess that's why she told the Heuriger owner no."

"What?" Felix asked.

"At your birthday party. She was so good on the violin.

The owner offered her a job playing for him on weekends. She turned him down."

"We're worried about her family," I went on. "Her mom and brother sent her a letter saying they were coming to join her here, but . . . they never showed up."

"Do you think your mom could help find them?" Felix asked.

Rasheed frowned. "I don't know," he admitted. "But I'll ask her."

"Thanks," I said.

ON THE WAY home, I could barely breathe as we wove through the traffic, but the scary part was over after about five minutes. The path through the park was easier. When we arrived at home, I took off my bike helmet and shook my sweaty hair free. And I felt, well . . . I felt like I had climbed a mountain.

CHAPTER 29

In Prague

THINGS WENT PRETTY smoothly for a couple of weeks after that. We went sightseeing; we biked to dance class; we ate ice cream. Dad announced he was taking us on a quick trip to Prague during the second weekend in August.

"I wish we had more time," Dad said. "But the plan is for us to leave on the train early Saturday morning. We'll get to Prague in the late afternoon and have dinner. Then we'll have all day Sunday to sightsee. Katarina and I have to work Monday, so we're going to get up super early and take the four a.m. train. You and Felix and Sara can sleep in and come back with Sara around eleven a.m."

"Sounds good to me," I said.

We took a taxi to the same train station where we'd dropped off my mom. The train we boarded was made up of mini-rooms with six seats, three facing forward and three facing backward. Dad said you could slide the seats together to make a little bed on an overnight trip.

Felix had a guidebook (of course). "In 1989," he read, "Czechoslovakia overthrew its communist regime in a peaceful transition of power commonly referred to as the Velvet Revolution. On January 1, 1993, it split into two independent countries, the Czech Republic and Slovakia. Prague is the capital of the Czech Republic."

"How exciting," said Katarina, "to visit a country that is only eight months old!"

"Another communist country that dissolved into independent states?" I asked. "Is it safe?"

"Yes, perfectly safe," Dad said. "This split was completely peaceful."

"Then why is the situation in Yugoslavia so different?" I asked.

The question hung uncomfortably in the air for a moment, until the door to our compartment slid open and the conductor arrived to check our tickets. Once he was gone, Sara pulled out a package of Leibniz biscuits—these were flat shortbread-like cookies. She'd gotten the ones that were dipped in chocolate on one side.

We all munched happily for a while, looking out the window at the scenery. After about two hours, the train stopped. "Are we there already?" I asked.

"No," said Katarina, "we're at the Czech border. It's just passport control."

Another conductor, this time wearing a Czech uniform, came into our compartment. "Pässe bitte. Passports, please," he called out.

Dad gave him ours. Katarina handed over hers and Felix's. Sara adjusted her purse strap and pulled her passport out of her little green bag.

The man didn't even open mine and Dad's, just nodded when he saw the little blue books with *United States of America* and the eagle on the cover. He opened Katarina's and Felix's, glanced at the pictures, then promptly closed them again.

Sara's passport was a dark maroon. There were multiple folded papers inside. "Guten Tag," Sara said pleasantly.

The man frowned at her. He examined the papers in great detail, looking over every single page. He stuck his head into the hallway and called another, older man in uniform over to ask him a question.

"It's just a weekend trip," Dad explained. "Then she'll be returning with us to Austria."

Finally, the older man said, "Alles in Ordnung."

The younger man sighed, frowned again, and reluctantly stamped her passport.

"Danke," said Sara. "Schönen Tag."

The man didn't answer, just handed her passport back. He closed the compartment door a little too hard on his way out.

I ate another chocolate biscuit, but it didn't taste as good this time. It seemed like the Czech Republic was worried about Bosnian refugees too.

When we arrived in Prague, we took another taxi from the train station to the apartment my father had rented. There was a living room and a full kitchen with a table big enough for six. It also had three bedrooms: one with a king bed, one with a double, and the other with two twins.

"This place must have been expensive," I said.

Dad shook his head. "Twenty dollars a night. I paid in dollars."

"Why is it so cheap?" I asked.

Dad shrugged. "People want hard currency."

"Hard currency?" I asked.

"It means money from a country that's politically stable, so the currency is unlikely to fluctuate in value," Katarina explained. "Like American dollars or German marks or British pounds. Remember the Czech koruna was only invented in January."

"In fact"—Dad took out his wallet and pulled out some bills—"the currency still says *Czechoslovakia*. They just put a stamp on the larger denominations."

"That's so cool!" said Felix. "I want to save one. Part of history!"

I remembered Sara's dream and how her mother had used German marks to go shopping. I glanced over at her now, but she was busy unpacking her backpack.

Once we were settled in, we went on a walk. Prague

reminded me a lot of Vienna, with the same style of grand buildings, the same cobblestone streets, even the same distinctive yellow paint from Schönbrunn. "It looks a lot like Austria," I said.

"That's because it was part of the Austro-Hungarian Empire," Felix said. "The Hapsburgs ruled over Prague as well."

We went to a nearby restaurant for dinner. I thought it was going to be super expensive—it had white tablecloths and waiters in tuxedos—but it came to only about ten dollars a person. Hard currency sure bought a lot.

"Tomorrow," Felix said as we walked back to our apartment, "I want to see the astronomical clock and Kafka's house and the castle."

"I want to see the Jewish cemetery," said Katarina.

Dad turned to Sara and me. "Ladies, any requests?"

Sara shook her head.

I said, "I want to get some ice cream."

Dad laughed.

EARLY THE NEXT morning, I was enjoying a leisurely breakfast of yogurt and muesli (which was like granola) when Felix realized the apartment clock was slow and we only had ten minutes to make it to Old Town Square to see the Prague Astronomical Clock. "Every hour on the hour, there's a little show," Felix explained as he hurried us out the door. "I don't want to miss it!"

We made it to the square with about twenty seconds to spare. Built in 1410, the clock had two big faces—one dial representing the sun's and moon's positions and another one showing the months of the year. Above the sun/moon face were two small windows. As the clock chimed nine, the windows opened and a bunch of apostle figurines paraded by. A grinning skeleton rang a bell, and Felix took about a bazillion pictures.

After the clock, we went to Kafka's house. Apparently, Kafka was the guy who wrote the book about a man who turns into a cockroach. His house was located on the grounds of Prague Castle, on a tiny street called the Golden Lane. The house itself was blue, with "No 22" written over the doorway. Felix posed proudly with a copy of *The Metamorphosis*, which he'd brought along from home.

The buildings that made up Prague Castle looked a bit like Schönbrunn, though in Prague they were arranged in a giant square with a cathedral in the central courtyard. We went on the one-hour English-language tour. We had lunch, and then Katarina's Jewish cemetery was next. Felix read from his guidebook as we walked.

"The Jewish community in Prague wasn't allowed to purchase land for a new cemetery, so they put soil on top of the old graves and reused the same piece of land. In some parts of the cemetery, there are as many as twelve layers of bodies. So much dirt was added, walls had to be built to hold the graves and the soil in place. Some of the headstones you can see today are for bodies many layers down."

The cemetery was way more interesting than I'd expected. For one thing, Felix was right. The ground was raised several feet higher than the rest of the street. The tombstones were crowded extremely close together, leaning at odd angles, as if a child had stuck stones into the ground at random. Some of the grave markers were covered in Hebrew; others had names that were so worn with weather and time, you could barely read them at all. Dad and Felix and Sara went off to try to decipher more tombstones, but my feet were tired, so I sat down on a bench next to Katarina.

"I'm glad we came," she said, fanning herself with Felix's guidebook. She wore a light silk blouse that looked like an impressionist painting, but it was hot. "I've always wanted to see the Old Jewish Cemetery."

"Why?" I asked.

Katarina shrugged. "I think it's important to visit meaningful Jewish sites and places that memorialize history. I've been to the Anne Frank house in Amsterdam. I've even been to the Wailing Wall in Jerusalem."

"Are you Jewish?" I asked.

"No." She was quiet for a long moment.

"Dad's parents were," I told her, "but they never went to synagogue. My mother was raised Methodist. We always just celebrated a little bit of everything."

Katarina was silent for a long moment, then added in almost a whisper, "I think my parents were members of the Nazi Party."

"What?"

"We never talked about it," she went on. "And they weren't concentration camp guards or anything like that. But they were party members. When I was a child, I found the papers in the attic, on a rainy day when my brother and I were playing hide-and-seek. I tried to ask my mother about it last year, before she died. She waved a hand in the air and said, 'It was just a piece of paper. It didn't mean anything. It was what everyone did. We had to join.'

"But it was wrong. My parents knew the Nazis were persecuting Jews and Romani and homosexuals. And they didn't do anything." She paused. "Do you know the word *Vergangenheitsbewältigung*?"

"That's one word?" I asked.

"Yes, and it means *coming to terms with the past*. Learning what it meant and how to live with it. For me, it means . . . I can't pretend I don't hear the reports about the ethnic cleansing going on in Bosnia now."

"Do you think Sara's family is okay?"

"I don't know," Katarina said quietly. "I hope so, but . . . what I do know is that I believe it's wrong to pass laws that make it nearly impossible to get asylum. You know, in Nazi Germany they passed laws so that it was 'legal' to require Jewish citizens to register, 'legal' to make them live in certain parts of the country. It was legal, but it was still wrong."

I thought about that as I looked around the graveyard. In the olden days, sure, sometimes laws were wrong. I mean, slavery used to be legal, and that was clearly wrong! But I'd never thought about it today. Modern societies had gotten rid of the bad laws. Hadn't they? I mean, was it possible that things we thought were perfectly okay and legal now would be considered illegal, even immoral in the future?

My thoughts swirled together like the yellows, blues, and greens in Katarina's blouse. "I really want to go to your candlelight vigil," I said. "The one in support of refugees. But I'm not sure Dad will let me go."

Katarina smiled and squeezed my hand. "I'll speak to your father."

CHAPTER 30

The Bridge, Part 2

THE LAST PLACE we visited was the Charles Bridge. Felix read more facts as we walked. "The Charles Bridge crosses the Vltava River, connecting Prague Castle and the Old Town. Construction began in 1357. Legend has it that King Charles IV himself lay the first stone at exactly 5:31 a.m. on the ninth of July. King Charles was a believer in numerology and thought this would be an auspicious day and time, as it formed a palindrome: 1 3 5 7 9 7 5 3 1—year, day, month, and time."

"That's cool," I said.

"Over fifteen hundred feet long and over thirty feet wide, the bridge is decorated by thirty statues placed at intervals along its span."

I stopped listening once we arrived at the foot of the bridge. It was late afternoon, and the sunlight was golden, giving all the stone a shimmery glow. The bridge was made up of sixteen stone arches, stretching gracefully across the river.

"Oh, it's a pedestrian bridge," I exclaimed. "Like Kärntner Straße." Along the edges of the bridge, I could see artists painting views of the river, vendors selling snacks, and people hawking souvenirs.

Felix, Katarina, and Dad rushed ahead, eager to see the view from the middle of the bridge. I was about to join them when I glanced back at Sara.

She stood frozen on the edge of the riverbank. "Come on," I said. "I bet Dad will buy us ice cream."

"I tired," Sara said. "I wait here." She pointed to a bench.

"We can sit on the bridge," I insisted. "Come enjoy the view."

Sara shook her head.

I didn't know what was going on with her. I was about to go join my father when a little white dog ran onto the bridge. It barked once, twice, and then began to whine in fear.

And I remembered.

In Sarajevo, there was a bridge outside of Sara's apartment. The bridge where she'd seen a dog get shot. The bridge where her mother had died in her dream.

I went and sat down with Sara on the bench.

"You not have to stay."

"I know," I said. "But I want to."

I couldn't find any more words, so we just sat and watched

people stroll on and off the bridge. Dad looked back at us, but I waved and he didn't come over to investigate.

The little dog sat down in the shade of one of the statues. A moment later, an old woman rushed up to him, scolding loudly in Czech. The dog jumped up and licked her face.

Sara was watching the dog too.

"Do you want to try?" I asked.

Sara nodded.

I took her hand, and we stood up together. Slowly, step by step, we made our way to the edge of the bridge. Sara paused. There was a musician playing a violin, his case open before him. I threw in a couple of coins, and we took a few more steps.

Felix glanced back at us then, and I guess he understood the look I gave him, because he ran back and took Sara's other hand. "Sara," he said, "there's a man on the bridge selling surplus Soviet Army items. It's so cool! You have to see it. He's got these gigantic fur hats. And Mama said she'd buy me one!"

We were on the bridge now. Sara was trembling, but she kept walking as Felix chattered on. I looked over at a woman painting. Her picture was beautiful—the bridge, the river, the red roofs of the houses, the green dome of the cathedral. Then I glanced up, and it was as if the drawing had suddenly sprung to life.

The late-afternoon sun sparkled on the river. The

cathedral spires reached into the sky, almost touching the wispy clouds. The statues of the saints stood protectively over us as we walked in and out of their shadows, approaching the center of the bridge.

Dad and Katarina were waiting there, next to a man with a portable freezer. "Do you want some ice cream?" Dad asked.

Of course we did. Sara let go of our hands to take her cone, getting ice cream on her nose with the very first lick. We all laughed, and as I handed her a napkin, Sara squeezed my hand and whispered, "Thank you."

And so the spell of the other phantom bridge was broken, and it was just a normal afternoon, and we were just a normal family. Felix wore his new Siberian hat until sweat ran down his face. Katarina got into a long discussion with one of the artists and decided to purchase a painting. The man carefully removed the canvas from its frame, rolled it up, and placed it into a cardboard tube for Katarina to take home. Dad bought an old-fashioned pocket watch and kept popping it open to check the time. Sara and I watched the people stroll across the bridge; no one felt the need to run.

We stayed on the bridge for a long, long time, until the sun started to go down. Felix, Sara, and Katarina were huddled over the guidebook, trying to decide where to go for dinner. Dad and I stood still by the edge, looking out over the water, a breeze cooling our faces. Maybe I was feeling good from helping Sara; in any case, I turned to my father and asked, "Dad, do you ever wish that I didn't worry so much?"

"What?" He turned to look at me, the setting sun making half his face glow, the other half in shadow.

"I mean, I know you love me. And we had such a great time today! But sometimes, I feel like you wish that I . . . that I was a girl who didn't need a Doomsday Journal."

"Rebecca, that's not true," he said gently.

"I know," I said, embarrassed, staring at the stones of the bridge. "It's silly of me to—"

"It's not silly of you either," Dad sighed and ran a hand through his hair. "I just thought I'd done a better job hiding my frustration. Becca, I was a lot like you as a kid. I worried about everything! And my parents were so impatient. I swore I'd never be like that. It's hard to see you worry, to not know what to do or say to make it better. So you're right—sometimes I *am* upset, but it's never at you. I'm only frustrated with myself."

"Oh."

Dad put his arm around me, and we looked up at the castle on the hill. It felt like we were in a fairy tale. "Becca," Dad said. "You can worry as much as you want. You will always be my most special girl."

That night as I crawled into the twin bed across from Sara, the last thing I whispered to her was "This was a day full of pig."

CHAPTER 31

Drinks on a Train

THE NEXT MORNING, Dad and Katarina were long gone by the time the rest of us woke up. Sara, Felix, and I got to the station an hour before our departure time, so we had plenty of time to buy sandwiches for lunch and pick out a bunch of postcards. The train wasn't full, so we had a compartment to ourselves. Sara and Felix pulled out the seats and pushed them together to make a little bed. We were all lying flat on our backs as if we were in a sleeper, giggling, when the train pulled out of the station.

"Let's call Mai and Rasheed when we get home," I suggested. "Maybe they'd like to go see the opera movie at the Rathaus tomorrow."

Felix made a face.

"What?" I asked.

"You want me to tell you all the things wrong with that plan?"

"You like Mai and Rasheed!" I pointed out.

"Yes, but . . ."

The Czech conductor came by to check our tickets. Sara showed them to him, then tucked them back into her green purse. Once he was gone, Felix and I continued our discussion. "I'm trying to make *more* friends at school, Becca," he argued. "I can't invite them to some lame event full of grandmas and tourists!"

"It looks fun!" I insisted. "And you liked that opera!"

"No, I didn't," said Felix.

"Yes, you did!"

"Kinder!" Sara interrupted. "Time for lunch. Let's get drinks from the café car."

"Fine," Felix said. "I'll stay here and watch the bags."

Which meant I had to go help carry the drinks. I wobbled a bit walking down the corridor. *Why is Felix still so hesitant to make new friends? It's sort of annoying.* When we got to the end of the car, Sara pushed a big metal button, and the door slid open. In the space between the cars, the train tracks whizzed by beneath our feet. I stood still, watching for a long moment. *What if I fall?*

"Gap is too small," Sara said, as if she had read my mind. "Come." She tugged at my hand, and automatically I stepped over the gap. I felt a little dizzy, but Sara kept walking and I followed her. There was a second door to open, followed by a second gap to jump. This time, I didn't look down and it wasn't quite as scary.

Finally, we reached the café car. Instead of compartments, this car had little booths by the windows and a bar serving drinks. Sara ordered a Coke (for me), an Almdudler (for Felix), and einen kleinen Braunen (coffee with milk) for herself. The sodas came in glass bottles. I watched as the saleswoman popped off the bottle caps before handing them carefully to me. Sara paid with money from my dad's envelope and put the change back into her purse. Then she picked up her coffee.

"Becca, you get door," she instructed. "Be brave. Jump over quick."

I had just opened the door between the cars when a small child of five or six came barreling through the passageway and ran right into me. We both fell to the floor, knocking Sara down as well.

The drinks flew everywhere. Coffee stained the front of Sara's shirt; the sodas missed me but spilled onto the table of an elderly woman sitting in a booth by the window. "Ach du meine Güte!" exclaimed the woman, standing up to avoid getting wet.

"I'm so sorry!" The boy's mother came forward. She spoke English with a thick accent. She jerked the boy by the arm and handed him off to a man who was standing behind her. "I tell him not to run."

Sara pressed a handful of napkins to her shirt as the boy's mother and I grabbed some paper towels and helped the old woman mop up the mess. The soda was all over her table, soaking into her newspaper. She folded it into soggy squares and threw it into the trash.

The child came back again, running into his mother this time. His mother grasped his wrist hard. "Nein!" she snapped at him. "My apologies. I pay for drinks." She threw down a hundred-schilling bill and marched the boy off.

We finished wiping down the table for the old lady. Sara exchanged a few words with her in German. The woman shook her head. "Nein, danke," she said. "Bin schon fertig."

"What'd she say?" I asked.

"I asked if she wanted another newspaper. She said no, she was already done."

"That's lucky," I said. "But your shirt's all stained!"

Sara shrugged. "I have a clean shirt in my bag. Let's get new drinks now."

We waited in line—again—and used the hundred-schilling bill to pay. I opened the doors more carefully this time, and we made it back to our compartment.

Felix had slid the seats back into their normal positions and gotten out our bag of sandwiches. "What happened to you?" he asked, gesturing to Sara's shirt.

"A little boy ran into me," Sara said, shaking her head. "Very naughty."

I handed Felix his Almdudler and took a sip of my Coke.

"Sandwich?" Felix asked gruffly.

"Sure." He tossed me my ham and swiss on a baguette.

Fine. If he wanted to be grumpy, I'd just write a few postcards.

Sara sat down and took a long sip of her coffee. Then suddenly, she jumped up. "Where's my purse?" she asked.

"What?" I asked.

"My purse."

"You had it in the café car," I said.

"Maybe I drop it," she sighed and put her coffee down on a little ledge. "Stay here. I go look. Be right back."

"Okay."

Felix and I ate our sandwiches in silence. After a few minutes, the train slowly came to a stop. "Are we at the border already?" I asked.

"I guess," he said.

"Where's Sara?" I asked. "Doesn't she have to be here?"

"No," he said. "They can just check her passport in the café car."

"I'd rather go get—"

At that moment the door to our car slid open. "Pässe bitte. Passports, please."

Felix and I dug our passports out of our backpacks and handed them over.

"Traveling alone?" the conductor asked me, opening my passport.

"No," I said, my heart beating just a little too fast. "Our au . . . friend went to the café car."

He nodded and glanced at Felix's passport before handing them both back to us. "Gute Reise!"

Then he closed the door and was gone.

Felix picked up his sandwich again, but my stomach was churning. I wished Felix would talk to me. I'd never thought I'd have to go through passport control by myself. It hadn't been that bad, but I would have been less anxious if Sara had been there. Wait a minute . . .

"Where's Sara?" I asked.

"She went to the café car."

"It's been a while," I said.

Felix shrugged. "Maybe she had to stop by the restroom on the way back."

"Maybe."

The train jerked and started moving again. Felix pulled out a book, but he didn't open it. I tried to focus on my postcards, but I kept glancing at my watch. Five minutes crept by. Then ten. Then fifteen.

"I'm going to go look for her," I said.

"She told us to stay here."

"You stay here in case she comes back."

"Fine!"

I wasn't sure what we were arguing about anymore. I picked up my purse and put my hand on the door.

"Becca?" Felix said more gently.

"What?"

"She's probably just in the bathroom. Right?"

"Sure," I said.

I left and started walking quickly. *I'm known for over-reacting, aren't I? I mean, her shirt was covered in coffee. She probably stopped to wash it out.* But my heart thumped in time with the clatter of the train on the tracks. Sara would not have left us alone for so long unless . . .

Something's wrong. Something's wrong.

CHAPTER 32

Polizei

I PUSHED THE BUTTON, and the door between the cars whooshed open. The ground spun by beneath me, but I barely noticed this time. *Sara will be waiting in the café car. She probably decided to buy us a chocolate bar or something, and the line was longer than she expected.* I walked through the next car and pushed the button to open the final door. I took a deep breath, stepping into the café car.

There was no one there.

Well, that wasn't quite true. The saleswoman behind the counter was still there. And the old woman who'd had the newspaper. A completely bald man with a briefcase sat in one corner. That was it.

Where's Sara?

"Excuse me," I said to the saleswoman. "Have you seen my au pair, Sara?"

Oh, shoot! I wasn't supposed to call her my au pair.

But it didn't matter, because the lady just shook her head and said, "Ich spreche kein Englisch."

"My friend Sara! We were just here. We spilled our drinks and—"

"Tut mir leid. Ich verstehe dich nicht."

The train went around a curve, and it felt like my world was suddenly completely off kilter. What was going on? I realized we'd been to so many touristy places, I'd begun to think everyone in Europe spoke English. But I was wrong. I was in a foreign country. Alone.

"Sara!" I looked around the room. "Has anyone seen her?"

The businessman ignored me, focusing on his papers.

Is there another café car? Did I go the wrong way? Someone grabbed my elbow.

It was the old woman. Her eyes were wide and worried. She began to speak in German, quick and fast.

"I don't understand," I said.

She kept talking, gesturing now. I knew she was trying to tell me something important, but I had no idea what. "I don't speak German," I moaned.

"Polizei," she said. "Polizei. Polizei."

Wait. I knew that word. "Police?"

"Ja."

My skin broke out in goose bumps, as if I had walked into a freezer. I felt light-headed and clutched the table to stay upright. *The police! Something happened to Sara.*

I needed Felix. "I'll be right back," I said to the woman. She nodded, but I wasn't sure she understood me.

As if in a dream, I walked through the two train cars, stopping in each bathroom, checking for Sara. In the last one before our compartment, I splashed some water on my face. I was reaching for a paper towel when I saw it.

A bit of green strap peeking out of the trash bin.

I grabbed the strap and pulled. Paper towels fell onto the floor to reveal Sara's little green purse. The strap had been cut, as if with a sharp knife. The straps lay like limp pieces of spaghetti to either side of the small green pocket.

I opened it quickly and looked inside.

The money envelope from my father was gone. Sara's passport was gone. It was completely empty, except for an old ponytail holder and a slip of paper. I pulled them both out.

The notebook paper was folded and worn. It was Sara's list!

I clutched the list in one hand and the purse in the other and ran back to our compartment. "Felix," I called out before I had the door fully open. "Something's happened to Sara!"

"What?" He was sitting extremely still, the book still unopened on his lap.

"I found her purse in the bathroom. Someone cut the strap and took the money and her passport."

"Maybe . . . maybe it just broke and Sara threw it away."

I held up the piece of notebook paper. "Sara would *never* throw away her list."

Felix touched the paper carefully, as if it were gold leaf that might dissolve on his hands. "No," he whispered. "She wouldn't."

"And the old woman saw something," I said.

"Which old woman?" he asked.

"In the café car. When the little boy ran into me, I spilled soda on this woman's table. We helped her wipe it up."

"Becca, what are you talking about?"

"She tried to tell me, but I didn't understand. She kept repeating, 'Polizei, Polizei.'"

Felix got even paler.

"That means *police*, doesn't it?" I asked.

Felix nodded.

"Come on. We have to talk to her."

We ran back to the café car, skipping over the gap between the doors like it was no more than a crack in the sidewalk. The man with the briefcase was gone, but the old woman was still there. She gestured to the empty seats, and we slid into the booth across from her.

The woman started to speak quickly again, in German. Felix listened, interrupting her every now and then to ask a question.

Time seemed to slow down as they talked. I felt so helpless and stupid. I started to notice random details: a patch of sticky soda on the table that we'd missed, an empty glass on a nearby table with a lipstick stain, a child's greasy handprint on the window.

Finally, the woman stopped talking. Felix's face was gray.

"What did she say?" I asked.

"In a minute," Felix said.

The woman murmured one more thing.

"Nein, nein," said Felix. "Unsere Eltern sind hier. Danke nochmal."

He stood up. I followed his lead. "Danke," I said too, even though I wasn't sure what I was thanking her for.

Felix practically ran back to our compartment. He was shaking.

"What happened?" I demanded, slamming the compartment door.

"The police took Sara!"

"What? Took her where?"

"Off the train. They arrested her!"

"Arrested her? Why?!"

"They said she didn't have papers."

"But she did have papers! She had her passport. It was in her little green purse."

"She couldn't *find* her purse," Felix reminded me. "That's why she went back to the café."

"But she had it when we paid for the drinks the first time!" I said.

"They didn't believe her. They saw her necklace and

knew she was Muslim and figured she was a refugee trying to illegally enter the country by avoiding passport control, sneaking from the bathroom to the café car and back again."

I looked at the little green purse on the seat. "But what happened to her passport?" I wondered. "It was in her purse. I saw it when she bought the sodas. And then the little boy ran into us and . . ."

I had a horrible thought. *Did that family rob Sara?*

"The woman said something about a little boy and a woman and a man," Felix said.

I described the scene to him quickly. "Do you think the woman told the little boy to run into her?"

"Maybe. In the confusion, she or her husband could have quickly cut the strap on the purse. And grabbed it."

"And if anyone noticed, they could have just said they were trying to help."

"And maybe they knew where the border was, knew the train would stop soon, so they could jump off."

"And hopefully, she wouldn't even discover the loss until they were gone."

"But why target Sara?" I asked. "Surely that businessman had more money."

"They must have heard you speaking English," Felix said. "American passports are worth a lot on the black market. They must have figured Sara had your passport in her purse." He shook his head.

"And when they only found a Bosnian one, they took that and the money and dumped the purse in the trash."

"That's what the old woman thought."

"Why didn't she speak to the police?"

"She did," Felix said. "But it all happened so fast. They wanted to get Sara off the train before it left the border." He paused. "They thought Sara might be a little crazy. She was yelling something about hair as she left. 'Green hair!' It didn't make any sense." Felix started to shake. "What do we do, Becca? What do we do?"

"Go talk to a conductor?"

"What can he do? All he does is take the tickets!" Felix was panting now, his breaths short and shallow. "I feel sick," he said. "I can't breathe!"

"You're just panicking," I said.

I sat down next to him and passed him the bag the sandwiches had come in. Felix took it and retched into it. I patted his back.

"Sorry," he said when he was done.

"Don't be," I said. "I've thrown up lots of times when I was stressed."

"Becca, what are we going to do?!"

Sara's coffee was sitting on the ledge, untouched. I picked it up and took a sip. It was only lukewarm now, but the taste was bitter and familiar. "I don't think we can do anything," I said. "I think we have to wait until we get back to Vienna."

"We can't just wait!" Felix protested.

"What are we going to do . . . jump off the train?"

"I don't know," Felix wailed.

My mind was spinning. I didn't have a page for this in my Doomsday Journal.

"I feel dizzy," Felix said.

"You're in shock," I said automatically.

Shock! I did have a page on shock. And I had my journal in my backpack. I stood on the seat and got it down. Quickly, I flipped through the pages.

"What to do in case of shock," I read. "Step one: Lay the person down and elevate their feet."

Felix and I looked at each other. Then he shrugged and sat down, putting his feet up on the seat across from him.

"Step two," I read. "Begin CPR (if necessary)."

"Not necessary," said Felix.

"Step three," I said. "Treat obvious injures."

Felix looked at his hands. "I have a paper cut."

I nodded, rummaged in my backpack again, and pulled out my first aid kit. I found the antibiotic ointment and a Band-Aid and put both on his finger.

"Step four," I read. "Keep person warm and comfortable."

"It *is* kind of cold in here," Felix said.

I unzipped his backpack and pulled out a sweatshirt. I handed it to him.

He put it on.

"Better?" I asked.

"Yeah."

The strange thing was, I felt better too. Going through my list had given me something to do. Something I *could* do. I took another sip of Sara's coffee. "We'll take the train back to Vienna," I said. "Then get off with all our bags. Then call our parents."

"Okay," said Felix.

We sat in silence for a while after that.

"Becca?"

"Yeah?"

"I lied," Felix said. "I did like the opera."

"I know."

"If something like this had to happen . . . I'm glad I was with you."

"Yeah," I said. "Me too."

I reached out and took his hand. It wasn't romantic, 'cause Felix, ugh, he was sort of like my brother. It was more like, let's hold hands so we don't feel so scared. And maybe it worked, because we held hands like that all the way back to Vienna.

CHAPTER 33

Words on a Page

IT TOOK TWO more hours, but at last the train pulled into the station. We gathered up our belongings and stumbled down the steps. Felix practically ran to a pay phone. He dialed and spoke in German a couple of times, with long pauses in between, before finally hanging up the phone. "Mama's not there," he told me. "She's out doing an interview."

I tried my father then, at the work number he'd given me for emergencies. I'd never called it before. My fingers trembled as I dialed.

"He's on his way back from a meeting," his secretary told me. "They're stuck in traffic somewhere. Would you like to leave a message?"

"Tell him to call me at home," I managed to blurt out. "It's his daughter."

Felix and I looked at each other once I hung up. We

hadn't thought any further than this. "Do you have your Monatskarte?" he asked.

"Yes." My pass for August was safely tucked away in my backpack. We'd taken a taxi to the train station, but it wasn't hard to study the posted map and find the correct streetcar to take us back to the bus. Sara's backpack got heavier and heavier as we lugged it along, taking turns holding it on our laps.

It took us almost an hour to make it back to the Julius Meinl grocery store on the corner by our bus stop. We were just passing the recycling bins when Frau Gamperl called out. "No one took out your trash last night," she scolded. "Tell your father he needs to remember to . . ."

We turned to look at her. Frau Gamperl caught a glimpse of our faces and stopped yelling. I imagined we looked pretty disheveled after being on the train for hours and trekking across town. She noticed the third backpack. "Where's Sara?"

"Gone," Felix whispered.

"Gone?" she asked, surprised.

I shook my head, desperately trying not to cry.

"Your parents?"

"At work," I said. "We can't get in touch with them."

Frau Gamperl nodded as if she understood. "Come with me. We'll talk at my place."

Of all the people I'd imagined helping us, Frau Gamperl was not one of them. As she led us up to her front door,

I glanced at one of her little gnomes in the grass. It had green hair and was riding a bike. I started to cry, big silent tears running down my face. Felix was crying too—from relief at being home or fear or frustration, I wasn't sure.

Frau Gamperl opened the door and gestured for us to step inside. "Please take off your shoes." The house was tidy, with simple wooden furniture that was old but in excellent shape. There was a small round wooden sign that said "Willkommen" with little flowers painted around the edges and a cuckoo clock on one wall. "Sit down at the table," she ordered. "I'll make some tea."

The tea was good, black and strong, and she added milk and honey without asking. It was warm and sweet, and by the time we'd had a few sips, we'd managed to stop crying. Frau Gamperl put a few cookies with jam on a plate in the middle of the table. "Now," she said. "Talk."

And we did. We told her about the train and Sara disappearing. Frau Gamperl was a good listener, nibbling on a cookie, stirring her tea, but not interrupting. We took turns talking, each telling parts, adding to and clarifying the story. Once or twice, Felix lapsed into German. I finished my tea, staring at the leaves at the bottom of the cup.

"You mean to tell me," Frau Gamperl said when we were done, "you two made it back here on your own?"

We nodded.

"Hmm," she said. "You're tougher than I thought." She stood up and wiped her hands on her apron, even though they looked spotless to me. "Give me your parents' numbers," she said. "I'll keep trying until I get through. Although it sounds like what we really need is a good immigration lawyer."

"Lawyer!" Felix said, suddenly looking up. "I have an idea."

DAD, KATARINA, AND Rasheed's mother, Frau Kumar, all ended up arriving at Frau Gamperl's within five minutes of each other. We had to tell the entire story again—only this time, Frau Kumar took notes.

"I don't understand," Katarina said when we were done. "Sara had all her papers in order. What about the passport thieves? Why didn't they arrest them?"

"They were probably gone, jumped off the train as soon as it stopped," Frau Kumar explained. "Maybe they had a friend waiting for them with a car. I've seen situations like this before. Sadly, the police rarely believe the refugee."

"What can we do?" I asked.

"The first step is to locate her," Frau Kumar said. "Are you sure she hasn't called?"

Katarina shook her head. "There's no message on the machine."

Frau Kumar sighed. "They are supposed to allow a phone call. I'll see what I can do tomorrow. The best thing now is for everyone to go home and get some rest."

We tried. No one ate much at dinner. My mom called while I was doing the dishes, but Dad talked to her for a long time first.

"What a traumatic experience!" Mom exclaimed when Dad finally handed me the phone.

"Yeah."

"Dad and I are so proud of you," Mom continued. "You didn't panic. You and Felix figured out how to get home."

As awful as it had been, I was a little bit proud of myself too. Felix and I *had* handled it. "Mom, we have to find her!"

"You will," Mom said. I wished I had her confidence.

I was exhausted by the time I finally crawled into bed, but I couldn't sleep. My limbs felt heavy and achy, as if I had the flu, though I knew I didn't have a fever. *This is what it feels like to be Sara*, I thought to myself. *To not know where your loved ones are. To not know if they are safe.*

It was so awful, I wasn't sure I could survive it. I was about to go ask Dad if he still had those pills from Dr. Teresa, the ones for an emergency. This was surely an emergency! And yet Sara had been in the same situation every single night since I'd known her. And she'd survived. But I wasn't as strong as her.

I got up and went downstairs to find Dad. He was still

sitting at the kitchen table in his pajamas, nursing a cup of tea, listening to the radio. "Couldn't sleep?" he asked.

I shook my head.

"Me either." He poured me a cup of tea. "I can't . . . I can't believe that happened." Dad sounded horrified. "I'm so sorry. I never should have let you go with Sara alone on the train."

"It's not your fault," I said. "It might have happened anyway."

"Yes, but . . . if something had happened to you!"

"But nothing did."

Dad sighed, but his shoulders were still tense. He drummed his fingers on the table, making the teapot rattle. "Becca, there's something else I need to tell you."

"What? Did Sara—"

"It's nothing to do with Sara," Dad said. "Remember when I told you I didn't buy the tickets to *Les Mis* because I was worried you might get nervous?"

"Yeah."

"That wasn't the whole story. The truth is, I was worried *I* might get nervous. That you might get upset, and I wouldn't know what to do. I was so afraid that the evening might not turn out exactly as planned, I decided that I'd rather not do it at all. That decision left me feeling so bad, I called Dr. Teresa and asked her to recommend another therapist. For me. So maybe I could deal with some of my own anxiety."

"You went to a therapist too?" I asked.

Dad nodded. "For about a year, once a week, after work. And it really helped! In fact, she helped me see that I'd been too hesitant to take some risks in my own life. *That's* what moving to Vienna was about. And I thought that maybe by moving, by dealing with some of my own fears, I could finally be a better parent to you."

"But Dad," I burst out, "you've always been a good parent."

"I don't know about that," Dad said. "Do you ever think about that first plane ride? The one when we went to visit your grandparents."

"Of course."

"Sometimes I think I shouldn't have rented a car to drive us all home. What if we had just taken our flight home as planned? Maybe you wouldn't have developed so many fears if I hadn't given in to them."

"Dad . . ."

"And the bike. When I tried to teach you back in Virginia, I was all, 'Watch out!' and 'Don't hurt yourself!' No wonder you found it hard to learn."

"It's okay, Dad. I did learn."

"Even the au pair! I'm mean, did you really need a baby-sitter this summer?"

"Yeah," I said. "I definitely needed Sara!"

Dad sighed.

"Dad, you did the very best you could!" I insisted. "But why didn't you tell me about the therapist before?"

Dad shrugged. "I don't know. I wanted you to think I had everything under control."

I thought about that. "You know, Dad, I used to think the purpose of my Doomsday Journal was to make me feel in control. I thought if I could just research and plan everything, I wouldn't ever feel nervous. But now, I don't think that's why it works. I mean, no way in a million years would I have thought to put in a page about what to do if your au pair gets kidnapped by the police because someone stole her passport."

"Yeah."

"Maybe the point is to know that whatever happens, I'll be able to cope. And somehow, putting my problems and fears down on paper makes them smaller. They're no longer overwhelming—they're just black-and-white words on a page. I think the thing I'm actually most afraid of is being too anxious to do all the things I really want to do."

Dad was silent for a long time.

"Say something," I urged.

"Tomorrow," Dad said slowly. "I'm going to have to go buy a journal."

I smiled.

"Think you can sleep now?" he asked.

"Yeah."

"Me too." Dad stood up and put our cups in the sink.

I reached over to turn off the radio, when something made me pause. The song on the radio sounded familiar. I listened a moment longer before it hit me—the station was playing *La Traviata*.

I got goose bumps again, just as I had at the opera. This was a sign. Everything was going to be okay. Sara would come back to us! Well, either that or she would die of tuberculosis. But we had antibiotics now, so that seemed unlikely.

The music swelled, washing away my fears. I turned off the radio, and Dad switched off the light. We walked silently up the stairs. Before I went into my room, Dad stopped and said, "Becca, I am so lucky to have a daughter like you."

And when I climbed into bed, I swear I could still hear the music.

CHAPTER 34

Waiting

FELIX AND I sat by the phone all day Tuesday and Wednesday, but Sara never called. On Thursday, Frau Gamperl announced she was going to take us into the city to visit the Hofburg. I knew she was trying to distract us from worrying about Sara. The Hofburg was the winter residence of the Hapsburgs. Like the castle in Prague, it had lots of rooms and tapestries and blah, blah, blah. We'd missed the 9:00 a.m. English-language tour, and there wasn't another one until 2:00 p.m., so we did the German one instead. Felix translated the important bits, half-heartedly. Every time I saw a funny painting or a cool piece of jewelry, I turned to point it out to Sara, forgetting again and again that she wasn't there.

After the tour, we walked around Heldenplatz, the big open space in front of the Hofburg. "This is where Hitler gave his infamous speech when he marched into Austria."

Frau Gamperl pointed. "He spoke from that balcony right over there."

It was hard to imagine. The plaza was fairly empty and peaceful. But fifty-five years ago it had been filled with Nazis. I shivered. We sat down at the base of a large statue, a man on a horse who was holding a rolled-up flag in one hand.

"In 1938, right?" Felix asked.

"Yes."

"How old were you?" I asked.

"I was sixteen when Hitler marched into Vienna," Frau Gamperl said. "I spent much of the next seven years passing what information I could on to the English. My English was always very good."

"You were a spy?" Felix asked.

"I like to think I was a good citizen. Part of the Austrian resistance."

"What?!" Felix exclaimed. "You were part of the O5?"

"Yes," she said. "I'm surprised you've heard of us."

"I like history," Felix said.

"There was only a small group of us. But we did what we could. I helped a few families escape when it was still possible. One night, we painted our slogan all across Vienna!"

"Did you paint the symbol on Stephansdom?" Felix asked.

"No. But one of my friends did," she said with a grin. "That was a long time ago." She stared at the Hofburg.

"What happened after the war?" I asked.

"I was twenty-three. I married an English officer—he was part of the Allied forces occupying Vienna after the war. He loved the city, and we settled here. He died when the kids were small, of a heart attack, and for many years I was too busy to worry about anything except getting the next meal on the table. But now my kids have grown up and moved on with their own lives. I spend most of my time now discussing politics and planting flowers in my garden."

Okay. Gotta admit. Old lady spy living next door to my father was *not* what I expected. She'd seemed so dull and old-fashioned, and yet there she was, telling us about sneaking information to the English. She'd been brave. Like Sara.

"You're coming to the Lichtermeer, right?" Frau Gamperl asked. "It's on Saturday."

"What's that?" I asked.

"The march against Haider's petition," Felix explained.

"Oh yeah, definitely!" I said. "But why did you call it a Lichtermeer?"

"Literally, it means *sea of lights*. Everyone is supposed to bring a candle and light it when the march starts. There are going to be speeches all over the city, speaking out against the hatred of foreigners. And the center is going to be right here, at Heldenplatz, where Hitler gave his own hate-filled speech."

I looked around the plaza, trying to imagine it full of people. I knew I wanted to be part of the sea of lights.

ON FRIDAY, FELIX and I rode our bikes to dance class. This was our fourth class, and I was getting pretty good at both dancing and riding my bike. But it didn't feel right without Sara there. Katarina had called the dance studio and left a message, but I guess Marco hadn't gotten it, because he came up to us as soon as we arrived. "Where's Sara?" he asked. We had to try to explain what had happened, right there in the waiting room. Marco got stiller and stiller until his face looked like a marble statue. "Missing?" he asked. "I not understand."

But it was time for class then, and we couldn't talk anymore. Frau Kovács had to demonstrate the steps herself, and she scowled the whole time. She even snapped at Marco when he accidentally messed up. Mai showed up late, and Daisy and Peter both had a cold, so they didn't come at all. Even Felix stepped on my foot three times. I tried really hard not to yelp, but it hurt! "Sorry," he mumbled miserably.

Yeah. That's how I felt too.

Felix, Rasheed, Mai, and I went to Giovanni's Gelato after class, but even ice cream didn't cheer me up this time. No one had much to say. "Is anyone else going to the Lichtermeer tomorrow?" I asked.

"Definitely," said Rasheed. "My dad is from India. He was here legally and met my mom at university. But even though my mom's Austrian, I was born here, and German is my first language, sometimes when I'm out with my father, people yell at us and tell us to go back home. So yeah, we will be there."

Mai wanted to go too, so we all made plans to meet in front of Felix's house the next evening. As we were finishing our ice cream, I heard Mai say to Felix, "You were so brave."

"No, I wasn't," Felix said. "In fact, I was terrified."

"Maybe," Mai said. "But you still made it back to Vienna."

Riding home, I kept thinking about what Mai had said. I'd always thought that I needed to be brave *before* I could do stuff, but maybe I had it backward. Maybe being brave was about *doing* things—getting on the bike or stepping onto the dance floor or boarding a plane—and the feeling of confidence came after.

In any case, as we put our bikes back in the storage room, I realized I'd been so preoccupied with the definition of bravery that I'd forgotten to worry about falling off my bike.

CHAPTER 35

Das Lichtermeer

THE NEXT EVENING, Saturday, August 21, we all met in front of Felix's house: Katarina, Felix, Dad, me, and Frau Gamperl. Rasheed and his folks joined us too. I was expecting the Kumars and Mai's family, but Peter and his parents and two little brothers also showed up, as well as Daisy, her mom, her dad, and an older sister.

Dad pulled me aside before we left. "Becca," he warned. "I probably don't need to say this, but they are expecting huge crowds. There's going to be no way to get out if you get scared."

"I still want to go," I said.

"Okay," Dad said. "But what if *I* get nervous?"

We both smiled. The streetcar was crowded, and I noticed other groups like ours. It was almost festive, like the Fourth of July (which, of course, they did not celebrate in Austria). When we got off at Schottentor, the streets were already packed. "Streetcar number one isn't running," Katarina said. "There are so many people, they are blocking the rails. We'll have to walk to Heldenplatz."

I glanced over at Frau Gamperl.

"I'm not that old," she snapped. "For this, I can walk."

The crowd got thicker as we walked. Dad and Katarina stuck close to Felix and me, as if they were scared to let us out of their sight even for a moment. By the time we reached Heldenplatz, it was so crowded, it was hard to move. Katarina flashed a press pass, and we all squeezed forward, into another section.

I gotta admit—I felt a little uncomfortable. Not because it was hot and I was thirsty (which I was) but because there were no easily accessible exits. *What if someone has a stink bomb? Or tear gas? Or a gun?* But every time I felt like giving up and running away, I touched the little green bag I wore across my body. I'd stitched the leather straps back together. It wasn't pretty, but it held. Inside, I had my Monatskarte, some money, and Sara's list.

Finally, we found a spot to stand, not far from the statue where Felix, Frau Gamperl, and I had talked two days before. Dad pulled a package of long white candles from his backpack and handed them out, one for each of us. Katarina had brought small paper plates with a hole cut in the middle of each and showed us how to pull them down over the candles to protect our fingers from the dripping wax. Frau Kumar passed out matches—from the Heuriger where we'd had Felix's birthday. There was a light wind, and Daisy's and Peter's candles kept going out, but mine burned strong and clear. I helped the others light theirs until they were all burning.

We were surrounded by people. Everyone seemed tall, giant-sized, and I could barely see a thing. We were crammed in so close together, I almost set a woman's long blond hair on fire. Another man had a jacket that brushed through my flame. I cupped my hand around the candle and held it closer. A drop of hot wax dripped from the plate onto my hand.

Will it leave a scar? What if I burn myself? Dad had my first aid kit in his backpack, but it was so crowded, I wasn't sure I'd be able to pull it out. I didn't like being jostled and squished. *What if people start to panic? Or riot?* I had a section in Doomsday Journal #3 about how to avoid getting injured by a stampeding crowd, but I couldn't remember what it said to do. I started to shiver even though it was a warm night.

"You okay, Becca?" Felix asked softly.

I shook my head. I held on to the candle with both hands, as if for dear life. *I will not panic. I will not.* I focused on the flame as it burned bright and clear. *Sara. Sara. Think about Sara.*

Felix stood on one side of me, and Dad somehow appeared on the other. I could see Ms. Madden with her camera crew on a platform near the speaker. She turned and scanned the crowd. Katarina waved dramatically, and Ms. Madden waved back at us. I felt a little better.

The first speaker began his speech, and I started to forget about being squished together like sardines. No . . . like bugs in a jar of paprika. Felix translated for me, whispering into my ear.

"We can't isolate ourselves; we can't close our eyes and ears from what is going on around us," the first man said. "We don't have a foreigner problem; there is only a problem between poor and rich, because no one has anything against rich foreigners. We must give the poor, the socially vulnerable in Austria the feeling that they are not worthless, regardless of whether or not they are citizens. That is the greatest goal."

A clergyman spoke next: "The belief in Jesus Christ and the hatred of foreigners are incompatible. Loving our neighbors knows no boundaries. Like Martin Luther King Jr. with his dream of a society where the color of your skin does not decide whether people have rights or not. Like this dream, we want to have equal rights for all people living here, regardless of race, religion, political beliefs, social class, and also independent of place of birth."

"We reject Mr. Haider's point of view," continued a member of parliament. "The truth is, his petition makes only one thing certain—that it will rile up emotions and leave our problems unsolved. Many sectors of our economy would cease to function if we no longer had any foreign workers."

Another government official went on: "We were happy here, on this side of the Iron Curtain, but we knew that on the other side of the border, our neighbors thought of our land as a harbor for refugees and hope. People are demonstrating tonight not for their own rights and privileges but for the rights of others."

"I don't believe that the lot of the unemployed in Austria can make us blind to the fact that outside of our borders, millions struggle simply to survive," a bishop told the group. "I don't believe that the majority of Austrians can take offense when there are problems in the schools with students who don't speak perfect German, and yet remain unmoved when children in other places are slashed apart by grenades.

"I simply don't believe that seeing Muslim women in their strange-to-us clothing irritates us more than the fact that in Bosnia thousands of Muslim women and girls are defiled, raped, mutilated, and killed.

"There are situations in which lines must be drawn. Staying quiet, observing, looking away, that may be more comfortable. But when the minority is threatened, the majority must show that they are ready to take them into their protection, to build a wall of people around them.

"I don't know how many Austrians will sign the Austria First petition. But I am certain that the majority of Austrians think differently. That for this majority, solidarity with people in need is not an empty phrase."

I thought again about *The Sound of Music*. About how the captain and Maria and the children sang "Edelweiss" at the music festival and how the other performers covered for them, extending their bows so they'd have a couple of extra minutes to get away. I thought about the nuns taking the spark plugs out of the Nazis' cars so they couldn't follow the von Trapp family up into the hills.

Is that what we're doing tonight? Nothing that seems very big. Nothing irreversible. Just for one night, taking the spark plugs out of a car.

I suddenly saw the beauty of the evening, the thousands of candles twinkling in the darkness. The people there were saying no, one politician and his followers did *not* represent who they were as a country. Did not represent who they wanted to be.

Yeah. I think a few less spark plugs could make a difference.

CHAPTER 36

Green Hair Dye

AFTER THE MARCH, we all went back to Katarina's house. We had cake and tea, and eventually, everyone started to head home. Right before Rasheed's family was ready to leave, Frau Kumar's pager buzzed. "May I use your phone?" she asked.

She disappeared into the kitchen, and when she returned a few minutes later, she was smiling. "They found her."

"Thank goodness," Katarina said. "Where is she?"

"In a detention center near the border."

"How do we get her out?" Dad asked.

"That's going to be trickier," Frau Kumar said. "Depends on what paperwork you have."

"I don't have anything," Dad said. "Katarina?"

Katarina looked down at her hands, tapping her red manicured nails against her palm. "Sara applied for asylum when she first arrived. It was denied, and she received

TPS. She didn't have a work permit. I was very clear that the au pair arrangement was a casual favor between friends. I didn't want her to get in trouble!"

"Did she have a driver's license?" Frau Kumar asked. "Or even a student ID card?"

Katarina shook her head. "Sara didn't drive."

"She has a student ID," I said. I'd seen her use it at a museum.

"But she kept it in her wallet," Felix added. "Which was also stolen."

Frau Kumar sighed. Her T-shirt and jeans were rumpled from the protest; her light brown hair was falling out of its ponytail.

"Sara was here legally," Dad said. "Isn't her name on a list or something?"

"Most definitely," Frau Kumar said. "But how do we prove she really is that person on the list?"

"But we know her!" Katarina explained. "Can't we just sign something saying we vouch for her?"

"It's doable," Frau Kumar agreed. "But it will take a while."

"Would it help if you had a copy of her passport?" I asked.

"Yes, of course. If we could prove who she is and that she was here legally, I could get her released quickly and—"

"Sara said she was going to make a copy," I interrupted.

"When we went to the police station to get the stamp she needed."

"I already searched her room," Katarina said. "There's nothing."

"I'd like to look," I said.

"Of course! Be my guest."

I ran upstairs. I'd never been in Sara's room before. It looked almost identical to mine: bed, desk, bookcase. Her violin was in the corner; a picture of her, a woman, and a little boy sat in a small frame on the desk. *That must be her family.* The room felt oddly bare. As if she hadn't let herself get too attached. As if she had felt she was only visiting.

I opened the closet and saw the fancy dress hung on a hanger. There were only a few other clothes, mainly black.

Where would Sara put something to keep it safe?

I searched the drawers of the desk, the bookshelves, and under the bed. All the obvious places. In a dresser drawer I found extra copies of the flyer Sara had posted at the airport: *Ich suche Petra Tahirović, 44, und Eldin Tahirović, 6.* Even though we knew where she was, it felt like Sara was lost too.

Finally, I returned to the closet. There was a shelf above the hangers. I didn't see anything on it, but I reached up and felt around just to be sure.

There was something there! I pulled it out and found a small box. I couldn't read the writing on it, but there was a picture of a woman with her hair dyed green. I was about to put it back when I remembered what the old woman on the train had said. Sara had yelled *Green hair!* as they'd dragged her off. My heart started to beat faster.

I shook the box. It felt empty. Of course it was. She'd used it to dye that streak of hair green when she'd first arrived. She'd kept the box only to remember her mother. Unless . . . Quickly, I opened it.

Inside were two sheets of paper. Two photocopies, folded into quarters. I unfolded them slowly, my hands trembling. The first was a copy of Sara's passport, the page with her photo and all her info. The second was a copy of the page with her TPS stamp.

"I found it," I called. But I was crying so hard, no one could hear me. I wiped my nose on my sleeve and tried again. "I found it!" I yelled.

And they all came running.

THE NEXT DAY involved waiting. Lots of waiting. It was Sunday, so the offices we needed weren't open. Frau Kumar told us she would call if she heard anything.

We tried to distract ourselves. Felix and I played so many games of Mensch Ärgere Dich Nicht, I was afraid I was going to be dreaming about little colored pegs. We went for a walk in the vineyards. Katarina made goulash again, and it tasted even better without the bugs. Over dinner,

Dad read us facts from the paper. "Approximately three hundred thousand people attended the march in Vienna last night. There were also demonstrations in Graz, Linz, Innsbruck, and Salzburg."

"Wow," I said.

"The population of Vienna is only 1.7 million." Felix made some notes on the edge of the paper. "That's almost eighteen percent of the entire city population."

"I'm glad we were there," Katarina said.

"Me too," Dad agreed.

"Do you think Haider will get his million signatures?" I asked.

"I don't know." Katarina sighed. "He has one week. Guess we'll have to wait and see."

A week? I was supposed to go home in just over a week. Next Saturday, August 28, was the ball. Sara and Marco were supposed to dance in the opening. We were all planning to attend, not only Dad and Katarina but Felix's friends and their families too. It had sounded like so much fun! But without Sara, I didn't want to go at all.

I was just getting ready for bed when the phone rang. I stood on the stairs, my toothbrush in my mouth, as Dad picked up the receiver. "Hello?"

He looked serious for a moment, then smiled. "Oh, thank goodness." He listened a moment longer. "Wonderful, we'll see you there. Thanks again."

"What happened?" I asked, trying not to spit toothpaste on the banister.

"Frau Kumar got through to a friend of a friend. We're supposed to show up at ten a.m. tomorrow at the detention center, take the papers we have, and hopefully, we'll be able to bring Sara home."

I didn't think I'd be able to sleep, but I must have, because I closed my eyes and next thing I knew, my alarm was going off.

We piled into the car, with Katarina driving because she knew the roads best. Dad rode shotgun, and Felix and I were in the back. I didn't think we'd all been in the car together since they'd picked me up from the airport. I remembered how squishy it had been then, with Sara in the back with Felix and me. I longed for it to be crowded again.

It was about an hour's drive to the detention center. We parked in a small lot out front and went inside. It was an ugly low concrete building, nothing like the massive police station we'd gone to with Sara to get her passport stamped. Frau Kumar was waiting for us when we arrived. She had on a tailored black suit and high heels, and her hair was pulled back into a severe bun. I almost didn't recognize her—she looked so different from the casual, friendly woman we'd seen two days before.

"Good," she said. "You're on time. Kids, stay here."

Felix and I were left on two folding chairs in the concrete-block lobby. Felix pulled out the copy of Lincoln's speeches we'd given him for his birthday. "Do you want me to read aloud?"

"Sure," I said.

Felix started to read something about a house divided, but I was so distracted, the book might as well have been written in German. I kept folding and refolding my hands in my lap, crossing and uncrossing my legs. *Was there ever a folding chair this hard and uncomfortable?* Finally, we heard the click of heels on the tile floor, and Frau Kumar appeared around the corner. "Come on," she said. "They are going to let her go."

We followed her down a corridor that seemed eerily familiar, though whether it reminded me of the police station or the opera or the school cafeteria back home, I couldn't quite tell. Dad and Katarina were waiting in a small room with a table and four chairs. We went inside, but before we could even sit down, the far door opened.

And there was Sara.

CHAPTER 37

The Heartbeat of the Universe

I T WAS HARD to believe it had been a week since I'd seen her. Her stained T-shirt was gone. Instead, she wore light-blue sweatpants and a sweatshirt, both too large. Her eyes were big and sad. Her green lock of hair hung like a new leaf on a branch over her forehead.

I ran and gave her a hug.

That's when she started to cry. "You came," she whispered. "You came."

"Of course!" I said. "You're family."

Everyone else wanted a hug too. Katarina had wisely brought some of Sara's own clothes and a hairbrush. She went to the bathroom to change and came out looking more like herself, in black jeans and a gray T-shirt.

"Oh!" I said. "I kept this safe for you." I handed her a folded piece of notebook paper.

Sara knew what it was without even unfolding it. "My list!" she exclaimed. "Where?"

"I found your purse with the strap cut in the train bathroom. It was empty, except for a ponytail holder. And your list. That's how we knew something was wrong!"

"List?" Dad asked. "What are you talking about?"

"We all made lists," I explained. "Sara wrote stuff she wants to do when she goes back to Bosnia and sees her family again. I wrote down stuff I wanted to try, like . . . *learn to ride a bike*."

"It's why I agreed to go to the Heuriger," Felix admitted. "*Have a birthday party* was on mine."

I could tell Dad wanted to ask more questions, but at that moment, a guard came in with some papers for Katarina to sign and a plastic bag full of Sara's belongings. *As if she had been in jail!* Sara opened the bag, pulled out her necklace, put it on, then threw her old stained T-shirt and jeans in the trash, as if she never wanted to look at them again. Another woman came in with a folder full of papers; she and Katarina whispered back and forth in German for a long time.

Finally, the woman stood up, and it seemed like we were all going to be able to go home.

But at the last moment, yet another guard came in and whispered in Frau Kumar's ear. "Wait a moment," she said. "I'll be right back."

Frau Kumar followed the guard out of the room. No one spoke. I reached out and held Sara's hand.

"Are you hungry?" Katarina asked.

Sara nodded.

"We made goulash yesterday. There's lots of leftovers," I said.

"And no bugs this time," Felix added.

Sara gave a weak smile. "Why taking so long?" she asked, in a voice so low I almost couldn't hear her.

"I'm sure it's just a formality," said Dad.

"They probably need another signature or something," Katarina added.

Still, it felt tense. It was an ugly little room, with nothing on the walls. *What if they changed their minds?*

Finally, the door opened again, and Frau Kumar entered.

"Everything okay?" Sara asked desperately.

"With your case . . . yes, yes. It's fine." Frau Kumar had an odd look on her face. "It's just . . . there's been a development."

"What kind of development?" Dad asked.

"Did they catch those thieves who stole her passport?" I asked.

"No, unfortunately not. However, there is a person . . ." She looked down at her notes. "Actually two people who claim to know Sara."

"I not understand," Sara said.

"Apparently, all the detainees have been talking about the young woman who speaks many languages." Frau Kumar glanced at the paper again. "Sara, do you know Petra and Eldin Tahirović?"

We all looked over at Sara.

Her green eyes were so wide. "That's my mama and my little brother."

"Well, they're here."

"What?" Katarina demanded.

"Where?" Dad asked.

"In a different section of the building. I think they've been here a couple of weeks." She flipped through her notes. "It's a little unclear."

"May I see them?" Sara asked.

"I can do better than that," Frau Kumar said. "There's a lot of overcrowding here. If someone were to vouch for them, agree to pay for the costs of housing and feeding them while they applied for TPS benefits, I might be able to get them released."

"Released?" Sara asked.

"Meaning they could go home with you. Today."

"Yes, of course. I'll vouch for them," Katarina said.

"You can put my name down as well," Dad said.

Frau Kumar smiled broadly then. "Okay, then, if you can be patient a few more minutes . . ."

She left the room. Sara was crying again. I went over and put my arm around her. "Sara, it's okay," I whispered.

"You're gonna see your mom again. And your brother. We can bake him a cake!"

"And your little brother can sleep on my top bunk," Felix offered.

Katarina nodded. "You can all stay as long as you—"

The door opened again, and we all jumped. But it was only Frau Kumar. She was grinning from ear to ear. "Sara, if you'd come with me. We thought it might be better not to overwhelm them with everyone at once. Your family is waiting in the next room."

SARA'S MOTHER, IT turned out, was short and thin, with an angular face and green eyes like her daughter. Her long dark hair was arranged in a messy bun, with streaks of gray spread across it like a spiderweb. She wore the same light-blue sweats as Sara. Katarina kept apologizing for not bringing her extra clothing, even though we hadn't known she would be there.

Sara's brother still had a baby face, with big round eyes and chubby cheeks. When I met him, he was holding Sara's hand and refusing to let go.

BY THE TIME we all made it home, it was late afternoon. We put a big spread on the table: goulash and rice and Semmeln. But the meal, which I'd been so eagerly looking forward to in the car, imagining it as a heartful reunion full of hugs and laughter, like the time when Jimmy was finally reunited with his twin brother, Johnny, on *Love on the Evening Tide*, turned out to be kind of awkward.

Mrs. Tahirović and Eldin spoke no German, so Sara had to translate whenever they wanted to say anything, even "Pass the salt." Eldin gobbled up everything in sight, stuffing goulash and bread into his mouth, until halfway through the meal, he threw up. Sara changed him into some of Felix's outgrown clothes, then settled him down on the couch to watch TV, where he promptly fell asleep. Mrs. Tahirović drank a cup of coffee but ate little and said even less. "Mama says her tooth hurts," Sara explained finally. "She broke it a couple of months ago and . . . she'd like to go lie down."

"Of course," Katarina said. "The bed has clean sheets. And I'll make an appointment at the dentist for tomorrow."

Sara carried her sleeping brother upstairs, her mother following slowly. "It'll be all right," Dad said as Felix and I cleared the table and helped with the dishes. "After all they've been through, they're just going to need some time to adjust."

🐷

SARA CAME DOWN in the early evening and asked Felix and me if we wanted to take a walk. The three of us headed off into the vineyards. The sun was warm, and the fields smelled slightly of manure. A light breeze rustled the grape leaves. We walked for a long time without saying a word.

"Do you want to talk about it?" I asked.

"No," said Sara. "And yes. It was so scary when they took me off the train! I'm sorry I left you there alone."

"It's not your fault!" I insisted.

"We were fine," Felix added.

"They were supposed to let me make a call, but . . . the border police said I be allowed to at the detention center. And at the center, they said I should have already made my call!" She shook her head.

"What was it like in detention?" Felix asked.

"There were two other women in my room, both older than me. One woman sat there and stared at the wall. Rumor was her daughter had been taken by the Serbian Army. I never heard her say a word. The other woman was nice, a little younger than my grandmother, but she spoke absolutely no German, so I had to explain what was going on. She did not even understand we were not in real jail, just Schubhaft."

"What's Schubhaft?" I asked.

"It means being detained because we had crossed the border illegally, not because we had committed any other crime."

Felix snorted. "Still sounds a lot like jail to me."

"I guess it was," Sara said. "The cell had wooden platforms for beds. There was a thin mattress and a blanket on each one. The blankets were kind of dirty, but we got three meals a day. We had to eat everything with a spoon."

"Sounds awful!" I said. "I'm so sorry, Sara."

"The worst part was that there was nothing to do. The older woman had a deck of cards, and there was one Heimatroman."

"That's like a romance novel," Felix explained.

"Yeah. A lawyer moves to a tiny Alpine village and falls in love with a milkmaid. It was pretty bad, but I read it three times."

"Did they ever let you out of the cell?" I asked.

"Once a day, we went outside and walked around in the courtyard. It was never for very long, but I got to talk to some of the other prisoners. Most of them were also from Bosnia, but I was the only one who spoke good German. I sometimes got extra time outside because the guards liked that I could understand them."

"You never saw your mom or Eldin?" Felix asked.

Sara shook her head. "They only let a few of us out at a time. But I asked everyone about them. I guess word got around that I was there."

We'd reached the top of the hill by that point. We could see the trees of the Vienna woods just off in the distance. After a moment, we turned around to go back home.

"Were you scared?" I asked.

"I was so scared," Sara said. "But I kept thinking about the bridge in Prague. I imagined you were both there, holding my hands."

We held hands again, Felix on one side of Sara, and I on the other. We walked back down the hill in the golden twilight.

"The worst part," Sara whispered, "is that Mama will not talk to me. All I know is that they only got my first letter with the old address. They decided to leave, and things did not go as planned." Sara started to cry. "I wish she would tell me more. Whatever horrible things happened, not knowing feels worse."

I squeezed her hand. We walked in silence for a long way. But it was a good quiet, not a bad one. Then Felix started to sing: *"Di quell'amor ch'è palpito dell'universo intero."*

Sara was so shocked, she stopped walking. "Felix, you have a beautiful voice!"

He blushed. "My father taught me to sing a little."

"You should sing more," Sara said.

Felix shook his head.

"Come on," I urged. "There's peppermint tea at home."

As we walked, Felix and Sara and I hummed bits of the opera, listening once more together to the heartbeat of the universe.

CHAPTER 38

The Riesenrad, Part 2

DAD HAD TO go back to work the next morning, but Katarina took the day off and drove the rest of us to the dentist. Eldin only needed a cleaning and one cavity filled, but the dentist decided Mrs. Tahirović needed a root canal. While Sara explained to her mother what was going to happen, Eldin ran around the waiting room, ripping the covers off all the magazines. Katarina suggested that since the dentist was near the Prater, maybe we should take Eldin on a little walk. "Stay as long as you want," Katarina said, giving Sara some money. "We'll meet you back at home."

I liked Eldin. Sure, he was a little naughty at times, but he reminded me of a puppy dog, running in circles around us. I'd thought escaping from a war zone might have made him shy; instead, he seemed to assume Felix and I were his best friends. He chattered away to us nonstop, although we couldn't understand a single world. Whenever I asked Sara to translate, she said something like "He said, 'Pretty bird.'" Or "'Lot of big cars.'"

"You're not translating everything!" Felix scolded her.

"He's young," she said. "Uses too many words. Repeats himself. I get to point."

At the Prater, Eldin liked the games and the rocket-ship roller coaster. But he kept grinning and pointing at the Riesenrad. Finally, Sara turned and looked at me.

It was my last week in Vienna. I was going home next Tuesday. I doubted I'd make it to the Prater again, and I really did hope to cross the Riesenrad off my list. Eldin obviously longed to go. I didn't want to be the type of person who prevented a little kid from going on a Ferris wheel.

"Let's try it," I whispered.

"What?" Felix asked.

"I'd like to go on the Riesenrad," I said a bit louder.

"You sure?" Sara asked.

I nodded.

Sara smiled and went to get the tickets.

We all stood in line, looking at *The Third Man* poster once again, just like we had done . . . had it only been seven weeks before? I'd like to say I waltzed onto that ride without the slightest twinge of anxiety, but I'd be lying. In truth, it was almost as scary as it had been before. But this time, I was able to say, *I hear you, heart. You're beating like there are bombs falling overhead. But it's only the bumper cars next door.* I took long, deep breaths, and Felix helped, counting, "One, two, three, four, in. Hold. Eins, zwei, drei, vier, out." As we got closer to the front of the line, I felt nauseous. *Fine,* I said to myself, *throw up. There's a trash can over there.*

What I didn't do was run away.

Finally, it was our turn. I held Eldin's hand as the man took our tickets, and his enthusiasm propelled me over the threshold onto the ride. The car was big, bigger than our compartment on the train. I estimated it could hold twenty people easily.

The conductor shut the door and locked it tight. I still felt dizzy, so I sat down on one of the benches along the side. Eldin ran to look out the window.

Twenty people fall to their deaths, my brain screamed.

Sara walked over, and I clutched her hand. I closed my eyes, and that's when we started to move. I was so surprised—it was such a funny motion, like an elevator but moving sideways—that I forgot to be scared and opened them again.

Felix and Eldin were standing by the window, looking out, and we went to join them.

The view was amazing! I could see . . . I could see my summer. Stephansdom, the streetcars, the opera, Heldenplatz, Schönbrunn—it seemed like every place we had gone was there, laid out before me in miniature. I was fascinated. It was like the music at the opera, only this time, it was the view that made my nerves fade away.

The Ferris wheel stopped at the top. I glanced at Felix, but he said, "They're loading more riders."

I nodded. Felix and Eldin were pointing things out to each other. They were smiling. My fear was still there, but so was I.

"You did it, Becca," Sara said. "You finished your list."

I thought about that. When I'd talked about traveling somewhere, I'd meant by airplane, but a train was close enough. I had eaten an egg, learned to ride a bike, and hung out in a couple of large crowds. And now I was on a Ferris wheel.

"Nah," I said. "You're wrong."

"Wrong?"

"I think you should say *we* finished my list."

"Yes." Sara smiled. "Very true."

ON THE WAY home, we stopped by the Julius Meinl so Sara could pick up a few groceries. She gave Eldin a package of candles and spoke a few words to him. He got so excited, he ran up and down the aisles, waving the candles in the air and shouting.

"What's he saying?" I asked.

Sara sighed. "He's yelling, 'It's my birthday!' It isn't, but I told him I would make him a cake."

We laughed and lugged the flour back to Katarina's, only to find Mrs. Tahirović working with Frau Gamperl in her garden. Sara exchanged a few words with her mother.

"She says she feels better now," Sara reported. "And she likes pruning flowers."

Eldin "helped" Sara make the cake, which meant he spilled a cup of flour and broke a glass measuring cup. But the cake was delicious.

CHAPTER 39

At the Ball

WE SPENT MOST of Saturday getting ready for the ball. Katarina was wearing a rich-red gown, and her hair was piled in an updo, with dark curls falling onto her forehead and neck. She looked amazing. For me, she'd found a purple dress she thought would suit me in the back of her closet. I spent Saturday afternoon standing on a box in her bedroom while she tucked and pinned and hemmed.

"So . . . a ball is basically a big prom for grown-ups?" I asked.

Katarina laughed. "Something like that. Most balls are held in the winter," she explained. "It's Vienna's version of Carnival. Kids are usually strictly verboten, but since this is a student ball—and the dance studio helped organize it—your class is being allowed to go. Sara's gone early to get ready to perform. We'll meet her there."

Katarina made one final adjustment to my skirt. "Done. Take a look!"

I stepped down off the box and turned toward her mirror. The purple dress had a tight bodice and lace over the shoulders and sleeves. The skirt was full and flew out when I twirled. I had a petticoat underneath, and Katarina had found me a pair of high-heeled shoes. (They were low-heeled high heels, because shoes that are too high are very bad for the tendons in your feet. See DJ #3, p. 31.) In any case, the dress made me feel like I had walked into a fancy party on *Love on the Evening Tide*.

"I love it!"

My dad took Felix to rent a tuxedo, and the two of them got more into it than I'd expected, coming home talking cummerbunds and cuff links. Even Sara's mother was coming, in another borrowed dress from Katarina, this one black and long and elegant. Eldin was way too young to come (and he'd probably break something), but Frau Gamperl had volunteered to watch him. "I've been to plenty of balls in my time," she said. "But you all have fun!"

The ball was being held at the University of Vienna, in a massive building that looked more like a palace than a school to me. We showed our tickets at the door and were waved through a hallway into a courtyard surrounded by curved archways on all four sides. A wooden dance floor had been laid out over the stones of the patio.

Sara and Marco came over almost as soon as we arrived. "You made it!" she cried. Sara looked beautiful. Her dress was white and as light and fluffy as a vanilla cupcake. She even had a tiny tiara sparkling on her head, right where her green streak should have been.

"It's gone!" I exclaimed.

"Yeah." Sara touched her hair gingerly, as if she could feel the change in color. "Mama is here."

Mrs. Tahirović smiled and kissed her on both cheeks. Katarina snapped a picture of them together, one all in white, the other all in black.

Marco wore a white tie and tails—he even had white gloves—and looked like he'd stepped out of *Masterpiece Theatre*. He bowed and kissed Mrs. Tahirović's hand, making us all laugh.

"We must go," Sara said. "Meet you after opening!"

Rasheed, Mai, and their parents joined us next.

"Hey," I said to Rasheed. "Looking sharp."

Rasheed pulled at his collar and muttered, "This thing is so uncomfortable."

Felix laughed. "Becca's dad took me for a professional fitting."

"That's why your tux looks so nice," Mai said.

I thought Felix was going to faint. Luckily, he was saved from having to respond, because at that moment, eight trumpeters appeared, poking their instruments out of the second-story windows, two on each side of the courtyard. A hush fell over the crowd.

They played a fanfare. A real gosh-darn-it fanfare, like we were in a movie. The orchestra, tucked away in a corner of the courtyard, started to play. The young women and men opening the ball stepped two by two onto the dance floor, then they joined together to march four by four, then eight by eight, and finally they made a circle around the courtyard. It took me a minute to find Sara in the sea of white dresses.

The trumpets played another fanfare, and then the orchestra played the first measures of a waltz. I couldn't take my eyes off Sara and Marco as they spun around the courtyard. The dresses swirled out like little tulle tornadoes. They seemed to float across the floor.

When the song was finally done, they all bowed, and a man in tails came onto the floor and called out "Alles Walzer!"

Immediately, people rushed onto the dance floor as the band started another song. Dad held his hand out to Katarina and asked, "May I have this dance?"

The rest of us stood awkwardly in a group for a moment. I was waiting for Felix to ask Mai to dance, but of course he didn't. "Hey, Rasheed," I said. "You want to try out some of those steps we learned in class?"

"Sure!"

Mai got the hint. "Felix, would you like to dance?" He nodded, and the four of us walked out onto the dance floor.

"Ouch!" I exclaimed as Rasheed promptly stepped on my foot.

"Sorry," he called out cheerfully. "Just like in class."

The dance floor was packed. Back in the United States, I'd only ever seen old people waltzing, maybe at a wedding or a stuffy restaurant. But most of the couples here were Sara's age, and they zipped across the floor, spinning like tops. It was kind of hard to avoid them. Actually, it felt like dodgeball in gym class.

"Ouch!" I exclaimed again.

"Oops!" said Rasheed with such a goofy grin, it made me giggle.

I stepped on his foot—on purpose. Then he stepped on mine, and it turned into sort of a game. A couple who totally weren't paying attention to where they were waltzing ran into us. They yelled at us in German, and we burst out laughing.

"Come on," I said to the others. "Let's go explore!"

The orchestra in the courtyard was playing traditional music—waltzes, polkas, and tangos. We found another band playing rock and roll in a smaller hall. Felix, Rasheed, Mai, and I watched for a while, smiling at the Austrians in formalwear dancing the jitterbug. "They are so good," I marveled.

There was another room with a disco ball and a DJ, and yet another with a magician doing magic tricks while people in ball gowns plopped down on the floor to watch. After a couple of magic tricks, we got up to explore some more and ran into Sara, Mrs. Tahirović, and Marco in the hallway.

"You were amazing!" I gushed to Sara.

Marco squeezed her hand.

"Did you see the magician?" I asked. "He's great!"

"No, we were just on our way to—"

At that moment, a waiter carrying a tray of drinks collided with a couple dancing their way out of one of the ballrooms. The glasses fell to the floor with a spectacular crash. Someone screamed.

Almost before the glasses had finished tinkling to the floor, two more waiters descended on the scene with brooms and a dustpan. Clearly, they were prepared for this, because a minute later, all signs of the accident had been erased, except for a small wet patch from the spilled drinks on the stone floor.

But someone was still crying out, as if in pain, as if they'd been hurt. I turned around and realized it was Mrs. Tahirović, her hands protectively covering her face. She was sobbing.

"Mama! Mama!" Sara called.

"Was ist los?" asked Marco.

"What's wrong?" I repeated in English.

Mai and Rasheed made a little wall, trying to block her from the view of the others passing by in the corridor.

"Did she get hit by a piece of flying glass?" asked Felix.

"I do not think so," Sara said. She and her mother had a brief, terse exchange in Bosnian. "The glass breaking reminded her of something that happened in Sarajevo."

"Let's get her outside," said Marco.

Our little procession led Mrs. Tahirović down the stairs and into a side garden just off the courtyard. It was a warm evening but much less stuffy outside than it had been in the crowded building. We found a secluded bench in one corner. Mrs. Tahirović sat down, and Sara put her arms around her mother. Mrs. Tahirović's mascara ran down her face, leaving a gray smudge on the shoulder of Sara's white gown.

"Could someone get some water?" Sara asked. "And find Katarina?"

"I get the water," said Marco.

"We'll find Katarina," said Mai, pulling Rasheed away with her.

Felix and I stood awkwardly nearby, unsure if we should leave or stay.

Sara gripped her mother's hands and began to plead with her in Bosnian. I didn't understand a word, and yet somehow I knew she was asking her mother again and again to please tell her why she was upset.

Finally, Mrs. Tahirović began to speak. I couldn't

understand her either, of course, but she spoke slowly and deliberately. Sara was crying, with silent tears running down her face.

Dad and Katarina ran up then. "What's happened?" Katarina asked.

Felix spoke softly. "A waiter dropped a tray of glasses, and Mrs. Tahirović started crying."

Marco came back with a glass of water and handed it to Sara's mother. She drank it in one gulp.

Mrs. Tahirović spoke again, then looked at her daughter to translate. "My mother apologizes for making a scene," Sara said in almost a monotone. "The glass breaking reminded her of . . . an incident back home."

"It's all right," said Katarina kindly. "Why, anyone could get startled!"

Sara translated again, and Mrs. Tahirović smiled weakly.

"Let's take your mother to the restroom," Katarina suggested. "She can wash her face, and she'll feel much better."

Sara translated, Mrs. Tahirović nodded, and the three of them walked off.

Dad, Felix, and I watched them go. Marco picked up the water glass and went to return it to the bar. I looked around.

No one was paying us any mind. A group of young women giggled as they walked by. A couple argued loudly in German. I couldn't tell what they were saying, but everyone ignored them too. Mrs. Tahirović had freaked out in a group, in public. The thing I had always feared. The fear that had kept me from fireworks and musicals—and yet nothing had happened. We'd had a good time before she'd gotten upset; could we even have a good time after?

I looked over at Felix. "What do we do now?"

He shook his head uncertainly.

"I think," Dad said slowly, "we should go to the disco."

So we did. The DJ was playing "Y.M.C.A." I knew a bunch of people on the dance floor: Daisy, Peter, and their parents had shown up. Even the stern Frau Kovács was waving her arms in the air. Mai, Rasheed, and Marco joined us. We walked out onto the dance floor. The others welcomed us into their little circle, and we all jumped up and down and waved our arms and called out "Y-M-C-A" together, pronouncing the letters with a German accent. I'm not sure I've ever laughed so hard.

When we tired of dancing, we wandered back to the courtyard. It was almost midnight. Waiters were handing out bubbly drinks in tall glass flutes. Dad, Marco, and Felix went to get some. I spotted Katarina, Sara, and Mrs. Tahirović sitting on a stone bench in a little alcove.

"Becca!" Katarina called out. "We are having a lovely time watching all the dancers." She jumped up, her red dress swirling like a rose in the wind. "Sit here, sit here. I'll get us some Sekt for our toast!"

I sat down next to Sara. Mrs. Tahirović looked better—still pale and wan, but she wasn't shaking anymore. "Everything okay?" I asked.

Sara squeezed my hand. "Mama started talking to me," she whispered into my ear.

Dad, Katarina, Felix, and Marco joined us, passing out glasses until we all had one. An old bell started to toll. Everyone cheered, and Dad and Katarina called out, "Prost!" We all clinked glasses and took a sip.

It was sweet and fruity. The bubbles tingled on my tongue. It tasted like a liquid flower, not like any sparkling cider I had ever . . .

"It's champagne!" I held the glass away from my body.

"Yes," Dad said.

I made a face and everyone laughed. Even me.

The ball was wrapping up, so the grown-ups paired off for one final dance.

"Felix?" I asked.

"What?"

"Would you like to dance?"

"Sure," he said. "Why not."

I took his arm like they'd shown us in class, and he led me out onto the floor. We had a fabulous time, stepping on each other's toes and laughing every time we messed up. "I'm so glad I came," I said.

"To the ball? To dance class? To Austria?" Felix asked.

"All of it," I said.

"Yeah," he agreed. "Me too."

AN OLD MAN in tails stood by the exit. "Fräulein!" he called out to me as I walked by. "Ihre Damenspende."

He handed me a gift bag with a little black box inside.

"What's this?" Dad asked.

"There's always a gift for the women at a ball," Katarina told him, taking her own bag. "Ooh, it's perfume!"

Sara walked arm in arm with her mother. Mrs. Tahirović opened her box and pulled out a little bottle of light-yellow liquid.

"Spellbound," I read off the side.

Mrs. Tahirović sprayed a bit of the perfume in the air. It was spicy and sweet.

Felix sneezed. "Magical." He sneezed again.

"Do you want to get a taxi?" Dad asked.

"No," Katarina said. "Let's take the night bus."

We all walked to the bus stop. There was a crowd of people waiting, all wearing tuxedos and ball gowns. Marco's bus came first. He hugged everyone and kissed Mrs. Tahirović's hand again before he left. Our bus finally came, and everyone filed orderly onboard. No one checked our bus passes.

Katarina and Mrs. Tahirović sat in the front of the bus.

Felix and Dad found a seat behind them. Sara and I sat across the aisle.

"Sara," I said. "I just thought of something. What was the first item on your list?"

"Play violin recital," Sara replied. "Why?"

"You did that at my birthday," Felix commented.

"And two?" I asked.

"Study language at Uni."

"You did that with Marco," I pointed out.

"Ballroom dancing was on the list too," Felix added. "I remember because I thought, *No way!*"

"I did that tonight," Sara mused.

"And Eldin got his cake! But I can't remember number five."

"It was," Sara said slowly, "'get ice cream with family and walk across bridge.'"

"We did that in Prague!" exclaimed Felix.

"Now you've completed your list too!"

Sara looked thoughtful for a long moment. Her eyes got so big and watery, I thought her mascara was going to start running down her cheeks like her mother's had done. But instead of crying, she broke into a grin. "Yes," she said finally. "I guess I have."

By the time we got home, my feet hurt and I had a blister. But for once, I didn't worry about applying antibiotic cream or taking a shower after being in a large group of people. I just tumbled happily into bed and fell asleep.

CHAPTER 40

So Long, Farewell, auf Wiedersehen, Adieu

I<small>T WAS MY</small> last morning in Austria. My suitcase was packed. My Doomsday Journals too. Only my Pig Journal remained on the desk, the sketch of the Riesenrad looking up at me like an eye. Today, I was going back to Virginia. And even though I was definitely excited to see my mom and my friends and catch up on *Love on the Evening Tide*, as I walked down the stairs, I sort of felt like crying.

Katarina was in the kitchen, wearing an apron, with powdered sugar on her nose. Felix sat with a book he was only half hiding under the table; Eldin raced toy cars on the tablecloth beside him. Sara poured coffee. As I looked out the window, I could see Mrs. Tahirović watering Frau Gamperl's flowers. Dad was standing at the stove, frying bacon.

"There you are, Schatzi!" Katarina called. "I made

Palatschinken. They're like Austrian crepes. Delicious. You sprinkle them with powdered sugar. Alas, something went wrong, but I'm going to try . . ."

I laughed. "The table is already covered with food! Let's just sit down and eat."

Just like on my very first day, there was a basket of round Semmeln fresh from the bakery. The butter, from mountain-pastured cows, was soft as always, since Katarina kept it on the counter and not in the fridge. There was apricot jam, ham, cantaloupe, coffee, and hot chocolate. Mrs. Tahirović brought in a bouquet of flowers. We all sat down, and then Eldin picked up his eggcup and pretended it was a hat, and Sara yelled at him, and Felix tried not to laugh. I ate a bite or two of pretty much everything—even the soft-boiled egg.

"Well, Haider didn't get his million signatures," Dad said, glancing at the front page of the paper. "He only got four hundred thousand."

"That's still a lot of people," Felix said.

"It is," Katarina agreed. "But there's a lot more that didn't sign."

We were just finishing breakfast when the phone rang. "Oh, hello, Frau Kumar," said Dad. They chatted for a bit while I cleared the table, then Dad handed the phone to me.

"Hello?" I said.

"Hey, Becca!" It was Rasheed. "I wanted to say good-bye. I'm glad we met."

"Me too," I said.

"I hope you come back sometime," he said. "I'm gonna keep taking dance lessons. Maybe next time we go to a ball, I'll only step on your foot once."

I laughed. "Sounds good."

"Can I talk to Felix? Peter and I are riding bikes to the park tomorrow for a picnic. Thought he might like to come."

"Sure," I said.

Felix looked surprised when I handed him the phone. But after a minute, he was chatting about what he was going to bring to the picnic.

Katarina came over then and gave me a big hug. "Thank you for helping him," she whispered in my ear.

"I didn't do—"

"Yes, you did," Katarina insisted. "And, Becca, you must come back soon! Maybe at Christmas? Oh, Christmas in Vienna is gorgeous! We have real candles on the trees. You've never seen anything so beautiful!"

"Real candles?" I asked.

"Yes," she said.

"On a dead tree? Inside your house?!"

"Yes, of course!"

"Do you know how many fires start from unattended candles?" I asked.

Katarina laughed. "That's just what your father said."

I glanced at Dad. He shrugged. "It's what they do here, Becca. I'll make sure we have a fire extinguisher on hand."

Katarina hugged me once more. "Just come back soon."

Sara and I went up to my room so she could help me finish packing. "Are you going to stay in Austria?" I asked.

"I want to. Frau Kumar said with my language skills, maybe she can get me a work permit."

"That's wonderful!"

"Nothing definite," she said, but she smiled. "For now, I stay with Katarina and take classes at the university in the fall."

"And your mom? And Eldin?"

"I not sure. She has a cousin in Berlin. And another one in New York. But for now, I think she's going to move in with Frau Gamperl."

"Really?"

Sara shrugged. "She has more room than Katarina. And she said she enjoys company. Your dad already helped enroll Eldin in Felix's school. I do not know how long they will stay, but for now, I'm glad we're together."

"So much uncertainty!"

"There's always uncertainty, Becca. We not like to think about it, but we never really know what is going to happen. What is the expression? *You could get hit by a bus?*"

"Or a Straßenbahn!"

Sara laughed, then her face turned serious. "I thought

a lot about this when I was in detention. It is important to prepare when you can, and of course you should always look both ways before you cross the street. But if you never cross at all . . ."

"You miss out on a lot," I finished.

"I think the best way to deal with uncertainty," Sara continued, "is to sit with it. Invite it in. Trust ourselves that we can handle it. And if we have family or friends to sit with us, well then, we are extra lucky."

"Stop acting like Fräulein Maria," I said. "You're making me cry."

"Who?" Sara asked.

"Never mind." I hugged her one last time.

🐖

FELIX WAS WAITING by the front door. "Hey," he said. "Want to go for a quick walk?"

"Sure," I said. "I've got time."

We headed out toward the vineyard. Felix stared at his feet as we walked, shy again, as if we had gone back to our first day. "You know," he said finally. "I called my dad last night."

"Really?"

"I wanted to tell him about the ball and . . . remember how I told you about that tap dance class he took me to when I was a kid?"

"Of course."

"I asked him about it. 'I can't believe you remember that,' he said. 'You were so adorable, standing in the back row, doing your best to follow along. I was so proud of you!'"

"What?!"

"Yeah," Felix went on. "I was so surprised. I'd thought he was disappointed in me; and yet it turned out he'd remembered it in a completely different way."

"That's wonderful!"

A wind blew through the grapevines, making them rustle. "I'm not sure I would have been brave enough to ask him about it if I hadn't met you."

"Aww, Felix. You should add it to your list."

"I did! Just so I could cross it off."

I laughed.

"I'm going to add some more things to my list too."

"Cool. Like what?"

"Maybe 'join the choir at school.'"

"That's a great idea."

"And at the ball," Felix went on, "Mai mentioned she liked Alfred Hitchcock. They are showing *North by Northwest* at the English-language theater next week. Think I should invite her?"

"Yes!"

He smiled. "I'm gonna miss you, Becca."

"I'm gonna miss *you*, Felix."

We hugged, a bit awkwardly.

"See you next summer?" he asked.

"Absolutely."

DAD DROVE ME to the airport. The rest of them wanted to come too, but I said I'd like a little time alone with my father. We didn't say much in the car; I just looked out the window. "I like Vienna, Dad," I said finally. "I like Katarina and Felix. And you picked a great au pair. I had a wonderful summer."

"Yeah," Dad agreed. "Me too."

"Oh, Dad!" I exclaimed. "Did I tell you about my Pig Journal?"

"No." He laughed. "What in the world is a Pig Journal?"

"I decided that instead of only focusing on what might go wrong, I want to spend some time remembering everything that goes right."

"Oh, pig!" Dad said. "Like *good luck* in German."

"Yeah."

"I love that, Rebecca. Maybe I'll start a Pig Journal too."

At the airport, Dad parked and checked my bag, and suddenly we were standing in front of the X-ray machine. I put my bag on the conveyor belt, and Dad walked right through. Too late, I realized I'd never told him how nervous I'd gotten going through the last time.

There was a moment—okay, a long moment—when I

wasn't sure I could do it. But then I noticed a nearby TV playing CNN. Ms. Madden was on the screen, interviewing someone. I glanced around the airport and noticed a kid peeling a hard-boiled egg. And a teenager putting a luggage tag on a bike. A woman was hanging up a tourism poster with the Riesenrad on it. There were crowds of people around me, and I was about to get on an airplane.

"Becca." My dad had stopped and turned, realizing I wasn't following him. "Are you okay?"

And even though my heart was pounding and my hands were sweaty, I nodded. Because I was nervous *and* I was okay. I took a deep breath, imagined my friends holding my hands, and just walked through.

Mom was waiting for us at the gate. She looked different. Her hair was longer—and messy. She wore a flowery orange-and-yellow dress with a ketchup stain on one sleeve. Her new bag was dirty and scuffed, her nose sunburned, and yet when she turned toward us, she looked so happy.

"Becca!" Mom exclaimed, running toward me. We hugged.

"You look different," I said.

"Yeah," Mom agreed. "I am different."

I smiled. "Me too."

Dad gave me a snack in a brown paper bag to eat on the plane. Instead of peanut butter, it was an Apfelstrudel from

Aïda. Mom snapped a couple of pictures, and I imagined getting them developed and sending them to Dad.

"You have a two-day stopover in New York, right?" Dad asked.

"Yup," Mom confirmed. "I thought it would be fun to show Becca some of the sights."

"Well," Dad said, handing Mom an envelope. "Make sure not to miss Broadway."

Mom opened the envelope, and a puzzled look crept over her face. "I thought we'd decided . . ."

I grabbed the envelope from her and peeked inside. There were two tickets to see *Les Misérables*. I squealed with delight.

"Don't worry," Dad said. "Becca will do just fine."

We grinned at each other.

A minute later, Little Red Riding Hood announced that the Austrian Airlines flight to John F. Kennedy International Airport was boarding. I gave Dad one last hug, and as Mom and I walked down the gangway, I realized, *Wow! I do have confidence.*

And I might have even skipped.

Between high school and college, I spent a gap year in Vienna, Austria, working as an au pair. I have long wanted to write about my time there. There was only one problem: I had a fabulous time in Vienna! Wonderful times are great to live through; alas, they are less interesting to read about. Conflicts and problems are what make for an exciting story.

Still, something about the time period—the early 1990s, right after the end of the Soviet Union—intrigued me. While rereading some old letters I had written to my parents, I recalled attending a demonstration in Vienna in support of refugees and asylum seekers, the majority of whom were fleeing the war in Bosnia. The year was 1993, and far-right Austrian politician Jörg Haider thought it was time to "put Austria first." The son of former Nazis, he was attempting to get a million signatures for a petition to limit the rights of refugees and foreigners in the country. The Lichtermeer, or "sea of lights," was a counter-protest—and ended up being the largest demonstration in Austria's history.

The details of that protest were very much as described in my book, except it was actually a cold night in January, not a warm summer evening. (Becca seemed much more likely to visit her father in the summer, so I took a little poetic license.) I'm not sure I realized at the time what an important occasion it was. My letter mentioned that the candles looked pretty, I got a hot dog for dinner, and then I went to the opera to see *The Flying Dutchman*, which I didn't like that much. (Although it is also true, as described in the book, that the standing-room ticket only cost me $1.50.)

My letters also made me think about what was happening in the United States almost thirty years later. Politicians vowing to "put America first" eerily echoed Haider's words. News reports about children being separated from their parents on the border and people being denied the right to apply for asylum reminded me of the Bosnian refugees. I remembered the other students in the German classes I took at the University of Vienna. Almost all of them were young women from Eastern Europe who had left their families behind in search of more opportunities. I recalled going to the police station to get my work permit and being waved to the head of the line because of my American passport. It was one of the first times I remember being so aware of my own privilege. I'd found my way into a Vienna story.

And yet, I still had a problem. Au pairs are usually eighteen or nineteen, much too old to be the protagonist of the type of middle-grade books I write. But at the same time I was mulling the idea of setting a book in Vienna, my twelve-year-old niece was struggling with anxiety. Many days, just the idea of going to school literally made her throw up. I watched in admiration as she and my sister searched for (and eventually found) techniques to help her cope. I had been a child with lots of worries too. My niece's struggle reminded me of how over the years, I have learned to tolerate anxiety—not to get rid of it, but to try not to let it stop me from doing the things that I want to do (most of the time).

So now I had two ideas, and in joining them together, *The Thing I'm Most Afraid Of* was born. I hope you enjoyed reading about Becca and Felix and their au pair, Sara, and how they all learned to handle their fears together.

Kristin Levine
ALEXANDRIA, VIRGINIA

Suggested Books for Learning More

The River Runs Salt, Runs Sweet: A Young Woman's Story of Love, Loss and Survival by Jasmina Dervisevic-Cesic. Part love story, part war memoir, this book was written by the first Bosnian refugee given permission to come to the United States to seek medical care.

The Bosnia List: A Memoir of War, Exile, and Return by Kenan Trebinčević and Susan Shapiro. This is a fascinating memoir of a man who escaped from Bosnia as a boy, then returned as an adult to confront some of the former neighbors and friends who had turned against his family.

Land im Lichtermeer by Martin Kargl and Silvio Lehmann. This book contains the text of the speeches given on January 23, 1993, as well as some background information. Unfortunately, I believe this book is only available in German, but it would be a fascinating part of a high school or college German curriculum.

Zlata's Diary: A Child's Life in Wartime Sarajevo by Zlata Filipovic. This book covers the first two years of the war in Sarajevo from a child's perspective; the author was eleven to thirteen when she wrote most of the diary entries.

What to Do When You Worry Too Much: A Kid's Guide to Over-coming Anxiety by Dawn Huebner, PhD. This book is a great resource for kids and families trying to gain the skills to deal with anxiety.

Guts by Raina Telgemeier. This graphic novel about a girl with anxiety is so relatable—my whole family loved it.

WEBSITES

Much of the joy in my book, from riding the Straßenbahn to standing room at the opera to having a birthday party at a Heuriger, came straight from my own experiences. I highly recommend curious readers google any of the locations or buildings mentioned in the story—nearly all of them are real places. An image search for "Lichtermeer Vienna 1993" will return many beautiful pictures as well.

For those struggling with anxiety: **adaa.org**—the Anxiety and Depression Association of America offers information and resources.

For those wanting to learn more about refugee issues (past and current): **unhcr.org**—a United Nations agency working to protect the rights of refugees; **globaldetentionproject.org**—a research center studying the use of detention as a response to migration and protecting the rights of refugees.

TURN THE PAGE TO READ MORE
FROM KRISTIN LEVINE

I USED TO THINK that life was like a puzzle, and if I was organized and worked really hard, I could make all the pieces fit neatly together.

Turns out, I was wrong.

This scrapbook tells the story of how I learned that. It's full of emails and phone conversations, receipts and flyers. Transcripts of old home movies that I typed up. It's the story of how we lost my dad and how we found him again, all organized in a binder with headings and labels, colored tabs and archival scrapbooking tape.

Because, if you ask me, there's nothing like a good list to make you feel calm and in control. Guess I'm just weird that way. I needed to put this all in one place, to see how the clues and pieces all came together to reveal the truth about me and my family.

And if there's only one thing you learn about me from this collection of documents (and I hope there's not just one, but if there is just one), it's this:

I really do love a good puzzle.

Claudia Dalton

From: Jeffery Dalton <jeffdalton327@gmail.com>

Date: Friday, June 26, 2015 4:55 PM EST

To: Claudia Dalton <claudiadalton195@gmail.com>, Jennifer Dalton <jennydalton431@gmail.com>

Subject: Will be home late

My favorite girls,

    Something came up while I was at work. Not quite sure when I'll be home. Don't wait up!

Love you both,

Dad

Claudia Dalton's Cell Phone | Friday, June 26, 2015, 5:03 p.m.

PHONE TRANSCRIPT

Mom: Hello?

Claudia: Dad said he had to work late. When are you going to be home?

Mom: Um, might be 7:30.

Claudia: But Dad was going to drive Kate and me to the movies! It starts at 7:30.

Mom: Do you mind missing the previews?

Claudia: Yes. And I can't sit in the front row because you know I get a crick in my neck.

Mom: Well, I'm sorry, Claudia, but my big conference is in ten days and . . . Why can't Dad take you? I thought this was his last teacher workday before summer vacation.

Claudia: I don't know. He just emailed that something came up.

Mom: Huh. Maybe Kate's mom can take you.

Claudia: She has a project she's trying to finish before she goes on maternity leave.

Mom: That's right! When's the baby due?

Claudia: Couple of weeks.

Mom: Give her my best.

Claudia: Okay. But what about the movies?

Mom: I can pick you up afterward, but—

Claudia: It's fine, Mom. We'll walk.

Mom: Sorry, sweetie. Text me when you're done.

Claudia: Will do.

Mom: Love you!

Claudia: Love you too. Bye.

Claudia Dalton's Cell Phone | Friday, June 26, 2015, 5:11 p.m.

KATE

Hey, BFF?

Sup

Itsy-bitsy change in plans

What?

How do you feel about walking?

Claudia!

Sorry
My dad flaked
Mom working late

Ugh. Mine too

Could your dad . . .

Haha
You know he's never home before 8

So we walk?

Yup

Meet at your place? 6:30?

See you then

6

WHEN I WOKE up the next morning something felt wrong, but I didn't know what it was. I walked into the kitchen and put some bread into the toaster. I got the paper from the front porch and glanced at the headlines: "Gays' right to wed affirmed," "For Obama, a day of triumph, grief and grace," "Dozens killed in terror attacks on 3 continents." (Why did we still get the paper anyway? Couldn't my parents read it online like everybody else?!) I smeared peanut butter and jelly on my toast.

And then I saw it. My father's favorite mug. The one he used for tea every morning. Sitting on the counter, clean and untouched.

From: Claudia Dalton <claudiadalton195@gmail.com>
Date: Saturday, June 27, 2015 10:30 AM EST
To: Jeffery Dalton <jeffdalton327@gmail.com>
Subject: Where are you?!

Dad,

Why didn't you come home last night?!!!

I'm really freaking out. Did you drop your phone in the toilet again? Did you have a car accident? Did you run away to join the circus?!

Mom says she's sure there's some really lame, normal explanation. Like maybe you went bowling with the young teachers from school and had too many beers and decided to crash on someone's couch and you thought you'd texted us, but there was no signal in the bowling alley and you didn't notice the message had failed to send. Even though I've shown you about 500 times how to check it.

But I think she's lying because Mom spent all morning scrubbing the kitchen floor. You know Mom. Unless we're having a party, she only cleans when she's angry or nervous.

Anyway, call us!!!

Love, Claudia

Claudia Dalton's Cell Phone | Saturday, June 27, 2015, 2:14 p.m.

PHONE TRANSCRIPT

Mom: Hello—

Claudia: Mom, has he called?

Mom: No. Are you still at the pool with Kate?

Claudia: Yeah. They invited me to stay for dinner too.

Mom: Okay. That's fine.

Claudia: Have you called the police yet?

Mom: Yes, Claudia. They said we have to wait twenty-four hours before filling out a missing persons report.

Claudia: Oh.

Mom: Wait, I'm getting another call!

Claudia: Is it Dad?

Mom: No. No, it's your grandfather. I called him earlier.

Claudia: That means you think it *is* serious!

Mom: I'm just covering all the bases.

Claudia: But, Mom . . .

Mom: I'll let you know if I hear anything. I gotta go.

Jenny Dalton's Cell Phone | Saturday, June 27, 2015, 2:16 p.m.

Mom: Have you heard anything, Walter?

Papa: No, I was just checking in with you.

Mom: Oh.

Papa: This is so strange. Was Jeff having any problems?

Mom: No.

Papa: You don't sound certain.

Mom: Well, he was acting a little distant lately. But I thought that was because of Lily. I thought it was normal.

Papa: Grief is normal. Disappearing is not.

Mom: I know. I need to call some more friends and . . .

Papa: Let me know if you hear anything.

Mom: I will.

Virginia Missing Persons Information Clearinghouse Report

INVESTIGATING OFFICER Maria Campbell	DATE REPORTED: June 28, 2015 8:14 AM DATE ENTERED VCIN/NCIC: VIC NO:

PART 1

*Agency Submitting Report:				*ORI No:	

*Last Name Dalton	*First Name Jeffery	Middle Name Robert	Suffix	*Sex M	*Race White

Place of Birth: Bakersfield, CA		*Date of Birth: 6/20/1974

*Height 6 ft. 2 in.	*Weight 205 Lbs.	*Eye Color ☐ Maroon ☐ Gray ☐ Multicolor	☐ Black ☐ Green ☐ Hazel ☐ Pink	☐ Blue ☒ Brown ☐ Unknown	* Hair Color ☐ Black ☐ Blond ☐ White ☐ Sandy ☒ Brown ☐ Gray ☐ Red ☐ Pink

Complexion	☒ Fair/Light ☐ Albino ☐ Ruddy ☐ Lt. Brown	☐ Black ☐ Dark ☐ Sallow ☐ Med. brown	☐ Medium ☐ Olive ☐ Yellow ☐ Dark Brown	Scars, Marks, Tattoos and Other Characteristics Scar on left leg under knee; no tattoos

Fingerprint Classification:		Social Security Number: xxx-xx-xxxx	

Operator's License Number B2987	O.L. State VA	Date of Expiration 6/12/19	DNA ☐Yes ☒No Location of DNA:

*Date of Last Contact: 6/26/15	*Originating Agency Case Number:

Fingerprints Available ☒Yes ☐No Location of the Fingerprints Richmond Public Schools	Photo Available ☒Yes ☐No Photo Received ☒Yes ☐No Photo sent to the State Police ☒Yes ☐No	Dental Records ☒Yes ☐No Location of the Dental Records Smile Time Dentistry

Blood Type: O+	Body X-Rays Available ☐Full ☐Partial ☒No	Location of the X-Rays:

Medication Required ☐Yes ☒No	Medication Type	Medical Condition ☐Yes ☒No If Yes, what type:

Person Who Is Reporting Subject Missing:

Last Name Dalton	First Name Jennifer	Middle Name Ann

Relationship to Missing Person: wife

Address: 3457 fast Run Trail Richmond, VA	Contact Telephone: 804-555-3948

Telephone # of Investigating Agency (accessible 24 hours) Area Code ( )	Authority for Release ☐Yes ☐No

Last Seen in Company of: NAME(S)		Sex	Race
(1)			
(2)			

MISCELLANEOUS DATA
(information which may assist in identification: nickname, associates, direction of travel, hairstyle, clothing, etc.)

VEHICLE INFORMATION

License Plate Number	State	Year of Exp.	Lic. Type	VIN
Vehicle Year 2010	Make Toyota	Model Prius	Style	Color Blue

Corrective Vision Prescription: Wears glasses

Jewelry Type and Description:

PART III

I certify the person described in Part I is missing and that the information I have furnished is true and correct to the best of my knowledge and belief.

Janfer D alt	6/28/15	wife
Signature	Date	Relationship

PART IV

I authorize any law enforcement official to use photographs and/or any other identifying information I have provided in any manner they deem necessary in attempting to locate the person I am reporting missing.

Janfer D alt	6/28/15	wife
Signature	Date	Relationship

Virginia Missing Person Information Clearinghouse
Virginia State Police
Criminal Justice Information Services Division
P. O. Box 27472
Richmond, Virginia 23261-7472

*** IMPORTANT ***

PLEASE ATTACH A CURRENT PHOTOGRAPH OF THE MISSING PERSON TO THIS FORM

E ARLY SUNDAY MORNING, so early it was still dark, I woke up
and couldn't fall back asleep. When I went into the kitchen
for some breakfast, I found Mom already there.

She was sitting at the kitchen table, picking slips of paper out
of a Mason jar. I knew what they were: messages my father had
left in my lunch.

Have a great first day of school!

Good luck on your science test.

Break a leg in your history skit!

Dad had put notes in my lunch for years, not every day, but a
couple times a week. I always brought them home and stuffed
them into the jar as I cleaned out my lunch box.

At least I had until a few months ago. Billy Peterson had caught
me reading one, snatched it out of my hand, and spent the rest of
the day repeating, "I love you, sweetie! Have an amazing day!" in
a fake, high-pitched voice. I'd marched home and told Dad I was
too old for notes in my lunch anymore.

I felt awful about that now. Had I hurt Dad's feelings? Was he
mad at me? Mom and I pulled note after note out of the Mason jar
until they covered the kitchen table.

When we were done, Mom finally admitted that she was
worried too. She cooked breakfast, eggs that neither of us ate,
and we filled out the missing persons report together. I looked
through my phone and found three current photos of Dad to
give to the police. I also found the following video, in case they
wanted to put it on TV or anything.

INT. KITCHEN—NIGHT

The room is full of people. Streamers hang from the ceiling and a bunch of balloons are tied to one chair. Claudia's father, Jeff, stands next to the balloon chair. His hair is dark and he wears brown glasses. He has on a blue dress shirt, khaki pants, and a novelty math tie that says $C = 2\pi r$. Jeff is chatting with Kate and her mom, Mrs. Anderson. Kate wears a silly hat with candles, which she takes off and puts on Jeff's head. Her mother wears a dark blue maternity dress that clings to her belly.

JENNY (Off-Screen)

Time for cake!

The lights suddenly go out.

Claudia's mother carries a beautifully decorated round cake with two number candles, 4 and 1, on the top. She looks as if she's come straight from work. She has dark blond, shoulder-length hair, and is wearing a silk blouse and a pencil skirt. Everyone starts to sing.

Jeff smiles patiently until they're done. Then he closes his eyes for a moment, making a wish. He opens his eyes and blows out the candles. Everyone cheers.

Jenny leans over and gives him a kiss.

JENNY (CONT'D)

Happy birthday, sweetie.

IT WAS STRANGE to see my father on the video. I couldn't help thinking that if I walked out of the kitchen and into the living room, my father would be there, reading the paper.

There were no other videos of my father on my phone, just a few clips of Kate and me and a couple of other girls from school at a sleepover, lip-synching to songs and trying out crazy hairdos.

I told Mom we needed to get out our home movies—the clip was kind of dark and a little blurry for television—but she said Dad had taken most of our videos to his parents' house when Nana was sick. She'd felt too bad from the chemo to do much except lie on the couch, and watching videos of me always cheered her up.

Mom promised to see what else she could find. But I still felt disappointed. I wanted to see those videos now. I wanted more notes in my lunch. I wanted to see my father again, even if it was only for a moment on a screen.

ACKNOWLEDGMENTS

E ACH BOOK HAS a whole village of people behind it—
and with each book, the village seems to get larger!

I'd like to start by thanking my historical information sources, including authors Jasmina Dervisevic-Cesic and Kenan Trebinčević, who took the time to correspond with me via email about their fabulous memoirs (see suggested books). Heather Faulkner and Luke McCallin from UNHCR: The UN Refugee Agency and Michael Flynn from the Global Detention Project patiently answered questions and pointed me in the right direction to learn more.

A special shout-out to Liserl (Elisabeth Kaplan). We were au pairs together in Vienna so many years ago, and she still lives there today. She generously read through my manuscript not once, but twice, making sure my German was as correct as possible. Any mistakes that remain are my own. I have so many fond memories of hanging out with Liserl—what a joy to reconnect online!

Likewise, this book would not have been possible without the love and generosity afforded to me by my host family in Vienna—Stefan Schennach, Eva Pfisterer, and their son, Philippe. They took in a homesick young lady and made her feel like she had a second home! I'll never forget all the wonderful times we had together.

There were so many other people who made my year in Vienna what it was. Paula, Susan, Daisy, Danae, and my fellow au pairs: Mollie, Meg, Jane, and David. The artist/ German teacher from the University of Vienna who took us to a fabulous modern art exhibit, and all my fellow students too. The ballroom teacher who taught me to dance—to this day, if I'm waltzing, I count the steps in German. Prentice and his fabulous music classes. All the random people I met waiting in line for standing room at the opera.

Back home, there was my formal writers' group: Caroline Hickey, Tammar Stein, Erica Perl, Katherine Marsh, and Pamela Ehrenberg, who read many of the early drafts. Then I have the friends and cheerleaders in my life: Debbie Gaydos, Jessie Auten, Anna Williams, and Marcos Bolaños all read drafts at various stages, and their comments and support were invaluable. Chuck Stevens and Rebekah Bundang never failed to ask, "How's the book going?" A special thanks to the ladies who planned a Zoom party (complete with Prosecco, left at my door) during the coronavirus pandemic to celebrate finishing copyedits: Anna, Liz, Diane, Maria, and Jessie. And my mom friends who kept me sane: Aimee, Polly, Diane, Maria, and Alison.

I'd also like to thank the schools, libraries, and readers I've heard from over the years. Thank you for all the invitations, letters, and discussions. Writing can be lonely at times; getting to see how it touches others in the real world makes it all worthwhile.

Next come the professionals: Stacey Barney and Kathy Green, I can't believe this is our fifth book together. You don't get better editors and agents than these two! Thanks for pushing and supporting me throughout the past ten-plus years. Caitlin Tutterow is an assistant editor extraordinaire, Tom Clohosy Cole created an amazing cover, and I'm ever grateful to Janice Lee and Cindy Howle for copyedits, Jamie Leigh Real and Ariela Rudy Zaltzman for proofreading, and designer Eileen Savage.

Finally, there's family. First, I want to thank my sister, Erika Knott, and her daughter, Julia, who honestly and bravely shared their family's struggles with anxiety. My parents, Marlene and Tom Walker, who also read drafts and offered support—like they have been doing for years. I'm grateful to my co-parent, Adam, who always helps out when I have a deadline. And finally, my wonderful daughters, Charlotte and Kara, who read a draft, helped me brainstorm titles, and generally believed in me. Love you both so much!